BEING BOLAN

BEING BOLAN

Neander Haig

T

Troubador Publishing Ltd
Unit E2 Airfield Business Park,
Harrison Road, Market Harborough,
Leicestershire LE16 7UL
Tel: 0116 279 2299
Email: books@troubador.co.uk
Web: www.troubador.co.uk

ISBN 978 1 80514 505 9

British Library Cataloguing in Publication Data.
A catalogue record for this book is available from the British Library.

Printed and bound in Great Britain by CMP UK
Typeset in 11pt Minion Pro by Troubador Publishing Ltd, Leicester, UK

If, for whatever reason,
you feel like you don't belong,
then this is for you.

SEPTEMBER 16, 1977

Keith savoured every inch of his surroundings, determined not to rock the boat. He watched Daniel kiss their purple heart trophy and raise it towards the early morning sky, readying an empty bottle of lager to use as a microphone.

'Please show your appreciation for the winners of Sothis Media's Rock Heaven, beating London's Narcissists and Yorkshire's Heaton Mourning. I give you Manchester's Magnesium Gurus,' he wailed, impersonating the head judge from the night before. He dragged Keith to his feet and wrapped his arm around his shoulder, kissing him on the side of the head. 'We'd never have done this without you. Our debut single, "Suicidal Summer", will be on the shelves before a Christmas filled with festive sex, but now, my friends, we celebrate before embarking on our meteoric rise to superstardom by becoming the next T. Rex.'

'Keith this, Keith that,' Bennett snapped. 'The next Beatles sounds well better.'

Daniel threw an empty cider can, hitting him on his elbow. 'Who asked you? All morning, not a single word from your miserable lips, yet now you decide to chirp up and piss on my chips.' He staggered forward, giving Bennett his impending death stare. 'Skin up.'

Oggy threw himself on the sand in front of his bandmates, grinning. 'Met this awesome chick, Judy. She works for some marketing company. And she loves the way I pronounce my R's,' he said, biting the top off a bottle of lager and downing it. '*She* reckons Marc Bolan is appearing at Fabricated Frequency tonight, and Sothis want us to stay and perform after signing our contracts.'

Keith spat out his champagne, and Bennett chuckled at Oggy's speech impediment. 'Careful. I smell a gold digger. She'll wob you, now you're a pwominent dwummer. Much prefer to be meeting Ziggy Stardust anyhow.'

'Bennett, you gobby sod. Marc Bolan is a musical demigod. Keith: Bolan or Bowie?'

'Neither. Daniel, we agreed. I need to get back. Me and Charlotte are going house-hunting.' Keith folded his arms, jamming his hands beneath his pits. 'It's all planned.'

'Are you deaf? Marc Bolan's coming to town.'

'Yeah.' Bennett cackled. 'You're punching well above your weight with that one.'

Daniel pushed him and winked at Keith. 'Do this for your best friend. Charlotte will understand. Since when does a bit of skirt come before our band?'

Bennett stuck two fingers in his mouth, pretending to throw up. 'Oh, Keith, you're the best teenage guitarist on the planet. Yes, Daniel. No, Daniel. Three bags full, Daniel.'

'Give your egos a rest.' Oggy stood and thrust his can of lager aloft. 'We have the world at our feet. The sky's the limit and we're all bickering like children. We should be talking about what we're spending our first million-pound paycheques on.'

'Money! We're on a musical mission. Life's about the journey, not the destination.'

'For once, Daniel, come down off your pedestal. We won. Here.' Oggy hurled a pile of paper at him tied together with women's underwear. 'Read through some of these.'

'*Daniel, you're so hot. I want your babies.* Okay. Guess I'm in there like swimwear. What about this one? *You make me hard, like a lump of lard.* That's a bit much.'

'A bit. It's not normal.'

Daniel scowled at Keith. 'Who gives a twopenny toss about normal? Who in this galaxy truly knows what it means to be normal, hey? You obviously don't, do you?'

'Chill. One more,' Oggy said, interrupting. 'They can't all be for you.'

'Don't see any with your name on, big man.' Daniel opened a small white envelope and unfolded the piece of paper from inside. '*You won't get away with hurting people any longer. You're an animal. Truth always comes out in the end. You'll get what's coming to you.*'

'Couldn't put that better myself,' Bennett said, sniggering. 'Just can't help yourself.'

'Shut your gob. Probably some nutjob.'

'Nah, sounds like they know you pretty well, if you ask me.'

Daniel, somewhat shaken, gazed at the words before stuffing the note into the pocket of his shorts. He warmed his hands in front of the toasty campfire and was drinking his lager when two stunning girls raced across and straddled him, snogging him before obtaining his autograph.

'Balls to this! I'm bursting. You two can sit here having five-knuckle shuffles over the dirty-dick Daniel show, but I'm off to party. See you at the contract signing, best friend, Keith.' Bennett stomped off, glugging half a bottle of cider, then twirled it high above his mullet, chuckled and flipped Daniel the finger. 'Oi, hotshot. Here's some rhyming slang. Turbulent tides are soon to come in. Fuck your chips, I'll piss on your chin.'

'Ignore him, girls; he's childish and rude. Jealousy fuels his foul attitude.' Daniel inhaled his joint, blew smoke up towards the starry sky and smirked. 'The feminine mind is a bewitched bouquet of white gardenias and pink cuckoo flowers. The more they're allowed to flourish, the greater their power. Tell you what, why don't you rescue your friends from the troupe by the pier? We can play spin the bottle and sup loads of beer.'

They stuck their tongues down Daniel's throat one last time, then dashed towards the bright lights of Fabricated Frequency. Bennett vanished altogether, and the minute Keith stumped up the courage to grab a quiet word with Daniel, scooter boys whizzed by, beeping their horns and revving their engines, ruining his opportunity to get stuff off his chest.

'Don't get up for us,' Clifford hollered from the open window of his green Beetle. His twin sister Becky and the Narcissists accompanied him. 'Congratulations. Well deserved.'

'Is that right?' Daniel leapt to his feet before Keith could stop him. 'Don't send me threatening letters if you're too chicken-shit to fight.'

'Eh?' Clifford climbed out, leaving his door wide open.

'You heard. Our remarkable rock band will record hit after hit, so piss off back to London, you sad, insincere tit.' Daniel pulled the nasty note from his shorts, ripped it to shreds and slung it up in the air. 'You lost, pontoon eyes. Keith, Oggy, say your goodbyes.'

Clifford shrugged. 'What's got into you? Is this a joke?'

'Okay, let's all relax.' Oggy stopped Daniel from moving closer to the Beetle with his fists clenched. 'Best you go, Clifford. Now. He's drunk. We'll sort this out later.'

Becky lost her mind, screaming expletives at Daniel before Clifford ragged through the gears en route to the pier. Keith could still hear her having a meltdown from afar as the lighter fragments of Daniel's note graced the sand. He sat clutching his bottle of lager with his heart still pounding. 'For what it's worth, I genuinely don't think Clifford wrote it.'

'Who asked you?'

'Stop! Daniel, that's enough,' Oggy bawled, flipping two buckets they'd used earlier for building sandcastles. 'Let's play something chirpy.'

Keith picked up his acoustic guitar and strummed it without saying a word. He loved performing with Daniel, no matter how ill-mannered he became. Oggy supported them on drums with plastic spades, turning the fretful mood on its head, and they sat in awe, listening to Daniel sing his own rendition of 'Summertime Blues' by Eddie Cochran.

'Been looking for you everywhere.' A sexy brunette wrapped in a grey woollen blanket, wearing a velvet stovepipe hat, lay down beside Oggy. She snogged the face off him, putting an unexpected end to their singsong.

‘Guys, this is Judy,’ he said, coming up for air. ‘Judy, this is Keith and that’s Daniel.’

Keith waved, but Daniel crept across the sand on his hands and knees, pretending to be a jaguar. He pressed his nose against Judy’s. ‘Only love can create a state of bliss. Allow me to introduce you to a real man’s kiss.’

‘You bastard.’ Oggy launched Daniel backwards. ‘We’re meant to be friends.’

‘I don’t need friends, especially ones who can’t talk properly.’

Keith butted in. ‘You’ve truly overstepped the mark this time. Apologise.’

‘Too late.’ Oggy thumped Daniel, giving him a gushing nosebleed. ‘Come on, Judy. I’m sorry he’s not what you expected. Can’t grasp it. Anyone would think we lost.’

‘And then there were two,’ Keith said, handing Daniel a beach towel. He rolled out two matching sleeping bags, grabbed two bottles of lager and shoved hardened white marshmallows onto sticks, listening to the neap tide drawing closer. ‘What you said to Oggy in front of Judy was cruel, uncalled for, and you got what you deserved. I don’t like you calling Charlotte a bit of skirt, either. So, you know I’ll be leaving in a few hours as planned. I also have an interview for an apprenticeship with a specialist engineering company.’

‘Run that by me again. What about your contract?’ Daniel scoffed. ‘If you don’t sign, you’ll no longer be a Magnesium Guru. That’s a fact.’

‘If this is what superstardom does to you, I want no part of it. In fact, I’m fine with it. I’ve been trying to tell you for weeks. We’ve changed. We want different things.’

'You mean Charlotte wants different things for you. What about our teenage dreams? You and me against the world. You can't just leave. I'm telling you now, getting a job, settling down – that's not living, it's existing.'

Keith rested his hand on Daniel's shoulder. 'We want to start a family. Can't you just be happy for me? I don't want to fall out. You'll find another guitarist.'

'Damn right I will. One that's not boring. And he'll be miles better than you, you watch.' Daniel brushed Keith aside, placed his bloody towel beside him and stuck rolled-up pieces of toilet tissue up both nostrils. He sat in silence for half an hour with his back towards Keith before speaking. 'Do you think love is a drug?'

'I reckon it's *the* most powerful drug known to man. That's why I want to go home.'

'Me too. I love when we perform. I love the electricity. I'm just so damn sick of suppressing my true identity.' Daniel lay on his back, gazing at the stars, and focused all his attention on specks of ash floating up to the sky before poking the fire with the end of his stick, listening to it pop and crackle. As the flames grew fiercer, the more relaxed he became, joining stars with the tip of his finger in between fiddling with the shiny silver locket hung around his neck on an old black shoelace. 'Egyptians reckoned it was best to stargaze close to sunrise. So wise. Us, we are but apes mating in the grass, praying our suffering will someday pass. Forged from the starry skies above and left to drown in the sea of love. One day, you'll see what I mean. Sailors of the skyway have me bursting at the seams.'

Keith rolled onto his front, firing a surprised look at him. 'You're not making sense.'

'I don't belong here. I don't feel free.' Daniel embraced their purple heart trophy, then pointed to the brightest star in the night sky. 'Now that's what I call rock heaven. What Bolan says is true. We all live in a zoo.' He leapt to his feet, gazing down into Keith's eyes. 'Don't you see? Life is all about the tree.'

Keith munched his yummy marshmallows and stood up. 'Think I'll stick some music on.' He approached Oggy's enormous silver ghetto blaster on the bonnet of his bright orange Mini, pressed play and 'Cosmic Dancer' by Marc Bolan and T. Rex bellowed out before the devastating news filtered through. *'Marc Bolan died instantly in the early hours of this morning when the purple Mini being driven by his girlfriend, Gloria Jones, skidded off the road and crashed into a tree on Barnes Common. Marc, unfortunately, took the full force of the crash.'* Keith passed Daniel a bottle of lager and a slice of bread on a stick. 'I don't know what to say. Shall I fetch Oggy and Bennett?'

Daniel shook his head and sunk to his knees, running glistening golden sand through his fingers. 'What if making Charlotte your wife becomes the biggest mistake of your life? You'll always be someone's puppet or slave unless you embrace your inner waves.'

'Stop! Please. You're in shock.' Sobbing and howling filled Keith's ears once the tragic news spread to nearby camps. The afterparty atmosphere transformed into a wake.

'Nobody understands Bolan like me. He knew what it meant to be free. Have you ever wondered what it feels like to take your last breath? Do you believe in life after death?'

Keith shrugged and cleared his throat. 'Think it's time we got some sleep.'

'Yes, can't be late for your life-numbing interview. I'll be fine. Where's your pillow? Here, have mine.' Daniel plucked handfuls of sand and clumped it together, patting it to make three pointed structures before singing 'Spirit in the Sky' by Norman Greenbaum.

'Now you're just being childish.' Keith rolled over.

***

He woke much later to the sounds of fairground attractions, but Daniel had vanished, leaving three sand pyramids replicating those at Giza. Oggy and Bennett were heading towards him from opposite directions.

'Judy is distraught over Bolan. So tragic. How's Daniel taken it? How's his nose?'

'Have I missed something?' Bennett asked. 'What's happened?'

'Marc Bolan died in a car crash. I woke up and Daniel was gone.'

'Them two tarts saw him half an hour ago legging it towards the sea in the buff by himself, hooting and howling like a wild animal.'

'We need to make sure he's okay.' Keith ran straight ahead, kicking off his sandals; Oggy veered to the right, and Bennett favoured the left side nearer the pier. The wind picked up and the sun disappeared behind a thick layer of grey clouds. They cupped their hands over their mouths and screamed as loudly as they could. Daniel could've gone to the arcades. He could've fallen asleep in a drunken heap somewhere else on the beach, but ahead, Keith glimpsed something black poking out of the sand.

He ran towards it and knelt, clutching one of Daniel's pumps, then cast his eyes out to sea, spotting the other on the sand some distance away. 'Oggy! Bennett!' Waving them over, he charged towards the other pump, grabbed it and held both close to his chest.

'There.' Oggy pointed to the tempestuous tide bringing a heap of clothes to shore.

Keith raced ahead and slumped to his knees, clutching Daniel's sky-blue T-shirt and black-and-white striped shorts. Shouting his name at the top of his voice, he searched as far as his eyes could see.

'Bennett, we'll carry on looking. Go get help. I can swim better than both of you. Go. Go now.' Oggy thrashed further into the sea, roaring and hurdling wave after wave.

Something shiny drifted past Keith's ankles. At first he didn't recognise it because of the murky water flowing back and forth over it. He scooped up Daniel's silver locket and flicked it open; inside lay a black-and-white photograph of him, Keith, Oggy and Bennett in their high school band. Images of Daniel running through Bournemouth naked were believable, but would he have done it without his locket? Keith, fearing the worst, bawled his eyes out with the water up past his waist. Diving in, he did his utmost to keep moving forward with mouthfuls of salty water, but the sheer weight of the waves forced him back to square one. 'Daniel, please stop messing about. It's not funny. I'm sorry.'

'Keith, get a grip. We need to go.' Oggy wrestled with him from behind till he had a firm grasp beneath his arms.

‘We need to move now, or we’ll drown. Kick your legs. I mean it. Faster. The current is too strong.’

Every time Keith called out Daniel’s name, squawking seagulls drowned out his voice.

ONE

Thursday, August 4th, 2011 - 20:00

Keith arrived at the Traveller's Rest in Levenshulme to find fellow construction workers slouched on stools at one end of the bar and a group of pensioners putting the world to rights at the other. He bought two lagers for himself and Oggy and a cider for Bennett, then placed his rucksack beneath his chair, keeping it safe. Draping his rain-drenched coat on the radiator in the corner, he laid his flat cap on top. The damp diamond-patterned wallpaper had peeled off in several places, large chunks of carpet were missing, and the ceiling hadn't had a lick of paint since before the smoking ban came into play. He flicked through his holiday photos on his phone alone, sipped his pint, and took a long-drawn-out breath when the landlady cranked up the volume on the TV.

'What an announcement in the last half hour. It's been over three decades since Sothis Media held a major competition, then out of nowhere: wham!' the news reporter said. 'Having been controversially victorious in their last one, Clifford, what will this mean for aspiring vocalists and musicians from all over the UK flocking to Manchester?'

Keith's chest tightened and he gulped down his pint, hoping to cure the same wretched emptiness he had experienced the last time they'd met, bawling their eyes out at Daniel's funeral.

'Well, Elaine, first and foremost, there was nothing controversial whatsoever about our victory. Listen, local bands will advertise for vocalists, new bands will be formed for this tribute competition and there's going to be an even bigger buzz flowing through this ambitious, creative city. Hotels and bars will be jam-packed with feel-good folk from all walks of life, spilling out onto the cobbles, enjoying themselves. It will be epic.'

'Some say you built your Dual Ventures empire off the Magnesium Gurus' misery. Would you say that's fair?'

'Daniel Saunders and I were good friends, so no, I would *not* say that's fair. I think you'll find I built my empire on hard work and commitment. There are no coincidences in life, only opportunities. We must grab them with both hands when they present themselves. Daniel's death was a tragic accident, and I believe he's in a much better place. Thank you.'

The camera zoomed in on Elaine. 'Magnesium Gurus, if you're watching, the wonderful people of Manchester would love to know what you're up to nowadays. Back to the studio.'

Keith relaxed his grip on his glass and wiped a tear from his face. He took one last glance at his former band members' drinks and had just stood to gather his belongings when Oggy appeared, scratching his scraggy beard. Squeezing his long grey ponytail, he wrung out his woolly Manchester United hat onto the filthy doormat and tucked it inside the pocket of his full-length black leather jacket. Keith acknowledged him with a nod and a false smile, knowing he'd blown his chance to escape, but hugged him regardless, getting a whiff of something unpleasant. 'Everything okay?'

Oggy fired a long, vacant look at him, hung his saturated jacket on the radiator, and plonked himself at the table. 'Sorry I'm late. You're looking fresh and tanned.'

'Wish I could say the same about you. Back from nine peaceful nights in Vilamoura.' Keith thrust Oggy's pint towards him and watched him knock it back without coming up for air. 'Do you honestly think Bennett will show?'

'Yes. Remember his dad shacking up with that young Nigerian dancer, Yolanda, from the Reno Club years ago? Well, they had a son, Jake. She kicked him out a couple of months back. He's coming too. Bit of a gobshite, apparently.'

Bennett, accompanied by Jake, ploughed in on crutches with his head shaved to the bone, a white goatee beard, and his right foot in a plaster cast. Jake helped him to the table, throwing his wet navy bubble jacket and matching bucket hat onto the seat. He ran his hand through his short spiky dreadlocks and grinned. 'Can't believe I'm drinking with Manchester's own none-hit wonders. You should've been legends. Your name crops up on all the pub quizzes.'

'Sit.' Oggy barged in front of Keith. 'I'll get these.'

'How many's that bum had?' Bennett asked.

'Going off his breath, I'd say he's topping up.' Keith tapped his knuckle on Bennett's plaster cast. 'What happened to you?'

Jake replied for him. 'Played snooker with his gay lover and came back a window-licker. I'm on my own now at the shop. Where's the pool table, pigeon-pube? Where's the sexy birds? You owe me big time.' He wandered off to the jukebox outside the ladies' toilets.

'What've I missed?' Oggy dumped the tray of drinks on the table before Keith could answer and wiped the sweat from his forehead with his sleeve.

'Jake was meant to go clubbing, but it fell through, and Charlotte let *him* out.'

Keith tapped his fingers on the table, ignoring Bennett's jibe, and spotted food stains on the bottom of Oggy's untucked denim shirt. 'She bumped into Judy at the fishmonger's the other week. Didn't seem her normal self. Everything okay at home?'

'Women for you.' His hands wouldn't settle. 'You see Clifford on TV? Seen his fat, fortunate face in a shop window. What's he got his mucky mitts into this time?'

'Nothing worth writing home about. The reporter gave him a hard time right enough. What possessed you to ever work for him in the first place?'

'Beggars can't be choosers,' Bennett barked, siding with Oggy.

Keith changed the subject pronto. 'So, where's Judy tonight?'

'Two more?' Oggy necked the rest of his pint and scarpered to the bar. Returning and handing out Jägerbombs, he raised his glass in the air and *clink* – their glasses clattered together. 'This is more like it. Daniel, here's hoping you made it to rock heaven. Happy fifty-second birthday, pal. For what it's worth, I'm sorry

I punched you on the nose all those years ago, and I'm sorry we didn't arrange to meet up on your fiftieth. I can't tell you how much I've regretted it of late.'

'Only the pensioners left. Ask Jake to put our song on,' Keith said. 'Oggy, Daniel knew he was out of order. You have absolutely nothing to apologise for.'

'And so it begins. I do, I suppose.' Bennett slammed his empty pot on the table. 'Can we leave it, hey? Can't be arsed playing the blame game again, fellas. He's gone. We all left him. End of. Shove your pathetic ritual and your depressing rucksack up your poo-chute.'

'Pardon. But—'

'But nowt, Keith. Drop it. Instead of being there for him, you beat off over Charlotte under your picnic blanket, Oggy slavered all over Judy's jugs under his, and I got shitfaced and stoned, hoping I never saw the dirty-dick bastard ever again. Any more and I'm off.'

Keith folded his arms and jammed his hands beneath his pits, blanking the selfish pig. He watched Oggy balance on the hind legs of his chair, drinking like a fish, instead.

'You lot gonna start scrapping?' Jake asked, sniffing. 'Who's not had a shower?'

Bennett pulled a small crumpled paper bag from his coat pocket. 'Anyone for a wine gum?' he asked, offering them out.

Keith ignored him and supped his pint, hoping he'd apologise for cutting him off, but he fiddled with his gold bracelet, grabbed his crutches and hobbled outside for a smoke, taking Jake with him. 'He hasn't changed one bit. Always has to have the last word. Still think he knows more about Daniel's death than he lets on.'

Oggy stood and trudged to the toilets in a trance.

'Did I say something wrong?' Keith waited a moment, followed him in and found him stooped over the sink, vomiting. He pinched his nose and waved at him in the mirror. 'I'm sorry, Oggy, but I can't sit with that unsavoury man any longer. One more, then I'm leaving.'

'Please don't go. Jude and I have split up.'

Keith exhaled. 'What? No.'

Oggy held his head in his hands. 'I caught the filthy cow in bed with another bloke. Four months it's took to say that out loud. Four bastard months.'

'No. Not Judy.'

'Stop saying no. Yes, scruffy, fucking Judy. The bastard leapt from my bedroom window for all the pissing neighbours to see. So embarrassing.'

'Are you sure they were—'

'Shall I draw you a picture? He ran like Linford Christie and had the lunchbox to match.' Oggy slammed his fists on the vanity unit. 'She called me a speech-impeded arsehole with a pin dick. Life was hunky-dory till she dived into my bed with a horse.'

Keith gazed at the tiled floor, praying Oggy wouldn't rip the cubicle doors off their hinges. 'Rinse and relax. Letting it out is the hardest part. Is there anything I can do?'

'Don't go home. I don't want to be alone tonight. And don't tell them plant pots.'

Keith left him drying his face with paper towels and returned to the bar, supping on his own. Blue flashing lights shot past the windows, accompanied by ear-splitting sirens, before Oggy emerged with the colour back in his cheeks, rubbing his hands together. Bennett, aided by Jake, slid into the seat beside him, and Keith checked his watch.

'There it is again. Can you smell that?' Jake asked. 'Either someone doesn't know what soap and water's for or one of them old codgers at the bar's jossed it. Can't we go to the next pub down? There's karaoke on. It's all going off. The old bill are storming the joint.'

'That's a great idea,' Oggy said. 'This pub ain't for the living, Keith.'

'You chose it. Besides, the Church is most definitely for the dying. Punters exit in body bags. Oh look, there go the ambulances. Charlotte would kill me if I stepped foot near that place.' Keith kept a watchful eye on Oggy, who was sulking and flicking beer mats off the edge of the table with Bennett, seeing who could catch the most. 'One Love' by the Stone Roses played on the jukebox, and Jake sang along, scratching his genitals.

'I'll get the last round in, then we'll see if anyone has a voice like Daniel.'

Keith stood to talk Oggy out of it and caught his leg in the strap of his rucksack. He tried to wriggle free but crashed to the floor, gawking at the yellow smoke-stained ceiling tiles spinning overhead. Bennett laughed at him nursing his lower back, and Jake, albeit amused, held out his hand and helped him up, plonking him in his seat.

'Here we go.' Oggy staggered to the table with a big smirk on his face and another round of drinks on a tray. 'Jake, you shouldn't be hanging around with us on a Friday night. Young lad like you should be in town with a bird on each arm.'

'Like you all used to,' he replied. 'You must have some top stories to tell.'

Keith pushed half a pint of lager into the centre of the table and burped, relieving his bloated stomach. He caught Bennett giving Jake the evil eye. 'Pardon me.'

'Here.' Jake showed Oggy photos on his phone of good-looking women from an online dating site. 'When you get in tonight, go on Pen Island. It's the best dating site going. The birds are up for anything. It's all by message, so they won't know you've got a lisp.'

'It's called rhotacism and dating sites are full of freaks,' Bennett grumbled, clipping him round the ear. 'You're the biggest one.'

'Lick my hoop.'

'Stick a song on and zip it before Oggy lamps you.'

Jake did as Bennett asked and dashed back to the table. 'You're just jealous coz I'm a young stallion and you're a Viagra-popping coffin-dodger put out to pasture. For someone who's gay, you spend a lot of time with Paula, the prostitute, on Saturday mornings after the bookies. Has she got gimpy guys chained up in her dungeon?'

'Watch your mouth. And keep your nose out of my business, you hear?'

'Married life isn't all it's cracked up to be. Sometimes takes a month for Charlotte to put her hand down my shorts. Did I say that out loud?' Keith hiccupped, realising Oggy's mind had shifted elsewhere. 'I need to eat. I'll be on the sofa tonight at this rate.'

'What's up, Ogg? You look like you've caught your Mrs in bed with another dude.'

Keith ran his thumb and finger along his eyebrows,

covering most of his face with his hand, and waited for the volcano to erupt in Jake's direction.

'Not just any man,' Oggy roared at the top of his voice. 'My Judy's been having extramarital relations with Leroy the length.' 'Suicidal Summer' by the Narcissists played on the jukebox and Oggy sang along. Swiping his leather jacket off the radiator, he stuck a cigar in his mouth and headed for the exit. 'Nobody to go home to. The Church it is.'

'Who put that God-awful song on?' Keith read a text off Charlotte, asking what time he'd be back, and sprang to his feet, taking command of the situation. 'We need to go after him. He needs our help.'

'We're off to the Church too. Go home, Keith.' Bennett needed Jake's support to stand. 'I'm serious. When Oggy and I needed your help in '77, you were nowhere to be seen. Rummage through your rucksack of remorse by yourself and leave us alone.'

***

Keith spotted Oggy marching past blue flashing lights in the car park of the Church close to the entrance. 'Don't go in,' he yelled, scurrying to where he'd last seen him. He kept his head down and his hands in his pockets, bypassing pools of blood and broken glass on the tarmac. Angry youths, swearing and threatening police, were being cuffed and bundled into the backs of vans, and paramedics were tending to those with facial wounds. His knees weakened; his phone vibrated in his pocket and he pulled it out, knowing full well it'd be Charlotte. He couldn't allow her to hear the commotion in case she dragged their kids from their beds to collect him.

'I wouldn't stand there if I was you,' a policeman said. 'This is the second time we've been called here tonight. The riot squad are on their way. They don't discriminate.'

'I think my friend's in there.'

'Well, if he's a true friend, I suggest you go find him sharpish, then continue your night someplace else. If not, scarper. The last thing you want is to end up in A&E or the cells with the rest of these animals.'

'Oggy, come on. Where are you?' Keith stepped to one side of a police car and checked the zips on his rucksack weren't open before wedging it between his legs on the concrete. He texted Charlotte, saying he loved her, but blamed the background noise for being unable to answer. Shoving his phone back into his pocket, he had just bent down to grab his rucksack when a youth shunted him to the gravel, stole it and darted through the hostile crowd into the pub. 'Thief! Help! He stole my bag.'

Nobody batted an eyelid, and, forgetting all about Oggy, Keith barged past the bouncers at the doorway, catching sight of the youth trying to blend in with the pack. He stopped to open the rucksack and Keith gripped him with clammy hands. 'That's mine. There's only sentimental value – nothing you can sell. I'll give you twenty pounds if you just hand it back. Please, I'm begging you. I don't want any trouble.'

The youth didn't reply. He held the rucksack tightly in one hand, opened the palm of the other and gawped at him, waiting for payment. Keith obliged, retrieved his property and even thanked the bandit before he took off.

Taking a deep breath, he checked none of his belongings were missing and continued his search for Oggy, hoping to escape before the premises became a war zone. Thankfully a thin, shabby bloke in a green-and-white bobble hat started to belt out 'Mustang Sally' by Wilson Pickett on karaoke, lightening the mood a little.

The pool table had been jammed between the wall and the banister and covered by a giant cloth; foil plates filled with sandwiches, crisps and sausage rolls had been spread across it, and the higher booth had a microphone, speakers and monitors set up. Keith wormed his way through more youths dressed in black hoodies and jeans, noticing photos of two teenagers pinned to the bar surrounded by 'Rest in Peace' floral tributes.

'Sorry for the disturbance earlier, ladies and gentlemen,' the shabby bloke said, addressing everyone. 'I need you all to look this way and listen to your good friend Paddy. Before last orders are called, I'd like you to put all your possessions, drinks and whatever down, then bow your heads for a minute's silence in memory of local boys Cade and Conroy. Their favourite song will begin after the silence, so tink of all the special memories you have of them growing up and give it everything you have. Dance, wave, whatever. I want this pub fucking rocking – peacefully, though, you hear? *Don't* break anything and *don't* give GMP's finest an excuse to chuck you in the pen.'

The lights dimmed and 'Jump Around' by House of Pain bellowed from the speakers. Not a single person kept still. Girls pushed their boobs together under the noses of police, and lads used their fingers as pistols one minute, then clutched their crotches the next, winding them up.

Everybody cheered and applauded at the end, but the minute Keith made eye contact with Oggy raiding the buffet, drinks were launched from the back of the lounge and all hell broke loose.

'Have some respect, Jesus. I said peacefully, you fucking eejits.'

Pints and bottles flew overhead, and Keith ducked for cover, bumping into overexcited teenagers swearing, pushing and shoving him into others. 'Sorry. Sorry. I shouldn't be here. Excuse me, I need to find my friend. Heavyset bloke, ponytail, black jacket; have you seen him?' He tripped into the back of someone, causing his specs to fall off, but as he knelt and grabbed them off the beer-soaked carpet, a knee met his mouth at pace before he got trampled on. 'Oggy, help. Somebody help, I'm bleeding.'

'It's me. On your feet.' Oggy's enormous arm gripped Keith through the volatile crowd and he dragged him up. 'You were right. This place is brutal.'

'What possessed you?' Keith flinched with every sound of breaking glass.

'We need to go.' Nearby police were whacking everyone they encountered, and one of them raised his baton to strike Oggy. 'I dare you. Can't you see my friend is wounded? I'm getting him out of here, so don't even think about using that on either of us. Feel me?' Oggy held Keith up and escorted him outside to safety without further interference. He propped him against the nearest wall the moment Bennett and Jake showed up.

'What happened to you?' Jake asked, handing him a tissue from his pocket.

'Welcome to the gates of hell. Believe me now?'

'Sorry I put your life at risk. I needed a pee. The sausage rolls were tremendous.'

Keith dabbed his thick lip and groaned, realising one arm of his spectacles had snapped off. 'Well, that's just great. It's time I went home to face the music.'

Bennett sniggered. 'When the going gets tough, hey?'

'The main thing is Oggy's okay. Besides, you said to leave you alone.' Keith staggered away, having witnessed more than enough confrontation for one night. 'Please don't invite me to another reunion. The answer's no. Charlotte's going to kill me.'

'So stop out. She can't kill you twice. Let's grab something to eat, go back to mine, play some music and reminisce. We can finish our ritual. What do you say? Come on, don't leave. Your adrenaline must be pumping like mad. Mine is.'

'I'm sorry, Oggy. I'm done.'

Two vans jam-packed with police dressed head to toe in riot gear parked up, and they dived out in square formation, ready to storm the pub. 'Bennett, you'll be happy to know I give up. This is the very last time we meet up for Daniel's birthday to celebrate his short but memorable life. See you around, guys, or maybe not.' Keith had sulked his way to the edge of the car park when the most amazing voice, singing 'Gone Too Soon' by Michael Jackson, filled him with an abundance of newfound energy. He looked both Oggy and Bennett in the eyes. 'I know you hear that. Tell me you hear it. It's Daniel.'

'You must've taken a knock to the head and your gob,' Bennett said, cackling. 'Sounds nowt like him, so save your cum-face for when you get home. Off you go.'

'Sometimes it's the darkest places where we find the brightest light.' Keith's heart pounded. Tingly sensations sprang up beneath his flesh, and he strapped his rucksack securely to his back, fastening the buckle at the front. He summoned Oggy to join him and scrambled back up the steps past the police but slipped, smashing his shin on the concrete.

'Are you crazy? You'll get us both killed.'

'Didn't seem to bother you a few moments ago. Help me up.' Keith had this incredible urge to keep going to catch sight of the vocalist. Snatching a pint of lager off the table and downing it in one, he shunted Oggy forwards, finding a magnificent spot to absorb the euphonious sounds he'd never believed he'd hear again. The vocalist's shirt had been torn, his left eye was swollen, and he too had a thick lip. Keith recognised him from the opposite block on his construction site but couldn't remember his name.

His performance had Keith wanting to rush home, dust off his buttercream Fender Player Stratocaster and build up some real riffs. His mind transported him back to a happy, hot sunny morning in Daniel's tranquil back garden on his eighteenth birthday. Planting himself on the wall in the shade, he raised his leg, resting his foot on a large rock, and angled the neck of his acoustic guitar upwards. His strap wasn't too tight; he maintained good posture and strummed chords to Daniel's mum's favourite song, knowing her son would sing and stop making fun of him. He could never resist, and Keith often wondered whether the softening of Daniel's tone at the end coincided with him drifting back towards consciousness.

Keith snapped out of it; everyone in the pub stood in silence, gawping at the young vocalist, and the moment he finished, they cheered, clapped and chanted his name. 'Finn! Finn! Finn!' Keith raised his arms in the air, engaging with those around him in a jubilant transformational atmosphere, and when Finn eventually opened his eyes, he recognised Keith and nodded before disappearing among the congregation. Like Daniel, he had the same charming yet mischievous glint in his dark brown eyes and a phenomenal range.

Paddy adjusted the microphone. 'Where did that come from, you talented little bastard? Who wants to come and top that? I might as well fuck off home. Have I got the perfect opportunity for him? Landlord, get him what he wants on me.'

The police left the Church to rapturous applause without making any more arrests, and the riot squad decided against storming the premises. Keith spun round to find Oggy standing beside him, gobsmacked. 'That was electric. Look, I've got goose pimples. Where'd he go? I want to say hello and tell him how good he is.' He saw Finn wriggling through a mass of cheerful faces, receiving rubs to the head and pats on the back. His rowdy friends handed out high-fives and fist-bumps, then lifted him off the floor in a drunken celebratory fashion.

'There's no way we're heading into the middle of them head-the-balls to introduce ourselves. Let's go. We're not stopping here a second longer, especially with no riot police. Body bags, remember. Now move.'

***

Keith, Bennett and Jake piled into Oggy's huge four-bedroom detached house, half-cut but drenched, seconds before the thunder and lightning struck. Keith closed the door, Bennett slumped on the stairs and Jake bounced off the walls, taking off his trainers.

'Why?' Bennett asked. 'How pissed are you? There's no carpet. You'll get splinters. About time he spent some of his mam's dosh and did the place up, though, God bless her.'

Oggy snatched the food, and the moment he opened his kitchen door, a foul stench hurtled along the hallway towards them.

'What the fuck?' Jake said, covering his nose and mouth with his bucket hat. 'Has someone broke in and took a shit in the middle of your floor?'

Keith heaved, trying to hang his coat on the rack. Bennett wrapped his jacket around his face and Oggy, oblivious to the pong, launched cans of lager and cider into the centre of the room before nipping to the loo. Keith darted in and flung open the kitchen windows. 'Fetch some plates from the cupboard, Jake. Hurry. We can crash in his back room.'

'Are you real? I ain't going anywhere till someone sprays some air freshener. What if he's killed his wife? What if she's under the floorboards? Rudy! Rudy!'

'It's Judy. Would you like me to write it down? Now shush. Don't be so melodramatic and get your chips ate.' Crushed beer cans made the worktops barely visible; pizza boxes had been scattered across the floor and the sink was full of unwashed pots. Keith shook his head and opted for one of four green patio chairs, reluctant to ask where the furniture had gone.

Oggy returned with puffy eyes and lugged out one of Judy's broken line dancing trophies from beneath a pile of cowboy outfits. 'She won this in Blackpool. Made my way to the top of the tower to watch that dancing dirtbag,' he wailed, lobbing it into a mound of tosh.

'Did you know slavery was invented by privileged maggot-dick white men who were shit-scared of their wives craving the black python? It ain't Rudy's fault. Just human nature.'

Oggy leapt from his seat, gripping Jake by the scruff of his neck. 'You!' They tumbled to the floor, grappling with each other, and Keith dived between them to split them up.

'Get off, you big mong.'

'You n—'

'Say it. Go on. You're one of those Ku Klux Klan-loving mo'fuckers. Martin Luther King Junior said, "We may have all come from different ships, but we're in the same boat now."'

'I am not racist. I was going to call you a numb-fuck.' Oggy swung his gigantic arms, aiming to catch Jake square on his chin, then squirmed about, trying to grab him. 'You haven't got a clue what love is.' His head went a dark beetroot colour.

'Don't I?' Jake looked genuinely wounded. 'It hurt like hell when I lost Peter.'

Nobody spoke for a good sixty seconds. There wasn't any eye contact between them either, only puffing and panting.

'Jake, we know first-hand what loss is and we're deeply sorry for yours,' Keith said, keeping them apart. 'We've known Oggy all our life. Bennett and I can assure you he is not racist. Was Peter your best friend?'

Jake nodded. 'Peter chocolate-button-eater was my bearded dragon. What? Love is love. Animals are much nicer than humans. I've never been white enough to be white or black enough to be black. I've always found it hard to make real friends. Think Bennett's right. I've had too much to drink.'

Oggy exhaled. 'It's okay. Me too. It's been a tough day.' Luckily enough, he had heaps of rock and pop memorabilia from the '60s, '70s and '80s stacked in a giant pile by the far wall. He allowed Jake to root through with his greasy fingers. 'Just be careful.'

Keith settled back in his chair and slogged his way through the stash of photographs from his rucksack of the Magnesium Gurus. 'That's from our high school days. Daniel has the same photo in his silver locket buried with him.'

Jake flipped one over from the back, showing a recent photo of Keith and Charlotte. 'You're punching well above your weight.'

Bennett chuckled. 'Told him that from day one.'

'And he was proved wrong. Get your mucky hands off and don't pay any attention to him. I think it's time for our ritual. Oggy, would you do the honours?'

'Count me out,' Bennett snapped. 'Play "Rocket Man" instead.'

Oggy rummaged through his CD collection, unearthing his Elton John album. Keith raised his can and together they sang 'Daniel'. His nerves responded to every beat and the lyrics truly hit home, but as he reached the line about missing Daniel so much, Jake distracted him by sniggering. Keith pressed the pause button hard. 'What's got into you?'

'*Me?* Look at *you*. It's like one of those self-help meetings. *You* can't walk properly, *you* can't talk properly, and I've heard *you* get beat up off your Mrs if you walk or talk without her say-so. He's right – it's sad.'

Keith flared his nostrils at Bennett. 'Is it now?'

'He gave me twenty quid to come out coz your reunions are morbid as fuck and another twenty for sticking that shit song on in the boozer. You should be out there telling your side of things, not hiding away. How much did that journalist offer you this morning?'

Bennett glared at Jake. 'Zip it for once, will you?'

'No, Jake, please continue.' Keith placed his hands on his hips. 'What journalist?'

'Her off Granada Reports. Elaine something or other,' Oggy said. 'She offered us a grand each. If we got you on board, she'd be willing to get us five for a TV interview and magazine article. We didn't ask because we know where you stand.'

'Pretty sure we all stood together and agreed never to profit from Daniel's death.'

Bennett leapt to his feet. 'How dare you? Easy to say with no financial worries.'

'Daniel would turn in his grave if he heard you spouting off about money. Why don't either of you visit him anymore? It's as if you've forgotten the good old times.' Gathering his food and cans together, Keith positioned them on his chair and dragged it to the window.

'*You* buggered off and ruined everything after Daniel's death. *You* robbed us of our good old times. We could've had a life like Clifford's. But what riles me most after all these years is you never once apologised or offered a straightforward explanation.'

'My best friend died.'

'No, you self-centred prick. *Our* best friend committed suicide, and you saw him last.'

'What if someone else killed him?' Jake asked.

Keith couldn't stop himself from trembling with rage. 'That's enough from both of you. The coroner's verdict was accidental death, as you well know, Bennett. What exactly are you aiming to insinuate?'

Oggy dived between them before Keith had a seizure. 'Drop it! We all wish we'd done more to save Daniel, but we didn't. Please, you both need to stop this now. Bennett, Keith has told us the truth. Accept it. This isn't the type of trip down memory lane I had in mind.'

'Now it *feels* like someone's died.' Jake scrunched his kebab wrapper into a ball, threw it into the already overflowing bin in the far corner and sprayed air freshener. He fiddled with Oggy's vibrant satin jackets spread along the wall, mauled psychedelic shirts with gigantic collars and tugged at a black silky robe with a matching wig. Shoving them on over his clothes, he added a pair of funky knee-high boots. 'I'm *well* fit.'

Bennett blanked him and lit a joint, fencing himself in with a cloud of smoke, whereas Oggy leapt from his seat with a blonde wig on, tapping Jake's head with his drumsticks.

'You look like a pair of drag queens,' Keith said, cracking the slightest of smiles. He frowned at Bennett, and with *his* bright red face, he fired back a scowl of utter disapproval.

Jake plucked a colourful flyer from an envelope on top of a box and read it aloud. '*Sothis Media presents Love Is the Drug, Manchester's '70s Rock Revival. Live tribute bands go head-to-head across town, competing for a lucrative recording contract.* If there was ever a second chance for fame and fortune, this is it. Put the Magnesium Gurus back together for Daniel. Gotta be better than that shit ritual. We could rehearse in the back of our shop.'

'No.' Bennett shot him down on the spot, then glared at Keith. 'Keep your braindead ideas to yourself. What's done is done. The past can't be changed.'

'It'll liven the place up. It's been dead the past few months.'

Oggy snatched the envelope off Jake. 'Don't remember this. It's from Clifford. There's a note. *Come visit weekend. You need to grab this opportunity with both hands.*'

Jake swanned about with genuine passion. 'Put your Zimmer frames and colostomy bags away and grow some balls. You'll be dead soon, you coffin-dodgers – just saying.'

'*You* will, any more of your lip. I meant what I said. Leave me and my store out of it.'

'Imagine if you won. You'd have no financial issues. You could do what you want, you wouldn't have to hide and you wouldn't be profiting from Daniel's death.'

'Daniel isn't here, God bless his soul. A band needs a singer, Jake. You heard us. I can't speak, let alone sing.'

Jake checked out Oggy's vinyl collection. 'But if we gave it a shot, who would we be?' He plucked records from the stash by the Who, the Rolling Stones, David Bowie and Gary Glitter. 'What's this? Are you a nonce? I'll check your cupboards for Haribo.'

'Dick. It's been in there ages. Bin it.'

Jake smashed the vinyl over his knee and chucked the lot in the fireplace.

'You don't wanna be in his gang, then?' Bennett said, chuckling.

Keith remembered his discussion with Daniel about love being a drug and shot from the opposite end of the living room, fascinated by Oggy's '70s compilation. He fished out Genesis, Deep Purple and the Beach Boys before wiping dust off *The Slider* by T. Rex. The predominantly black-and-white sleeve with Marc Bolan sporting his stovepipe hat, surrounded by the forces of nature, reminded Keith of Daniel's bizarre connection with him. 'Daniel would love this.'

'How many times?' Bennett asked. 'Bowie's well better. Now drop it.'

'Marc Bolan was his hero. He's never been given enough credit or the recognition he deserves for his exceptional music, lyrics and poetry. It still baffles me to this day. He wasn't some designated follower of fashion. Bolan was a glam rock pioneer. He showed the world it was okay to be yourself, and the media inexcusably called him "The Glittering Chipolata".'

'T. Rextasy are brilliant. I've seen them live, but let's be realistic for a second. We have a drummer, two guitarists and—'

Jake creased up with laughter at Oggy's speech impediment.

'Have you finished? What is it you play again?'

'Bongos. Tambourine. Maracas. And I found the flyer,' Jake said, buzzing with pride.

‘Sorry: two guitarists, a drummer and a cross between Steve Peregrin Took and Mickey Finn. The music shouldn’t be an issue, but without pissing on Jake’s parade, who the hell would we get to sing and play like Marc Bolan?’

‘Keith or Bennett could play lead,’ Jake replied. ‘We’d just need a top-notch singer.’

Oggy’s eyes lit up. ‘I could be Legend, Bennett could be Currie, Keith could play like Bolan and that young kid we saw tonight in the Church, *he* could be Marc.’

‘The midget? Give over,’ Bennett said. ‘Heard the old bill chatting at the window. Them gangsters who got gunned down near Deansgate, that’s who they were bouncing about for. Did you see his monster mate with the huge scar down his face? He didn’t get that at uni.’

‘The vocalist you’re referring to is Finn, and he works in the opposite building on my construction site,’ Keith said, sticking up for him. ‘Yes, he’s rough around the edges, but it doesn’t make him a member of the Quality Street.’

‘He’s a thug. And what makes you think Keith is up to playing lead, Oggy?’ Bennett asked. ‘Rumour has it he hasn’t strummed a guitar since Daniel died. Is it true?’

Keith held his broken specs over his eyes and whipped out his phone to find Charlotte had texted him multiple times. ‘Back to reality. Taxi for anyone? Thanks for our very last reunion. Maybe we’ll bump into each other again if we’re not all dead. Cheers for that, Jake.’

‘We’ll stay here tonight if it’s okay, Oggy,’ Bennett said.

‘Balls to that, you boring bastards. I’m not stopping. It honks.’ Jake dropped his wrappers and empty cans on the floorboards. ‘I’d rather eat my own shit than stay here. Keith, I’m in the taxi with you. Is your sexy wife home?’

TWO

Friday, August 5th, 2011 - 03:00

Finn woke up sweating. His head buzzed with high-pitched sounds and a flowery scent filled his bedroom. Navy neon lights from his alarm clock projected the time onto his sky-blue wall and his curtains blew back and forth in the breeze. He shuffled to the edge of his bed naked and sipped water from the bottle on his chest of drawers before standing to close his window. Distant voices swished past his ears. 'Hello. Is someone there?'

Convinced his mind was playing tricks on him, Finn opened his wardrobe door and grabbed his favourite photograph of himself with his parents on holiday in Cornwall. 'Mam, is that you? Whoever said it gets easier with time was full of shit. Sorry for swearing. It's just, I wish you were here. Went out for my eighteenth birthday. Absolute madness. People wouldn't stop fighting. I'm okay though. Mace got cuffed ready to be thrown in the back of the van. I couldn't just stand there and watch. I hid in the toilets, humming minor and major pentatonic scales, then sung melodies via lip trills, making loud sirens. Nobody even heard me. I carried on singing my way through the vowels, exhaling on a hiss, then made my way to the microphone, tapping it three times, listening carefully to the beat like you taught me. A strange warmth formed at the base of my spine, words leapt from my lips, and I lost all sense of time and place. It wasn't till I sang my last word with the music fading that I opened my eyes to find everyone in the pub gawping at me. It erupted. Nothing like our competitions. Hope you got to see it and you're not annoyed with me for performing without you. Might have some explaining to do. Think a guy from work recognised me. He seemed impressed, though. If you see Cade and Conroy, can you make sure they're okay? They're not bad lads really. Paddy would've made you laugh. He called me little-legs and had to lower the mic. You get what you're given, right? Mace, Tommy the landlord, teenagers off the estate and even the police stopped brawling to show their appreciation. It was insane. Then Paddy tried roping me into some stupid singing competition.' Wiping tears from his face, Finn dragged his belt from his jeans and wrapped it around his knuckles, glancing at his doorknob. 'I can't remember the last time I sang in front of a live audience.'

A soft male Cockney voice accompanied by a choir called out to him. 'Don't tell fibs. I can. It was at the *Manchester Voices* primary school singing competition in your ninth year. Pretty sure that's how long my career lasted. Wonderful performance, by the way. Bravo. You won't be needing the leash.'

Every single hair on Finn's body pricked up. He launched his belt across the carpet, switched on his lamp and clutched his old rounders bat, swinging it in the middle of his room. 'Show yourself.'

Nobody replied.

'I'm not afraid to use it,' Finn said, bricking it. Raiding his sock drawer for his inhaler, he took four puffs with a two-minute break in between, gaining control of his breathing. He checked behind the door, then under the bed, and rested his bat against the wall. Dashing to the bathroom to get a drink, he placed one hand on the frame of his mirror and splashed cold water on his face, watching it trickle down his cheeks. His glazed pupils flashed red, orange and yellow, forming kaleidoscopic patterns, then off he went back to his room once they had returned to normal.

'Please, do not be afraid. Be excited. I am not here to frighten you. I am here to enlighten you. After all, the greatest part of sharing your true talent is you never quite realise who's watching. Fantastic song choice. Truly heartfelt. Kudos, my friend.'

'Am I dreaming?'

'I've upped the aura a little. Breathe slowly. You shan't be needing your medication. The night fever will subside, and respiratory issues shall no longer be a concern. Take it in. There you go. Now, when you're ready, calmly make your way to the mirror.'

Charmed by the rhythm of the male voice, Finn stepped in front of the glass and found an elf-like man with dark corkscrew-curly hair gazing back at him. Dressed from head to toe in a tight-fitting bright white shiny suit, he had a plunging neckline, flared bottoms and a pink fluffy feather boa around his neck.

'Pleased to meet you again. Well?' he said, pointing to his matching ballet shoes.

'What've you done to me? I feel weird. We haven't met.

I'd remember. How did you get in here? Are you wearing lipstick? Who are you?'

'Liberation at last. Do you know how dark it is in there? I have chills due to a complete lack of energy. Please, allow me to introduce myself. My name is Marc, and I am one of many quintessential sailors of the skyway,' he said with a cheeky grin. Full of beans, he performed a curtsy. 'What you can smell, my Mancunian teeny bopper, are gardenias dipped in something kind of magic. They shall make you feel more at ease.'

'I'm defo dreaming. No one breaks into people's houses dressed like that, and real men don't wear makeup.'

'*Real men*, huh.' Marc picked up Finn's hoody. 'If I put this on, will I transform into a real man? Somebody's mind is in dire need of expansion by means of a much-needed splash of further education.'

'Don't think so.'

'The boy I once knew had the most beautiful dreams merged with an overwhelming drive and ambition to become a rock star. Feels like a lifetime ago. What happened to your self-assurance?' Marc exhaled and clapped his hands. 'We are where we are, I guess. You have a red, orange and yellow radiance about you, but it's not enough. You can learn so much more about yourself from your dreams than in everyday life, you know. Probably best you take it down a notch with the alcohol from here on in.'

'It was my birthday.' Finn held his glowing hands out in front of him, watching fancy patterns swirl beneath his skin. 'What's happening to me? What's a teeny bopper?'

'Bless. First, my electric warrior, feel free to take a seat whenever you're ready.'

Finn did as Marc asked. He pulled out his foldaway chair and sat facing the mirror with his hands on his lap.

'I've been so looking forward to this,' Marc said, exiting the glass. He flicked through the pages of Finn's notebook. 'You have been busy. Sketches *and* poetry. Magnificent.'

'Oi.' Finn snatched it from him. 'That's private.'

'Not from me. There is rather a lot missing, if I say so myself.'

'Like what?'

'Your feelings on life. Your feelings on loss. From now on, treat your notebook as a journal. Writing about life experiences not only helps you, it helps those who may read your words in the not-too-distant future. Tell the world how this life of habitual repetition makes you feel. Tell them your story.'

'I'm nobody. My life's boring. Who wants to read that?'

Marc pulled a colourful flyer from Finn's jacket pocket. 'What do we have here? *Sothis Media presents Love Is the Drug, Manchester's '70s Rock Revival. Live tribute bands go head-to-head across town, competing for a lucrative recording contract.* Every single band in this competition would be lucky to have you as their lead vocalist. You should audition.'

'You should leave. You've read my notebook, been through my pockets. What now? You gonna rummage through my underwear drawer?'

'How rude! All journeys are important, however trivial they seem. I'd very much like to assist as you work your way along life's prismatic path. Do you wish to continue existing, or would you prefer to live life to the full?'

Finn scowled. 'I'm good as I am. What makes you think I need help?'

'Moping, sobbing and feeling guilty for breathing.'

'What would you know?' Finn snapped. 'You're not even real.'

'If I help prepare you for your audition, your journey may well turn out to be an exciting one. So you must choose. Nine, eight, seven, six, five, four, three, two—'

'Pretty sure I just did.' Finn spun, raising his voice, hoping Marc would back off. 'I'm not auditioning, because my mam's dead, my dad's a dick and I don't need anyone's help.'

Marc leapt onto the desk in front of him. 'Life has many obstacles. This one is no different. All journeys must be logged physically and mentally, so jot down what you remember from here on in. Keep your journal close by and record everything. Get a stranglehold on your emotions. Reflection is key. We are in Manchester, are we not? A diverse city where revolutions begin. It's been a long time since I last visited. I fell off the stage, if I remember correctly, and one of my best friends found it rather amusing. Free Trade Hall '71, Belle Vue '72. Although I'm a London boy – Hackney, in fact – I've always had a soft spot for Manchester. So much creativity skulking beneath its spectral surface.'

Finn threw his arm in front of his face to block the multicoloured lights flashing inside his mirror. 'What's going on?'

'I'm leaving. The greatest part about reaching eighteen is you get to choose who you take advice from, then decide for yourself what's best. Happy birthday for yesterday.'

The lights dimmed, and Finn dropped his hands away from his face, opening his eyes. 'Does this mean I can go back to sleep?'

Marc rested his hands on his hips and sighed. 'Some might say for the past nine years, you haven't been awake. Although attached to our orb of animation via our collective cord behind the third cerebral ventricle in the brain between reflective hemispheres, your vessel is dormant. Your primitive neurotransmitters have called it a day, your natural melatonin curtain has fallen, and I have risen from the depths of our vast interior ocean, drawing on universal knowledge, creativity and previous experience to help if required. But hey, with a splash of luck, I'll have time to visit family and friends, then see the sights in this fantastic suffragette city. Rest in the knowledge you are not alone. You may now return to more primitive procedures,' he said, directing his attention to the bed. 'Ciao for now.'

***

'Daydream Believer' by the Monkees vibrated from Finn's phone through his chest of drawers, chiselling deep into his skull. He reached over to switch it off, knocking it onto the carpet, and spotted chilli sauce and sweetcorn relish stuck to his bedside cabinet. 'Shit.' Dying to bury his head in his pillow, he leapt from his bed with donkey breath, a dose of morning glory, a massive bruise on his right knee and cuts to his elbows.

'Stop taking my covers,' Leanne said.

'Get up. I need to shoot.' He had a quick slash and, despite shoving clean socks and boxers on, plucked his work clothes from the pile in the corner, made sure they didn't honk and threw them on. 'Did you hear me?'

'What time is it?' Leanne shot up, more aware of her surroundings, looking like she'd been dragged through a hedge backwards by her hair. 'Fuck have I done?'

'That good, yeah? You know you said that out loud, right?'

'I'm so dead.'

'That makes two of us. My foreman's gonna lynch me. I'd make you a brew but—'

'I don't want a brew.' She stole his covers, leant back on his Marc Vivien Foé poster and tied her hair back with a bobble from her wrist. 'I shouldn't be here.'

Finn folded his arms, unsure what to say in case he came across as a proper whopper. 'Can I get your phone number – you know, maybe take you on a proper date?' The alcohol had worn off, but his hangover not so much.

'Are you mad? I had a massive row with my boyfriend in the car park before I heard you sing. With a voice like yours, I never expected to wake up here. He's gonna kill me.' She climbed out of bed naked and plucked her black lacy underwear off the floor. After throwing their used condom wrappers in the bin, she got dressed and gathered her belongings.

'You want me to order you a taxi, then?' he asked, rooting through his jacket pocket for his house keys. He pulled out a colourful flyer and read it aloud. '*Sothis Media presents Love Is the Drug, Manchester's '70s Rock Revival. Live tribute bands go head-to-head across town, competing for a lucrative recording contract.* Did you put this in here? Leanne?'

She'd taken off without even saying bye.

He stuffed the flyer into his pocket, grabbed his keys

and had just locked up when Moon-Head's scruffy mongrel with a gimpy leg hopped from the fly-tipped entry with a shitty nappy in its mouth. Dropping it in front of him, it growled, baring its sharp teeth, and blocked his path to the pavement with its eyes locked on him. He plucked a handful of stones from next to the hole left by the stolen grid and lobbed them close enough to scare it off. It took some time, but the neglected mutt scarpered off along the street, barking, leaving him to jog on.

'If it isn't Liam fucking Gallagher.' Moon-Head tipped her husband's clothes from her bedroom window into the front yard. She had scraggy hair and massive bags under her eyes. 'I'm a mess coz of you bleeding singing in the street, you piss-head. Where's your fancy-piece – buggered off already? Can't say I blame her. If you throw any more stones at my dog, I'll report you to them clowns down there.'

'You wanna try feeding it. It's living on baby shit.'

'Yeah, guess what? You can't sing for shit.' She slammed her window shut.

He horsed on to the end of his street to find the police camped outside the squatters' place on the opposite corner, which had been boarded up with sheets of metal for months. One officer peered through the cracks, banging on them with his fists, and the other leant on the bonnet of his car, eyeballing Finn. 'Had reports of antisocial behaviour round here last night,' he shouted, puffing out his chest. 'You see or hear anything?'

Finn shook his head, determined not to stop. 'I'm late for work.'

'Rough night? Here, you dropped something.' The

officer picked up Finn's flyer, glanced at it and looked him up and down before handing it back. 'You in a band?'

Finn shook his head. 'Someone shoved it in my pocket last night at the boozer.'

'I've heard decent things about this competition, but singing in the street in the early hours of the morning isn't an ideal place to rehearse. Now, I'm not saying it was you, but if it was, keep it down, hey. Off you go. Brilliant performance in the Church, by the way.'

The 197 bus arrived twenty minutes late and dropped Finn off outside the office refurbishment in Manchester Piccadilly. His normal working day meant starting at eight o'clock, but the fresh air hit him on his way up the side of the building in the operative's hoist shortly before nine. After crouching and puking in the corner, he rammed his fingers as far down his throat as possible, bringing up every bit, leaving him with a foul aftertaste of Red Bull and doner meat.

'Fuck sake.' Gibbo, the hoist operator, stopped without warning on the fourth floor. 'You filthy little twat.'

'You want knocking out?' Finn glanced between the gaps in the cage floor, sending him woozy, and grabbed hold of the mesh before wiping his mouth on his hi-vis vest.

Gibbo yanked the lever, forcing the metal ramp to slam hard on the scaffold boards, and the luminous yellow doors sprung open. 'Out! I'm not having you threaten me.'

'Stop gobbing off and thinking you're hard, then. I'm working on the ninth.'

'I ain't working with that,' he yelled, pointing at the vomit. 'Take the stairs.'

Finn didn't have enough energy to argue and left Gibbo heaving like hell behind him. He removed his hard hat and wiped heaps of sweat from his forehead on his way to the central staircase to find Bowden and apologise for being late. The moment he reached the lifts, Bowden sprang out from behind the door, towering over him in his bright red overalls with his beady eyes bearing down.

'Sorry. My alarm didn't go off. A dog tried eating me, the police stopped me in the street and my bus was late.'

'Give over. Look at the state of you,' he screeched in his high-pitched Scouse accent. 'I can smell the booze on you. *One* – you knew how important it was to have all hands on deck this morning. *Two* – you ain't nicknamed the boomtown rat for nothing. And *three* – get your arse down to them shitters. There's a blockage. Find it and fix it or fuck off.'

'What? But—'

'But fuck all. There's a long queue of punctual young men after your job. Men who want to be here. Men who want to learn instead of fighting the world. Tell me the truth, hand on heart. Do you even like this job, yes or no?'

Finn hesitated.

'That's precisely what your body language tells me every time I see you. Now sober up, sort your bloody lip out, pull yourself together and do as you're told. This is your last chance. Fix the bogs or you're sacked.' He traipsed upstairs without glancing back.

'Bowden, please,' he begged through gritted teeth. 'I had a few drinks for my eighteenth birthday. You can't have me cleaning up other people's shit. It's not right. I'm not doing it. I refuse, you fuckin' bully.'

'Hope it was worth it then, la.' You're sacked.'

Finn booted two red plastic cones at the breeze block wall and slung his hard hat with real venom against the concrete stairs, deeply regretting going to the Church. He slumped down on the third step with his head in his hands for a good fifteen minutes, then leapt to his feet, gripping his hard hat before wandering off between pallets of plasterboard to have a sneaky toot on his joint. He stubbed it out on the nearest wall when he spotted Trevor, the site manager, fast approaching in a grey suit and bright orange PPE.

'Who do you think you are? I saw the smoke. Can't you read?' Trevor pointed to the *No Smoking* sign. 'Are you listening to me? Look at me when I'm talking to you.'

'I'm not in the mood.' Finn stepped out of range of his dog breath.

'Show me your hands.'

'Piss off.'

'What's with the attitude? I'll remove you from site if you don't show me them.'

'Whatever, Trevor.' Finn turned his back on him. The hoist arrived and Gibbo opened the doors to let the other site workers out. One of the rusty bars made a loud screeching noise, startling Finn enough to make him drop his joint. 'Shit.'

Gibbo picked it up, handed it to Trevor and stood face to face with Finn, giving it the *big I am*. 'This is him. You're not coming in.'

'Take me to the ground, you bellend.'

'This yours?' Trevor sniffed the joint, gawped at the company logo on Finn's hard hat and jotted something in his notepad. 'Bowden warned me about you. *This* is for smoking illegal substances on site,' he barked, brandishing a yellow card.

'It's not mine. You can't prove shit.'

Trevor showed Finn a red card. '*This* is for threatening behaviour. I want you off my site as soon as you land, or I'll have you escorted off by security. I used to be a bit of a wide boy like you with a chip on my shoulder. Nothing was ever my fault. You can either end up in the gutter or be successful and well respected like me.'

Finn burst out laughing and dived into the hoist, hauling the metal ramp up with the lever. '*You?* No way am I taking life lessons from the ship's cat. What do you know about anything, you complete waste of oxygen?'

Trevor sniggered. 'Best of luck for the future. Off you go, little boy. Jobcentre's that way. We'll give you one last ride in the hoist for free.'

'Clean your own shitters. You couldn't run a bath, never mind a construction site. Tell Bowden he's a noncey old age pensioner who stinks of piss.' Finn pulled stupid faces through the mesh, and once his feet touched the ground, he flicked them both the finger before storming through the gate in the pouring rain. Barging into Keith accidentally, he knocked him on his arse. 'Watch where you're going.'

'Pardon. Your lip's bleeding. Can you at least help me up?'

'Why should I?' Finn asked, glaring down at him. 'I was late – so what? It was my eighteenth birthday yesterday. That nasty bastard in there just bulleted me.'

Keith climbed to his feet, dusting himself off, and

picked up his 24″ Stillsons. 'Take a breath. It was my best friend's birthday yesterday too. Happy birthday. Let me drop these off and we can have a calm, constructive conversation.'

'What can you do, you pussy? You won't change shit,' Finn roared till his voice broke. He marched off towards the café. 'You're just another one of Bowden's fuck puppets.'

***

Finn visited several building sites in the city centre. He even trekked through Salford to Media City, handing out his mobile number to as many project managers as possible before receiving a text off Mace telling him he'd pop round shortly. Reaching the end of his street, he pulled out his creased-up competition flyer, reading it aloud, and when he lifted his head to cross between two parked cars, a giant fist sent him flying backwards. He lay in a heap, blood trickling from his nose and down past his lips into his hand.

'I'm Leanne's boyfriend. Go near her again, Gary Barlow, and you're dead.'

Finn climbed to his feet, raising his hand to make it clear he didn't need the hassle, picked up his damp flyer and walked by Leanne, shaking his head.

'Sorry.'

'What're you saying sorry to him for?' Leanne's boyfriend snapped. 'It's me you should say sorry to. We need the coin, you useless bitch. You better not have put out.'

Finn heard an almighty thud and spun to find Leanne

sprawled on the pavement in tears with her boyfriend throttling her. 'Oi.' He sped towards him with his fists clenched and let fly with a decent punch of his own, followed by another, then another. Leanne wasn't strong enough to drag Finn off, but Mace was.

'Stop. Leave it. He's done. Leanne, get that prick out of here now. He goes to the old bill, I'll turn up at your gaff later and end him, you hear? Finn, let's get you cleaned up, man.' Mace fist-bumped him.

'You see what he did to her?'

'They're always knocking holes out of each other. Why didn't you call before you disappeared last night? She targets cash cows to pay off her sniff.' Mace sniggered. 'Guess she lowered her standards for one night, hey?'

'Don't make me laugh.' The cut on Finn's lip had reopened.

'You need ice, man. Looks like a shiner too.' Mace snatched Finn's keys, unlocked his front door and ran his hand through his twisted curls before lifting his short sleeve right the way up. Tensing his muscles, he showed Finn his new tribal tattoo, offering a glimpse of the stab-proof vest beneath his T-shirt. 'Mint, hey? Sun's out, guns out,' he jeered, tossing him a flannel ran under the cold tap for starters.

Finn's dad had set out a Manchester City birthday cake on his dinner table, complete with eighteen sky-blue candles and paper plates filled with sausage rolls, cheesy Wotsits and roasted peanuts just like his mam used to. He'd hung a large, colourful banner with the words *HAPPY 18th BIRTHDAY SON* from his living room wall too. Finn threw his hard hat and hi-vis vest into the cupboard under the stairs, whipped off his boots, kicking them to one side of the settee, and slung off his clothes, launching them into the washing basket. Swiping the tracksuit bottoms and T-shirt draped over the banister, he noticed his mam's belongings from her favourite handbag laid out neatly on the coffee table. 'Dad,' he shouted, sprinting upstairs. He banged on his bedroom door, raising his voice even louder. 'You in there, Dad?' His mam's favourite song, 'I Want to Break Free' by Queen, played in the background.

'Come in,' his dad said.

Finn stuck his head in to find him in his biscuit factory uniform with red, puffy eyes and his elbows on his knees at the end of the bed. He knelt in front of him, getting a strong whiff of booze from his breath. 'Why won't you ever talk to me?'

'You're eighteen once. I wanted to see you, not hear you through paper-thin walls.'

'You're never in.' Finn wouldn't look him in the eye. 'I texted to say I was going out straight after work. No reply. Just didn't intend to stay out that long.'

'What happened to your face? Why are you home early?'

'Job and knock. Mace is downstairs getting ice. What's happened?'

'Nothing.'

'I'll crack the jokes.' Finn had a good scope of his dad's room and noticed *FINAL REMINDER* in big red letters had been stamped on most of the bills spread across the floor. 'What's this one? Are we behind on the rent?'

Finn's dad snatched the letter off him. 'I'm dealing with it, but redundancy notices are being posted out in the next few weeks. I'm losing my job, son. Fifteen years for what? Might need more board off you in the coming weeks, so don't lose that job, whatever you do. I'll fill you in when I know more.' He passed him a snow-white bag from his mam's bedside drawer, which had a fluffy blue case inside with a shiny silver pen and two refills. 'Her favourite. I've seen you jotting stuff down in your notepad like she used to. She'd have wanted you to have it. Happy eighteenth birthday for yesterday.'

'Thanks. And cheers for my buffet.' He made his way to the door in a daze.

'Caught half a conversation in the canteen this morning. Some young lad had the Church rocking last night with his vocals. Wouldn't know anything about that, would you?'

'Must've missed it.' Finn left his dad's bedroom and closed the door with an enormous sense of guilt hanging over him as the importance of his situation hit home. He messaged Mace to find out what had happened to his ice pack, spread his flyer on the bed and crumpled to the floor with his back to it, dabbing his nose and wrestling with his conscience. Glaring at his mam's pen, he bit his knuckles to stop himself screaming the house down.

'You decent?' his dad asked, pushing the door open. He spotted the flyer and dashed in, grabbing it before Finn could stop him. 'What's this?'

'Nowt. Someone stuffed it in my pocket last night. Give it here.'

'Must've missed it, my arse! Please tell me you're not thinking about throwing your whole life away on this bullshit. What did I just say in there? You have a good steady job that pays well. What more could you want?'

'A life.' Finn shot to his feet and snatched his flyer back, opening his wardrobe door. He pointed to his family photos. 'You didn't think this was all bullshit back then. Mam didn't think it was bullshit either. Look how happy we all were.'

'That was a long time ago, son. Look where it got her. Look where it got us. Close it.'

Finn slammed the door. 'I'm never going to be happier than in those photos unless I'm doing what I'm good at. I miss singing. I miss doing something I enjoy. I miss Mam.'

'We can't always have what we want in life. You'll learn that as you get older.'

'I'm eighteen as of yesterday. Looking at my buffet, you seem to struggle with that. It's time I made my own choices. I'll happily take your advice, but I'm not taking orders.'

'This is my house and if you want to keep on living here, you'll abide by my rules.'

Finn shook his head. 'Is that what you said to Mam?'

'Christ, no.' Finn's dad stepped back with tears in his eyes. 'You know nothing about mine or your mam's life. You were a kid.'

'So fuckin' tell me,' Finn bawled. 'Why won't you tell me anything about her?'

'Lower your voice and stop swearing under my roof. Your mam wouldn't want you anywhere near that stupid competition. That I do know. Have *I* made myself perfectly clear?'

Finn stood nose to nose with his dad. 'You don't get it. I'm sick of seeing that day pop up in my mind. I need fresh memories. Mam would want me to do what's best for me. I need to experience life for myself. Not my fault the only thing you've ever won in your life is a pack of custard creams.'

Mace peered around the bedroom door with his gym bag over his shoulder and a gigantic piece of birthday cake in his gob. 'Now then.' Handing Finn his ice pack and a banana milkshake, he launched a crumpled-up McDonald's bag at him. 'Got your favourite.'

Finn continued eyeballing his dad till he barged past Mace and left the room without saying another word.

'Cool buffet! How old are you, five? Heard you having a heart-to-heart, so I buggered off to a couple of drop-offs. Can't beat a Maccies, mate. That custard cream diss was cold, man. He looked ready to belt you one.'

Finn dropped his Big Mac meal beside his bin and sat on the edge of his bed, sliding his mam's pen into his sock drawer.

'Chin up. At least you got a shag off the local bike. Hope you bagged up. What's with the boozed-up biscuit man this time?'

'He's being made redundant. We might lose the house. I got sacked again. The bastards wanted me to unblock the bogs. You got any jobs going?'

'Are you real? Have you forgotten what went down last night?' Mace grabbed Finn's meal and tucked in, lowering his tone with a gob full of gherkins. 'Wade and his crew from last night are Khan's foot soldiers. They killed Chad and Conroy. I might be next. So do me a solid and give your head a wobble. How did your chat go with Paddy? You find the flyer he gave me? I stuffed it in your pocket.'

Finn tried straightening it out and handed it to him. 'My dad saw it and flipped his lid. You know it's '70s rock? Costumes and shit.'

'You could always go back to cleaning up other people's shit. Rock stars get away with murder. Paddy reckons Love Is the Drug will be sick. You need to give it a shot.' Mace slouched on Finn's beanbag, emptied a sizeable amount of cocaine from a bullet-shaped keyring onto the back of his hand and snorted the lot. 'Well, what you think?'

'I think you're mad. Put that away before he comes back.'

'You wanted a job selling it a minute ago.' Mace glared at him. 'It's time you stood up to that cock and bolted. He's holding you back.'

'Shut up and finish your food. He'll hear you.'

'Your voice is your golden ticket out of this dump. What would've happened if I hadn't shown up before? You ain't got no cash. You ain't got no bird. It kills me watching you piss your talents away.' Mace chucked his rubbish into the bin and slurped his milkshake. 'All I'm saying is we got to see the real you last night and everyone in this shitty neighbourhood loved it. That was the first time you sang since your mam died. Am I right?'

'Drop it. I mean it. Not another word about my mam.'

'Or what?' Mace stood in the centre of the room. 'You gonna do me in like Leanne's boyfriend? You gonna stare me down like your bitch-arse dad? That wasn't you in the street. I don't have a clue who that dude was.'

'What if I'm not good enough? Then what?'

'Then at least you tried, man. You think I love selling this shit? Tell you what, how's about I give up dealing and use my contacts to help you get an audition if you promise to give it everything you got. We be like Dre and Eminem.' Mace pulled a sky-blue envelope and a brand-new grey hoody from his rucksack filled with bags of skunk. Placing his birthday card alongside the competition flyer on his chest of drawers, he tossed the hoody to Finn. 'Didn't wanna give you your presents in the Church.'

'Thanks, mate.' Finn hugged Mace. 'You serious about helping me?'

'Only if you're serious about getting us both the fuck outta Dodge. If you need to, stay at ours to rehearse. First, I need to get rid of these bags. All or nothing, mate.' Mace held out his hand. 'Promise me you won't back out.'

Finn bounced about with genuine excitement and shook on it. 'Promise.'

THREE

Friday, August 5th, 2011 - 10:30

Loud voices resonated from Keith's hallway and his lounge door flew open, bringing with it an enormous gush of wind. He cleared his throat and opened his eyes to find Charlotte hovering above him, brandishing her hairbrush.

'Knew you'd make me late. You should've told Bowden to get lost.'

'He needed my Stillsons. I couldn't say no.'

'Look at you. You're still an absolute mess.' She threw a cushion at him and headed to the kitchen. 'Get up, your lover's here. And that vomit in our front garden won't clean itself.'

Keith didn't possess enough energy to argue. He wiped slaver from the arm of the sofa with his shirtsleeve and spotted Oggy, well dressed and clean shaven. 'Morning,' he said with a harsh croakiness to his voice. 'It's been ages since you last showed up here. Has something happened? What's with this transformation?'

Oggy glanced around the lounge. 'One heck of a crazy night is probably the best way to describe it. I lay awake for most of it. Amazing how fast you sober up when deep in thought, reflecting on what might have been.'

'Did you learn anything?' Keith asked, rubbing his bruised shin.

'Yes. I'd like you to accompany me to Clifford's place to find out more about this so-called great opportunity.'

'Still feeling wheezy from our trip to site.' Keith lay back with his hands behind his head. 'So no thanks. I'll give it a miss.'

'What doesn't kill you makes you stronger. We're lucky we made it out of the Church in one piece.'

Keith scrambled forward with his finger pressed against his lips.

'Could you run that last bit by me again, please?' Charlotte asked, dashing in.

Oggy wouldn't keep schtum. 'We ended up in the middle of a riot. It was all my fault. I only nipped in for a pee.'

'Oh my God! That hellhole is never off the news. Were you trying to get yourselves killed? It's full of gangs, knife crime, drive-by shootings. Hang on, were you fighting? Is that why you're in such a state?'

'He got kneed in the chops and trampled on.'

'I give up.' She stormed off back to the kitchen.

'It wasn't that bad, love. The police had everything under control. We were in and out in a flash,' Keith shouted, glaring at Oggy. He stretched his arms in the air and yawned aloud, making Oggy yawn too. 'So, gob on legs, what happened to bad-tempered Bennett? I'd be happy if I never set eyes on that neanderthal ever again.'

'You know to ignore him when he gets like that. Shot off about nine. I offered to make him breakfast and give him a lift to town. Got the impression he couldn't wait to leave.'

Keith pictured the state of Oggy's house in general, but

when he blew his nose on a tissue, he remembered the foul stench that had drifted along his hallway, slapping him straight in the mush. 'What are we having for breakfast, love? I'm famished.'

'Had ours,' she roared from the kitchen. 'And stop calling me love.'

Oggy pointed to the side of Keith's head and whispered, 'Did she clobber you one? You've got a big red mark on your face.'

'No, she did not. Like you blurted out earlier, it's probably from when I got trampled on.' He rubbed his cheek but didn't feel any pain.

'Bennett must've fallen over at least three times in the night trying to find the toilet. Said he had a big surprise for that prat Jake today at the store. I've got a bone to pick with that strange little ferret. Pen Island.'

'Make sure you tell that idiot he's not welcome here ever. I mean it,' Charlotte yelled. 'You and that halfwit woke the neighbours, beeping in the taxi and laughing like hyenas.'

'We need to talk about Clifford's note,' Oggy whispered, pulling it from his jacket pocket. 'Don't say you were too drunk to remember. I never once blamed you for our predicament, but I know you blame yourself. Love Is the Drug could wipe our slate clean. What if we get to retrieve our fame and fortune? What if Clifford's mellowed with age and wants to help us make a comeback?'

'From where? We're the none-hit wonders. Top of the flops. You're deluded if you think Clifford regrets profiting from our misery.'

'People change. How well do you know this Finn youth? Did you dream about him?'

Keith groaned. 'Pardon? For the love of God! I don't know him at all. And after this morning's episode, I don't think I want to. He's an angry, troubled young man with a potty mouth. Now put that note away and stop this nonsense or I'll ask you to leave.'

Oggy sulked, tucking the note in his inside jacket pocket, and Charlotte brought in two cups of tea, handing one to him with *I luv my daddy* written on the side in large green bubble letters. She sat opposite Keith, teasing him by drinking the other. 'You can have half of this *after* you've cleaned the front garden.'

'Rotten.' Oggy sipped his tea. 'Has he told you Jude cheated on me?'

'He mumbled something about it, yes. I'm sorry to hear that.'

'From her line dancing class.' Oggy bopped in his seat, slapping his thighs. 'God knows how many more guys. Maybe five, six, seven, eight.'

Charlotte rolled her eyes at Keith, passed him his tea and started folding bath towels on the arm of the chair, changing the subject. 'Right, we're off to my mum's *finally*. We've sorted out their holiday gifts. No point you coming now, looking like that.'

'If it's okay, I'd like to take this smelly creature off your hands for a few hours.'

Keith scowled at him. 'I'm not moving. Need water. Think I'm going to puke again.'

'Don't you dare do it in here.'

Oggy rushed to the kitchen, returning with a bottle of water. 'We need to make sure you drink plenty of fluids. Here, I'll look after you.'

'Like you did last night,' Charlotte screeched. 'Kids, come and say bye to your dad. Do not kiss him on the lips.'

They raced downstairs like a pair of elephants, hugged Keith and kissed his cheek.

'Love you both. Behave for your mum.'

Charlotte finished brushing her hair in the mirror and threw her hairbrush at Keith. 'Clean up your sick. Clothes in the washer. Shoes in the cloakroom. Oh, and feed the fish. Now Oggy's here, he can help you put them shelves up in the conservatory you've been promising to do for the past six months.'

'Will you both leave me alone? It's my last day's holiday, for Christ's sake.'

Oggy's eyes locked on to Charlotte's bottom, and he didn't even attempt to look elsewhere till she slammed the front door on her way out.

'Do you mind? You better not be dreaming about my wife. Now take the hint. I am not coming to meet pontoon eyes today or any other day? You heard her; I have things to do.'

'Drink your water and listen. Last night did me the world of good, and that's what today is about.' Oggy sprang to his feet, raising his voice. 'We're moving onwards and upwards. We must take the bull by the horns and find out more info. Please.'

'Oggy, it's great to see you so upbeat after what you've endured, but you're behaving like a man possessed.' Keith glugged the last of his bottle but couldn't grasp how fast Oggy had rediscovered his drive and determination. 'Judy been back in touch?'

'Enough with changing the subject.' Oggy grabbed him

another bottle of water from the fridge. 'After everything we've been through, we deserve a second crack at a recording contract. This opportunity of Clifford's might be our last one.'

'Oggy, Bennett was right. I haven't played in donkey's years. I'd love nothing more than to wave a magic wand and change what happened after Rock Heaven, but we don't have one. I'd love to help you get back on your feet, I truly would, but I will not stand face to face with that man with him gloating and saying "Look what you could've won". I refuse to give him the satisfaction. I'm sorry, I don't trust him. The answer is no. And that's final.'

Oggy placed his hands on his hips and stared beyond the kitchen and conservatory at the back garden for a full two minutes. 'I understand if you feel rusty. I get it if you feel you might not be good enough anymore. Guess Jake and I will just have to find another lead guitarist to give Bennett a run for his money.'

'Stop. You're better than this.' Keith scratched the back of his neck and undid a couple more buttons on his shirt.

'We'd all love nothing more than to wipe that patronising, smug grin off Clifford's face, but he might genuinely want to put the past behind us.'

'My head's spinning. Sounds like yours is too.'

Oggy knelt in front of Keith on the sofa with his hands together, looking him directly in the eye. 'Daniel's death put an end to our teenage dreams. I'm begging you; I need this. I've lost my wife. I've lost my sense of direction. I'm stuck in a rut.'

'We've all lost so much.'

'Sorry, Keith. I didn't mean—'

'Hey, I know. Why not register yourself on one of those dating sites, join a gym, go for long walks in the countryside or read a book, even?' Keith's eyes glazed over, causing him to pull away from Oggy's gloomy gaze. He wiped a strange metallic taste from his mouth as a low-key humming sound surfaced in his ears. 'Can you hear that? How bizarre!'

'Are you alright? Here. Have another drink.'

Keith sighed. 'Bit dizzy. Need food. Tell you what. If you help me with my chores, clean up my sick and take me for breakfast – which you must pay for, by the way – I'll come to Clifford's, but I'm staying in the car. I'll happily give you some advice after your meeting, but I will not be getting involved in any way, shape or form, do you hear me?'

'Loud and clear.' Oggy threw a cushion at him. 'Chores, yes. Breakfast, yes. Sick, no chance, you repulsive rascal.'

'Non-negotiable, I'm afraid.'

'Preferred it when Charlotte was a laid-back hippie,' Oggy said, wrapping her scarf around his face before picking up her mop bucket. He grabbed Keith's remote control for his CD player. 'Get a move on, then, or I'm going to play Brenda Lee at full pelt and give you an even bigger headache.'

Keith clambered to his feet, sniffed his armpits and breathed on the palms of his hands, close to barfing. His breath stunk of garlic bread combined with chilli sauce, and he had a disgusting yellow crust caked across his tongue. 'I need to brush my teeth. Actually, I could do with a couple more hours' sleep. Can't you go see him tomorrow?'

'Get a shower, you tramp. It's high time the none-hit wonders took back their teenage dreams.'

***

Keith traipsed behind Oggy onto the top floor of a posh new apartment building near Spinningfields in Manchester city centre. He was clutching an empty bottle of water. The sweet scent of fresh flowers swept throughout the landing, making him sneeze. 'Give me your keys. I'm using his toilet, then I'm off. I refuse to get in a lip-lock with him when I'm still on holiday.'

'So you keep saying. I've got a great feeling about this. At least hear him out.'

'No chance.' Keith went all woozy. 'My tongue's like sandpaper. I need a lie down.'

'Just think how pleased Charlotte will be when she arrives home to find a nice clean garden and her new shelves fitted. Now try to keep your emotions in check. Be polite, let me do the talking and whatever you do, do not mention Finn's name.'

'Why would I?' Keith had no time for sprightly, colourful décor or fancy contemporary lighting. He lacked sleep but pulled tongues in the mirror, scraping the crust off with his bottle top. 'I'm about to pee my pants.'

'Not surprising really with all the water you've supped. Tuck it in.' Oggy pressed the loud, irritating doorbell and stuck his face in front of the peephole.

'Please, not again. My head hurts.' Keith leant against the radiant turquoise wall, unable to stop yawning. 'We should've called at a café first. He's not in. Let's go.'

Oggy pressed the bell again, only this time he left his finger on it. 'Stop with your griping. He must be, I can hear classical music.'

'Maybe it's his butler.'

Clifford unlocked his door and appeared with thick designer specs on, wearing a smart black-and-white pinstriped suit. His cheeks were a lot chubbier, and his wonky eyes bulged like a frog's. 'Ogg, how the devil are you?' he said in a posh voice, with a look of sheer excitement on his face. 'You look well. Miles better than last time we met. Thanks for testing the bell. I'm pleased to inform you it works.'

'Sorry. You remember Keith?'

Clifford looked him up and down before folding his arms. 'Thought you'd died. Evidently not. Rough night? You seem to be in a bit of discomfort.'

Keith sighed and bit his lip, giving him the silent treatment.

'I'd give you a big squeeze, Ogg, but you'd crease my suit. I've left tons of messages. Thought you still weren't talking to me.' Clifford had photos dotted about of him with a host of celebrities, a memorial to a Judy Garland lookalike above his mantlepiece and ornaments of men and women engaged in sexual activity. 'Would you like a glass of red wine?'

'Sorry to interrupt.' Keith scowled. 'Oggy, keys. Clifford, I could do with a pee.'

'Of course. You should've said. Visitor's toilet down there on the left.'

Keith found the bathroom, pulled the toilet seat up, then stood with one hand on the shower cubicle, aiming his pee from side to side in the fancy pan to the sound of Mozart. 'Oh look, one has landed on Earth from Mars. One must use the visitor's toilet.' The music switched to the Narcissists' 'Suicidal Summer', the scent of fresh flowers grew stronger, a sour taste filled his mouth and what sounded like an old dial telephone resounded in his ears.

'Has someone stopped taking their medication? Marvellous. Let's build a den.'

Goose pimples sprang up throughout Keith's body and he spun in the voice's direction, dribbling before zipping up his fly. 'Daniel.'

'I know you were busting,' he replied, giggling, 'but peeing on the floor: come on, Keith, you know it's frowned upon as well as disgusting.'

After pressing the posh silver button on the cistern, Keith searched high and low for something to wipe it up with and swiped an extravagant flannel. He dabbed his puddle, then set it back neatly on the shelf. 'This isn't happening.'

'Although Oggy and Clifford suffer from verbal diarrhoea, Love Is the Drug is a fantastic idea. Told you so. You're not living. You're existing.'

Keith washed his hands and slapped himself across the face many times before returning to the lounge. 'Nice place. And thanks for the perfectly timed composition.'

'My pleasure. You didn't touch anything, did you?'

Keith swung Oggy's car keys around his index finger and was heading towards the door when he noticed the purple heart trophy in a glass cabinet beneath a large tree painting titled *September 16th* by René Magritte. Beside it was a photograph of the Narcissists, Heaton Mourning and the Magnesium Gurus at the closing ceremony of Rock Heaven. Seeing Daniel holding their trophy aloft sent an almighty shiver down Keith's spine.

'You okay?' Oggy asked.

'Bit dizzy. It'll pass, but the sickly feeling I have in the pit of my stomach most likely won't go till we leave.' Keith staggered towards the windows, which spanned from floor to ceiling, offering an excellent view of Manchester's skyline. In the centre of the lounge lay an enormous cream circular rug, which he wanted to curl up on.

'Are you on your way out?' Oggy asked Clifford.

'Being picked up shortly. I have a meeting at the Midland Hotel. Did you receive my note and flyer for Love Is the Drug?'

Oggy pulled them from his pocket and unfolded them. 'These.'

'Enjoy writing brief notes, do you?' Keith muttered under his breath.

Clifford turned his back on him. 'Sothis Media's Love Is the Drug is all about performance and togetherness. Audiences want to feel part of something. We all need to be loved, we all need to belong, and we all need our fix. Over the years, I've learnt it's best to give the audience what they want. If your energy arouses them, their energy can carry you to places you've never even dreamed of.' He glanced at Keith, licking his lips. 'There's a powerful presence here. Not only can I feel it, I can taste it.'

'Look at him, Keith, with that smug, spiteful grin. We know what you are, Clifford – you're a self-absorbed cretin.'

Keith cleared his ears with his finger, wiped them on

a tissue and put it in his pocket before making himself comfortable in Clifford's chocolate-coloured leather recliner on the opposite side of the room. When he pressed the button on the side, the bottom flipped up. 'Ta da.'

'So glad you're easily amused. Moving swiftly on. Sothis will place notices in the windows of premises across Manchester in the coming weeks, letting everyone know which they'll be monitoring. Their judges will remain anonymous as they build up a portfolio of tribute acts. Bands must enter on their website, which will soon go live, give their contact details, and let them know where and on what nights they'll be performing. Those with the most potential will be whittled down to three by a secret panel and announced live on TV and radio at the Printworks, where they'll receive their magical rainbow invitations to compete in full costume with props in the grand finale on Bonfire Night at a venue still to be confirmed.' Clifford clapped his hands together and inhaled a vast amount of oxygen. 'The winners will receive this purple heart trophy, which you briefly became familiar with many moons ago, two cheques for twenty-five thousand pounds – one being for a chosen charity – and a lucrative recording contract, which again you nearly got to benefit from. Fancy it?'

'Yes. Yes. That's why we're here, isn't it, Keith? We'd like to thank you for this opportunity to win back our trophy.'

Clifford's look of excitement changed to a look of exasperation. 'You've lost me.'

'Your note. Grabbing opportunities. We'd love to reform the Magnesium Gurus and continue our rivalry with you at Love Is the Drug in a battle of the bands type scenario.'

Keith's jaw dropped, and Clifford burst out laughing. 'Is this a joke? Let's come back to the real world for a second. When I said do you fancy it, I meant *you*. Oggy, I asked *you* here to see if you'd straightened yourself out enough to mentor my nephew Antoine and his immensely gifted band Physical Graffiti at Love Is the Drug. It'd be a conflict of interest for me because of Dual Ventures and Sothis Media's ongoing working relationship. I intend to keep my trophy, so obviously I'll be involved in the background. We have a state-of-the-art rehearsal space kitted out with brand-new instruments and specialist equipment.'

Keith held back from firing his told-you-so look at Oggy in case he broke down.

'Maybe you should have put everything you just said in your minor note. It would've saved us the journey and embarrassment.'

'Not my fault you were reaching. Who in their right mind wants to see the Magnesium Gurus perform today? You'd be a laughing stock. You don't have a chance in hell of winning this competition, especially with the likes of that deserter.' Clifford pointed at Keith. 'It's abundantly clear you haven't straightened yourself out enough.'

'How dare you insult my friend? You know nothing. Apologise right now.'

Keith flipped his recliner back to how he'd found it and sat forward, glancing around the lounge. No matter which way he faced, an ornamental nipple or penis pointed at him. He closed his eyes for a moment, presuming they'd leave him alone, but the lavish, freaky furniture wouldn't stop stalking him. 'Time we left, I think.'

'Ignore him! Oggy, think about this. It's a great opportunity.'

Keith buried his head in his hands, trying his best to blank Clifford from his mind.

'True music lovers know how good we were, and so do you. We were the best.'

'Precisely. *Were.*' Clifford burst into laughter. 'When's the last time he played, hey? When's the last time you played together? Kids nowadays would wipe the floor with you. You'd struggle to raise the bar to Bennett's standards, let alone anyone else's. You're not teenagers anymore. You're a bunch of old washed-up has-beens with no vocalist. I can help with your drink problem, Ogg. I'll even pay for counselling and hand you a hefty bonus when Physical Graffiti win. You look like you need it. The harsh reality is, the Magnesium Gurus were nothing without Daniel. I don't blame you for running away, Keith, but I doubt it had much to do with loss.'

Keith sprang to his feet. 'Now, you listen here. You're nothing but a sad, jealous old sod. And, so you know, we've always been better than you and we always will be. That trophy's ours. You won Rock Heaven by default. Admit it.'

'Face it, your musical ambitions died the same day Daniel did. Are you really about to destroy Oggy's dreams once more? Return to your mundane life. You wouldn't even make it through the heats.'

'Is that right? You think Daniel was talented.'

'No, no. Now it's time we left.' Oggy tried to shove his hand over Keith's mouth and usher him towards the door. 'Stop talking. That's enough. Stop now.'

'Get off. Our vocalist along with us washed-up has-beens will destroy your nephew's band. You took Oggy and Bennett's livelihood away from them, not me. You're to blame, pontoon eyes, and its time someone taught you a lesson. Not only are we entering this stupid tribute competition, we're going to win it in style. Wait till you hear our new vocalist.'

Clifford chuckled. 'If you had a decent vocalist, I'd know. I'm glad I never saved you the embarrassment. It's been so much fun. Now you can leave. Say hi to Bennett for me if he's still alive.'

'You'll hear our vocalist soon enough. Audiences will chant his name right across the UK, mark my words.' Keith pointed at Clifford over Oggy's shoulder. His breathing speeded up, his muscles tensed and sweat spouted from his pores. 'If you wrote that hurtful note to Daniel, you're to blame for his death. You.'

'You're barking up the wrong tree, but challenge accepted. In six weeks' time, Sothis Media's judges will make their rounds. September 16th – a date we're all familiar with. Genuine singers want to be in genuine bands. They want a career. You can't offer either.'

Oggy dragged Keith to the door and waved. 'We won't keep you any longer, Clifford. Thanks for the info. Shove your counselling and bonus where the sun don't shine.'

'If you walk out that door and side with that amateur musician, that's you and I done forever. Do not come crawling back for handouts. Probably best you put *him* on a leash.'

'Keith has more talent in his little finger than you've ever had, you poisonous frog-faced fraudster.'

'Air. Now. I need fresh air.' Keith dashed off, yanking

the chain on the door and spinning the lock, rushing out, dropping Oggy's keys. He made a beeline for the open window in the corridor beside the lift, stuck his head out and vomited onto the car park below.

***

Keith sat with his hands covering his face in the front passenger seat of Oggy's black Jaguar on Tib Street in Manchester's Northern Quarter. Once affectionately known as pet shop paradise, the first industrial suburb had gone through substantial regeneration over the years. Derelict buildings had been transformed into fine bars, shops and trendy little cafés, oozing with diverse and delightful cultures, whereas Bennett's music store found itself fenced in by seedy sex shops and adult bookstores.

'Shall I go first? Okay. Well, that was eventful,' Oggy said, facing straight ahead. 'What happened to keeping your emotions in check and being polite? I gave you my keys.'

'I'm truly sorry. I don't know what came over me. I'm tired, I'm still drunk, never mind hungover, and it feels like I've just woken up in the middle of a nightmare. Is today let's-take-Keith-to-visit-everyone-he-doesn't-really-like day?'

'Out of all them posh motors, how is it I end up with regurgitated kebab and chips on my bleeding roof? Talk about throwing the cat among the pigeons.'

'Said I was sorry. Let's go back. I'll apologise and say it was all a big mistake. I fully intended to leave. I did. Till I saw that photo. Why the one of us winning Rock Heaven?'

'Clifford's nothing but a creepy narcissist. We can't go back, Keith. He'll have made a hundred calls by now, making sure I never work in the industry again. That's how much influence he has, but on the plus side, watching his wonky eyes nearly pop from his skull was fabulous and long overdue. That's the first time you've ever acknowledged Daniel may have committed suicide. Do you think that note may have contributed to his death?'

'No! I was just blowing off steam. Is it true? Do you have a drink problem?'

'Until last night I did. That's why Clifford sacked me. Look, I'm sorry if it feels like I've dragged you about today, but I'm sick of waking up and looking in the mirror to find a lifetime of regret staring back at me. I'm tired of being a laughing stock, aren't you?'

Keith's bowels loosened. 'Dragging me about isn't the issue, Oggy. Dragging up the past is. You know precisely what Charlotte will say if we go through with this.'

'I want something to keep my mind occupied. Please. I need *this*.' Oggy patted Keith's knee. 'You remember the buzz the four of us used to get performing. Daniel said we fed off each other's electrical energy, and once connected, we could take on the world. Let's give it our best shot for old times' sake. You must miss it. *I* do. Nobody knows more than us what it's like to miss out on a great opportunity, Keith, especially when we crossed the finish line in first place only to be stripped of our medals. The way I see it, we have three hurdles. Let's concentrate on clearing one at a time and go from there. The first one's Bennett. He has the talent and rehearsal space we need, but going off his stubbornness last night, he'll need some convincing.

Again, whatever you say, mention nothing about Finn. As far as Bennett's concerned, he isn't even an option.'

Keith's stomach churned, and he sighed. 'Do you know what you're asking?'

'I know what Bennett will be asking. He'll want the truth and nothing but the truth.'

Keith scrambled onto the cobbles beside Oggy, and the bell above the main door rang, giving him an almighty fright. Clutching their ham sandwiches, a young Asian man in a bright yellow T-shirt with the words *EAT ME* scrawled in purple greeted them. He had short dark hair with bouncy curls, a stud beneath his bottom lip and navy-blue eye shadow with matching lipstick.

'Bennett in?' Oggy asked, turning down the volume of 'Little Red Corvette' by Prince.

'I am Farooq,' he replied, stomping towards them in his tight leather trousers and designer winkle pickers. He shook their hands. 'They are out back. They are expecting you. You must be Oggy. Pleased to meet you. Bennett has told me all about you. Pleased to meet you too, Keith. Not so much about you. Go through. Go through.'

Keith didn't have time to browse the store. Instead he found Bennett in the back room sprawled across a filthy brown sofa. He had chewing-gum-white underwear on, a joint in his mouth, and his broken foot rested on the arm.

'Who's your new friend?' he said, chuckling and blowing smoke rings.

'Very funny.'

The chain flushed in the downstairs toilet next to the open-plan kitchen and Jake exited, drying his hands on a tea towel.

'Pooh.' Oggy opened the door to the back yard. 'Are you familiar with the saying "Don't shit where you eat"? That's wrong.'

'Is Stig of the Dump being serious? Had a wash and shave, have we?'

Oggy pointed at him. 'I ended up with tons of cock on my laptop screen this morning because of you. White ones, brown ones, black ones, big ones, small ones. Pen Island. Piss funny. You sent me to Penis Land, you prat. I could've got a virus.'

Jake burst out laughing. 'I didn't tell you to touch 'em.'

Keith added his twopence worth and waved his finger at him. 'Charlotte's gunning for you too, beeping in the taxi. What possessed you?' He gazed at the artwork sprayed on the brickwork. One wall had flying saucers dropping cages on apes in the grass and the other read *MADCHESTER*, along with the names of famous Manchester bands. 'Who's the artist?'

'Well, it ain't me,' Bennett replied.

Keith lifted dustsheets in the corner and rooted through buckets filled with spray cans. 'You should do this for a living. You're like Ancoats' very own Banksy.'

Oggy pointed to the store. 'Love the new Prince lookalike.'

'It's our kid's new bum chum playing shit pop music. Can you afford to pay him?'

'Farooq's your surprise?'

Bennett kept a watchful eye on the door to the shop. 'He's a dance student, recently evicted from his home for boogieing to Cyndi Lauper wearing only his sister's burqa.'

'Interesting. We need to talk about Sothis Media's

Love Is the Drug. Clifford just threw us out of Pontoon Palace. Keith lost his rag. He couldn't even stomach a free breakfast.'

'Still can't. Here.' Keith handed his ham sandwich to Jake. 'Something about that man makes me sick. He was his usual condescending self, begging Oggy to mentor his nephew's band, Physical Graffiti. He turned him down.'

'Was that wise?' Bennett asked. 'What's this got to do with us?'

Oggy shrugged. 'The competition final is a full costume and props event with the venue still to be confirmed, but if we're serious about forming a T. Rex tribute band, our best chance of finding Marc Bolan is attending more karaoke nights. What do you reckon?'

'Shouldn't the music side of things be sorted first, Oggy, before gallivanting in search of a vocalist?' Keith asked. 'Where would we rehearse?'

Bennett gripped his crutches and staggered to his tiny kitchen, where he filled the kettle.

'Shall we put it to a vote?' Oggy called out. 'Let's see those hands. All in favour of forming a T. Rex tribute band in memory of Daniel and entering Love Is the Drug.'

Jake flung his arm in the air and Keith supported him, putting up his.

'Have you heard yourselves? You're like a pissing double act. I saw you on the cameras. You've been sat out there over half an hour.' Bennett tapped his fingers on his worktop, launched tea bags into each cup and slammed the cupboard shut.

'Can we borrow Jake and your van, go to mine, have a clear-out and bring some gear back to sort through?'

'No, Oggy. You're not clearing your cesspit and dumping your shit at mine. This is our home. Your lives won't have to change if we rehearse here. I enjoy my peace and quiet, so if you want me to join and use my rehearsal space, what's it worth?'

'Money isn't everything, Bennett. Daniel taught us that. A record deal is what we always wanted. You especially. We put the past behind us and get revenge on Clifford in the process.'

Bennett returned to his resting position on his sofa, supping his tea. 'You can add your own milk,' he said, aiming his crutch at Keith. 'He knows precisely what I want. Three conditions. One – did Daniel say anything on the beach to suggest he was about to top himself, yes or no? Two – apologise for disappearing off the face of the earth after he jossed it, telling us why and where you went. Three—'

'You can't keep blaming Keith,' Oggy roared. 'That ship has sailed many times.'

'I want assurances. He can't just bail again if the going gets tough.'

'He won't, I'll make sure of it, but if you choose not to grab this opportunity, you can no longer blame Keith for the bad things in your life. This will be on you.'

Keith looked at Oggy. 'It's okay. Bennett, I'm deeply sorry I left.'

'And?' Bennett folded his arms.

'As I've said a million times, Daniel was looking forward to meeting Marc, and he wanted to apologise to Oggy for his inexcusable behaviour. I wish I hadn't fallen asleep, but I did.' Keith whipped off his spare set of specs, wiped them clean and pinched the bridge of his nose, cherry-picking the truth. 'People deal with trauma in different ways. Daniel's *accidental* death, his funeral, his mam's death shortly after … it all took its toll. I stayed with relatives in Devon and didn't know about Clifford stealing our record deal till Oggy told me months afterwards, I swear. I'm so sorry. Daniel and I would often rehearse in his cellar. I'd play his vintage 1974 Blue Sparkle, and he'd sing. We'd always pretend we were Bolan and Bowie. How could I continue playing after Daniel's death if I couldn't bear the thought of him not performing by my side? Hopefully one day you can both forgive me, but I'll never be able to forgive myself.'

Oggy rushed towards Keith and hugged him, Jake patted him on his back and Bennett nodded three times. 'Daniel loved that guitar. Still can't believe his mam gave it to the rag and bone man. If only we had his journal. We can't bring him or his possessions back, so what happens if you still can't play without him by your side?'

'We'll cross that bridge if we come to it.'

Farooq strolled in with his hands on his hips. 'Benny, the decorators phoned a couple of moments ago. They will be here Thursday along with the electricians.'

'What are you having done?' Oggy asked.

'Lick of paint in the shop, new indoor and outdoor speakers and a brand-new sign out front. Jake's designing it.' Bennett lit a joint at the back door. Him and Farooq took their conversation outside and Keith, Oggy and Jake earwigged in the kitchen.

'That went surprisingly better than expected. They're coming back. Pretend you're busy.'

Bennett hobbled in, shaking his head at the floor. 'This is nuts. Look at us. We're old and goosed. You,' he said, glaring at Jake, 'you're young and even more goosed. I know I'm going to regret this. Don't dress it up and say it's for Daniel, though, coz it's not. This is plain madness. Grown men wanting to be young again.'

'Does that mean you forgive me?' Keith asked, hoping to focus on the two remaining hurdles left to clear.

'It means you must agree to my additional and final condition or this ridiculous journey ends here and now. We commit to proper auditions, and we all have a say in who's worthy enough to fill Daniel's shoes. Do we have a deal?'

FOUR

Friday, August 12th, 2011 - 19:15

Finn sank four cans of lager on his way home from Mace's hospital bedside and found a note on his dinner table saying there was nothing in for tea. His dad had gone to the Labour Club again, and he'd be back late. He trudged upstairs, flung his soaking wet clothes onto the bedroom floor, booted his bin full of wastepaper across the room and pressed play on his laptop. Punching his wardrobe, he collapsed onto his beanbag in tears, listening to 'This Is How It Feels' by Inspiral Carpets.

'Why?' He gathered his winning trophies together, and one by one he launched them at the wall before crashing to the floor, gripping a photograph of himself and his mam at the amusement arcade in Blackpool on the weekend before she died. 'I lost my job, Dad's losing his, and it looks like I might lose my best mate now too. We were about to audition for Love Is the Drug and take the world on together. Dad'll be chuffed. Should fit nicely into his plans for the rest of my life. Have I done something wrong? What did I do to deserve all this? Dad hadn't mentioned you for ages till my birthday. He gave me your favourite pen, but I haven't had a chance to use it yet. I'm supposed to be an adult. Give us a clue. What am I meant to do with my life in this shithole of a planet? I wish I wasn't born. I don't belong here.'

Someone knocked on Finn's front door, causing his adrenaline to kick in. He dropped the photograph, wiped his face, grabbed his bat from the wardrobe and legged it downstairs, unsure if Wade and his gang had followed him from the hospital to stove his head in too. Peering through the net curtain, he saw a bloke in a flat cap with a rucksack on his shoulder and his back to him loitering at the gate. 'Who is it?'

'Keith from work.'

Finn rested his bat by the stairs and opened the door, glaring at him, but Keith grinned as if they were best pals. 'You stalking me? I saw you eyeing me up in the Church, then you ran into me in Piccadilly. Who sent you?'

'No. Sorry. Nobody. I seem to remember you calling me some rather unsavoury names. Feel free to apologise.'

'Why? Are you here to give me my job back?'

'Afraid not. A guy on site gave me your address. I told him I owed you some money. Have you been crying?'

'Tell me what you want or piss off. I'm not messing.'

Keith handed Finn his competition flyer. 'I'd like to offer you the opportunity to audition for our T. Rex tribute band. We're entering Love Is the Drug. You may have heard of it. We reckon you have what it takes to be our lead vocalist, Marc Bolan, handing us the best chance to win this lucrative, life-changing record deal. Your performance in the Church blew us away. You have the finest teenage vocals I've heard in thirty-four years.'

'Mate, I really don't wanna be a dick, but I've had the

worst night ever. Singing in some lovey-dovey rock tribute competition, pretending to be someone I've never even heard of, is the last thing I need. The Church was a one off, and as of ten minutes ago, I'm never going to sing again, so find someone else.' He made as if to close his front door.

'Wait! Why would you decide something as drastic as that?'

'I'm cursed. All I do is bring bad luck to everyone around me. It's contagious. You better do one before you catch it. Leave me alone.'

Keith whipped off his rucksack and held it in front of him. 'I brought this. There're books, DVDs, CDs, all kinds of material relating to Marc Bolan and T. Rex. It'll give you an idea of who we are too. Look, please. I'll leave it with you. All I ask is that you take good care of my belongings and don't walk away without giving this opportunity some real consideration. Our drummer, Oggy, is well known in the music industry. Here.' Keith passed Finn another flyer from his jacket pocket. 'We rehearse at Bennett and Jake's music store on Tib Street in town. Auditions are on Saturday, August 20th, one week tomorrow, and the following Saturday, August 27th. Nine a.m. till eleven a.m. both days. The address is on the bottom, and I've scribbled my mobile number on there too in case you have any questions. Oh, and if anyone asks, I was never here, we don't know each other, and you found this flyer in your local café.'

Finn checked up and down the street as well as the rooftops, stumbling forward with a false grin. 'If you're working for MI5, you better go. Sure I just saw a sniper up there.'

'Are you drunk? I see you've still got a bit of a shiner from the other night. How wild was that, hey? Oggy and I were lucky to make it out alive.'

'This one's from the day after.'

'Ah, right, okay. Do you think there's a slight chance you might change your mind about singing again and maybe audition on either day? Believing you're cursed is nonsense. I could pick you up. Be more than happy to.'

Finn knew Keith wouldn't let it go. Crazy revenge thoughts sprang up in his mind and he pointed to a burgundy Citroën C4 Picasso. 'That's yours, I take it. Is it safe?'

'Well, it belongs to my wife, Charlotte. Of course it's safe. Are you sure you're not drunk? I smelt alcohol, and you sounded a little tipsy then.'

'I'm not promising owt, but I'll have a look in your creepy rucksack and think about auditioning if you give me a lift to get some scran.'

'Great. No problem,' Keith said. 'I'm peckish myself. I'm driving, though.'

'I don't have a licence and never will, so chill. Be out in a sec.' Finn snatched Keith's rucksack, gripped his bat and took off upstairs, where he dropped them on the floor next to his bed. Digging out a pair of dark jeans, black trainers and a scruffy dark hoody from his wardrobe, he got changed and grabbed his inhaler. Leaving the house with a cold can of lager from the fridge, he climbed in the passenger side.

Keith wouldn't stop fiddling with the radio. 'A Change Is Gonna Come' by Sam Cooke played, and he cranked up the volume, singing and performing a cringeworthy dad dance. Finn made sure his seatbelt was securely fastened, clutched the door handle with one hand and gazed at the airbag symbol in front of him. Checking behind, he noticed a pink *Best Dad in the World* cushion on the back seat, then closed his eyes.

'A gift from my youngest.' Keith turned his music down. 'Are you okay?'

Finn's heart was racing. He downed most of his can and wiped the sweat from his forehead with his thumb. 'Fancy a curry? I'm thinking Rusholme – Khan's is meant to be cracking.'

'That's Charlotte's favourite. We haven't been for ages. Didn't it go up in flames a while back? Sure I heard something on the radio.'

Finn wasn't in the mood for small talk. He squashed his empty can between his thighs and gripped his inhaler with a trembling hand. Opening one eye, he watched Keith drive past Khan's in the busy traffic and spotted Wade, battered and bruised, hovering outside the entrance on his phone. 'Stop! I need to get out. Park there behind them taxis,' he said, diving out on the kerb, choking.

Keith did as he asked and somehow twigged. 'Do you need a doctor? You're not here to buy food, are you?'

Finn's temperature rose and his chest tightened. Taking two puffs of his inhaler, he stuck it back in his pocket. 'My best mate Mace is dying in hospital, and that sick fuck put him there. Drive off if you want, I'm not forcing you to stay, but if you do, keep your engine running and get ready to put your foot down.'

'What if you don't come back?' Keith muttered, glancing in his side and rear-view mirrors. 'Charlotte will kill me if she sees me on Crimewatch.'

'She won't, you're out of sight. I'll leave my door open.' Finn threw his empty can into the bin, flexed his fingers, clenched his fists in the large pocket of his hoody and smashed them together on his way past dating couples. He tilted his head forward, keeping his eyes fixed on Wade, then drew his fists from his pocket.

Keith leapt out in front of him. 'Don't do this. If you do, you're no better than he is.'

'He needs to pay,' Finn bawled, bursting with rage. 'I don't have a choice.'

'Yes you do. Please get in the car, and I'll take you home.'

'*Home*. Funny.' Images of Mace being tortured flashed through Finn's mind, causing a single tear to get the better of him. He wiped it on his sleeve. 'Go back to your fancy *home* and enjoy your time with your nice *cosy* family. Charlotte and the kids must be missing you. What are you even doing here? Soz, I forgot, you don't give a flying fuck about me – you need a singer for your stupid girly band.'

Keith folded his arms, looking genuinely wounded. 'Nobody's lives are perfect, no matter how good or how fortunate people seem on the outside. You can have a dig at mine all you want. It's far from perfect, but I'm not leaving here without you.'

Finn stepped forward. 'You don't even know me, but you turn up at my gaff like we've known each other years. Is there something wrong with you? Are you roofed in right?'

'You're drunk, you're angry and you brought me here under false pretences, so I'm sorry. I know you're hurting. I get it, more than you'll ever know, but I can't stand here and watch you ruin your whole life. He's not worth it. Please. Would Mace want you to do this? Would your parents? I highly doubt it.'

'Fuck would you know? You don't know 'em. You don't know me. Mace was about to help me audition for that same competition you're entering. He wanted us to take the world on. Now shift.'

Keith held his arm out in front of Finn. 'You still can. My band and I can help you achieve whatever it is you want. All I'm saying is revenge doesn't have to be administered by you. You may feel like a winner for a few hours if you go through with this, but in the long run you'll end up a loser just like them. What goes around comes around.'

Finn continued striding onward, glaring at Wade, knowing he could've pushed Keith aside easily enough and gone through with it, but deep down he was right. He climbed back into the Picasso and left the door open, choosing not to speak, but as soon as Keith sat beside him and started the engine, he dived out, slamming the door behind him.

'Wait!' Keith said, opening the passenger window. 'I don't know you, and perhaps I shouldn't have come, but I had this overwhelming urge to. Standing on the outside looking in, you need a change in direction, and it seems Mace and I are in complete agreement. This competition could be just the opportunity you need. If I was you, I'd give it my best shot, but who am I?'

'I know who you're not,' Finn said, walking away.

Keith sighed and climbed out. 'Understood. I won't *stalk* you, as you put it. It's your life, and it's entirely up to you what you do with it, but you have raw talent within you. Believe me, I know talent when I hear it. Your voice is out of this world, and with the right guidance, you could make a life for yourself and those around you which many of us only ever get to dream of. By the way, I'm getting a takeaway from there and I'll sit here and eat it, so don't get any daft ideas about returning, or I'll phone the police. Good night, Finn. I'm truly sorry about Mace, I am. I sincerely hope he pulls through.'

***

Marc sprang up in the mirror at three a.m. dressed in a sky-blue suit with matching glossy lipstick, waving a white feather boa to grab Finn's attention. His teeth gleamed, and glittery silver stars lit up his cheerful face. 'Would you mind if I shunted this a little?' he asked with his hands on the glass. 'Only fleeting flashes of red, orange and yellow within your central nervous system, but no green. Negative thoughts could lead us towards the land of nothingness. Tell me you still feel the universe lurking beneath your indigenous hair?'

'I don't have any hair,' Finn sobbed, setting one pillow on top of another before rolling onto his side. A much stronger scent of gardenias filled his nostrils.

Marc reached across and laid his feather boa across Finn's shins, plucking his mam's pen from his sock drawer. 'I see your day hasn't been the most fruitful. In fact, one might say your journey has taken a downward turn since we last spoke and you're in need of a helping hand. I'm a superb listener, you know.'

'Why does everyone want to help me? Why now?'

Finn wiped tears from his face with the palm of his hand. 'And what are you doing with my mam's pen? Put it back.'

'Are you actually going to use it?'

'Go away. I'm tired of fighting.'

Marc placed it gently on the chest of drawers and loosened his necktie. 'All humans suffer, but surely it's best to find meaning in the suffering rather than suffer in silence.'

'You can't help me. Nobody can. Please leave me alone, Marc. I'm goosed. Feels like I've only just nodded off. *One* might say I've had nothing but bad luck since you showed up.'

'No need to be facetious. Guessing you chose to exist, then?'

Finn buried his head beneath his pillows. 'Just do one.'

'No can do, I'm afraid.' Marc bopped on the spot. 'I am void of all negativities, you see. Pure positivity, me. It's Mace, isn't it? It's fine by me if you need to let it out and have a good cry. I shan't judge. Boys don't cry enough.'

'Don't think I'd stop. Found out tonight his girlfriend's three months pregnant. His mam blames me for what happened to him. He was about to turn his back on that life. He wanted to help me change mine.'

'Please come out of hiding. Everything you require to change your life is within you. You must find those who can help draw out the best in you by learning to trust them.'

Finn threw his pillows in Marc's direction and sat on the edge of his bed in his boxers. 'Them animals tortured Mace. They put him in a coma, and now he's rigged up to monitors with tubes and cables hanging out everywhere.

What if he ends up paralysed? What if he doesn't pull through? He's the only mate I've got.'

'So not true. I'm your friend.'

Finn shrugged. 'But you're not real.'

'I find truth to be much stranger than fiction. Every life is a journey. Every journey once recorded is a story. Each story has a beginning, middle and end. If it wasn't for your imagination, you'd still be swinging from tree to tree. How can you live a fulfilled life if you don't understand who you really are or how you came to be?'

'Men and women have accidents. That's how I came to be. Drunken nights with no protection. Why would anyone want to start a family in this painful world on purpose? I don't get it. Why are you here? Why am I here? I never asked to be born.'

'Neither did seven billion others, yet here we are. Have you heard the story about the Magnesium Gurus?'

Finn shook his head.

'The Magnesium Gurus were a tremendous teenage rock band, who lived not too far from here, as it goes. They won Sothis Media's last UK-wide competition, Rock Heaven, in 1977, but shortly after hearing about the tragic and untimely death of Marc Bolan, their lead singer, Daniel Saunders, passed away during their afterparty on Bournemouth beach.'

'See. More pain. More suffering.'

'The poor lad drowned. Rumour has it he didn't feel like he belonged to this world anymore either.'

'What are you trying to say? Stop looking at me like that. I'd never do that.'

Marc folded his arms. 'Anyhow, the Magnesium

Gurus' lead guitarist, Daniel's best friend, vanished shortly after his funeral and the band lost their trophy and the recording contract they'd worked so hard to win. All rewards went to the Narcissists, who finished runner-up in the competition.'

'What's that gotta do with me?'

'It's so easy to become caught up in the physicalities of life when showering in harmful chemicals and artificial light. As you say, heartache and pain unavoidably occur along life's winding path towards truth, and that's why every individual story is crucial. We take our feelings with us in our hearts and minds but leave hard copies behind to help others. This isn't the first time you've questioned your own life. Mace wanted to give his all, so you would too. All or nothing. Tell me, when you look in the mirror, what do you see?'

'A deep '70s fashion victim.'

Marc laughed. 'Look through me – past me, even. Do you see hope? Do you feel a burning love? Do you have a craving to stop the suffering? Be conscious of this each time you look in the mirror. Learn to trust yourself.' He boogied on the spot. 'Now tell me: who is it you've always wanted to be?'

Finn wrapped himself up in his duvet. 'Like I said, I'm nobody. Always will be. Right now, I just want to sleep. What do *you* want?'

'I want you to be brave. I want you to believe in yourself. I want to see your true colours shining through. Have you jotted down any of your thoughts and feelings? Freedom is within, and poetry is a fantastic way to release negative energy.'

'I've done *some*.'

'Groovy. Please try writing with your mother's pen. There are no limits to what you can achieve. If you wish to make this planet a brighter place, take a look at yourself and reshape. Have you had a gander through your friend's bag yet?' he asked, gawping at Keith's rucksack. 'You were very harsh on him.'

'No, I wasn't. He's not my friend. He's like everyone else.' Finn gripped Keith's rucksack, dropped it into his bin and dived onto his bed. 'He'll get my hopes up, then leave.'

'I beg to differ. He's rather fond of you, and he's right. Simply because someone looks happy and in control of their own life on the outside does not mean they are feeling like that on the inside. This you know to be true. As for being cursed and the bearer of bad luck, I must agree with him once more. It's absolute nonsense. With your permission, may I please exit altogether and find a suitable seat? I have the perfect surprise for you.'

Finn didn't know what to expect and kept one eye open. 'Do what you want.'

'Let's lighten the load.' Marc exited the glass with his acoustic guitar and positioned Finn's foldaway chair in the centre of the room. He took a seat and slipped off his sky-blue ballet shoes. 'Ready? Those who have ears, let them hear. Having one either side of your orb unites us intimately through vibration. Listen carefully to my voice. One. Two. Three.' Strumming his guitar with a clear crystal pick, he sang 'Half the World Away' by Oasis.

Finn wiped tears from his face and sat up, wanting to thank Marc, but he'd already left. 'Are you still there? You never told me what happened to the lead guitarist.'

'Why don't you peek in his bag and find out? But be warned. Your new journey will have begun, and what will be, will be.'

Finn leapt from his bed, switched on his lamp, dragged Keith's rucksack from the bin, unzipped it and pulled out the first book he grabbed: *Bolan: The Rise and Fall of a Twentieth Century Superstar* by Mark Paytress. Gobsmacked to find Marc on the back surrounded by nature, he read the blurb and had a quick flick through before turning it over.

'Do you like my feather boa?' Marc asked, seated in the mirror.

Finn jumped back. 'You're Marc Bolan?'

'I am indeed. Rock 'n' roll comes from the soul. I don't do normal. Never have. Normal is primitive. Normal is boring.'

'That's mental,' Finn said, smiling. He sipped his bottle of water, screwed the top on and stared at him. 'Why are you in my dreams?'

'Well, we have touched on physical recordings. Brace yourself for what's truly mental. Minds are split into three tiers of consciousness, and humans can be susceptible to all three without realising. The orb of animation is very much like an aeroplane's black box. It develops early in most vertebrate species, storing collective accounts of our previous lives and our present-day personal journeys, which primitive conscious egos seek to suppress. Societal stress and trauma cloud over them, causing many to shrink, and some vanish altogether, denying us illustrious adventures. However, music, visions, voices, signs and symbols from our memories trickle through our orb and are then transported via platelet crests and troughs in the bloodstream. If impaired under immense pressure, circadian rhythms flip the ship upside down, causing internal floods of mixed messages, triggering considerable distress. Night becomes day, day becomes night, and our voices are passed off as symptoms of our mental afflictions. Frustrating, to say the least, but meeting beneath routine melatonin cloaks of darkness is our safest method of communication, salvaging said voyages.'

'Just so you know, that went in one ear and out the other.'

'What I said was, I would very much love to help convert the built-up negativity you have working its way through your body of late, if you allow me. Too much stress can be catastrophic. Your sleep pattern has been disrupted, meaning this nautical trip shall be brief. The longer I'm here, the more time we have to steer you from the rocks and get you ready.'

'For what?'

'Love Is the Drug, of course. Life's all about internal and external waves. I remember recording my debut single "The Wizard" with the Ladybirds in '65. The feeling stays with you forever; so too when meeting Telegram Sam and his relatable feline, Flute, in Paris. The wizard knows why we laugh and cry, why we live and why we die. We play upon his golden shores, till the day we bang on his magic door.' Marc grinned. 'Although we've had a minor setback with your inner spectrum, revolutions often begin in bed. Rest. You have much to absorb in a short space of time, so back to the question in hand. Would you like my help?'

Finn nodded. 'Please, yes. Soz for being a—'

'Finding one's true self is difficult. Remembering and keeping true to oneself even more so. This shall not be easy, and you mustn't attempt to do this alone.'

'But I am alone. If I wasn't, I wouldn't be talking to you.' Finn emptied the remaining items from Keith's rucksack onto his bed and made two separate piles, one relating to the Magnesium Gurus and the other to Marc and T. Rex.

'Like I said, you were very harsh. Our time starts now. I'm off to call in on Ringo. Good night, Finn. Please, no more excessive amounts of alcohol, but much more feel-good music, and if you can, get some natural sunlight, preferably as it dawns and sets.'

'I'll try. Night, Marc, and thanks.' Finn read the first few pages of *Bolan*, listened to Keith's T. Rex CDs with his headphones on and read newspaper articles relating to the Magnesium Gurus' rise and fall, regretting everything he had said to Keith. He got the sad parts of both stories out of the way first, running through photos of Bournemouth beach and Barnes Common before watching documentaries on his laptop, hearing from some of Marc's friends and family. While reading about the circumstances of Marc's death, goose pimples sprang up all over him. He found it fascinating how both Marc and Daniel had started off as poets, writing about their emotions, alternate dimensions and out-of-body experiences.

Marc's self-assurance and passion for life inspired Finn enough to watch his interview on *The Russell Harty Show*. When Russell asked, 'Do you ever wake up in the middle of the night and think, in another twenty or thirty years I'm going to be fifty, or sixty, what shall I be doing?', Marc shook his head and replied, 'I don't think I'll live that long.'

***

Finn spent the following week running through his vocal exercises, jotting down his feelings in his journal using his mam's pen, and reading about the Magnesium Gurus and T. Rex in between visits to Mace in the ICU. He'd moved on to his next book: *Cosmic Dancer: The Life and Music of Marc Bolan* by Paul Roland, and not only did Marc's life interest him, it drew him in like a magnet. Planning to arrive at Bennett and Jake's music store on Saturday around 10.30 a.m. to apologise to Keith and get a feel for his band, he grabbed his bus pass, shot downstairs and legged it to his front door.

'Where are you off to?' his dad bawled. 'I've made a brew. We need a chat.'

'*You* want to talk. Right this minute. Haven't got time. I need to be somewhere.'

'Sit. I'll make it quick.'

Finn exhaled and sat with his elbows on the table, swigging his tea. His dad hadn't said a word to him all week, and he'd never once asked about Mace. 'Talk, then.'

'I'll be away for a couple of days from Monday. I told you about the redundancies at work; well, I had a meeting Thursday. The same position as mine has cropped up if I'm willing to relocate. The job's in Glasgow.'

'You might move to Scotland?'

'No, son, *we* might move to Scotland. Our piece-of-shit landlord wants us out. My boss said it'd be no problem getting you a start. We'll be working together.'

Finn's jaw dropped. 'Are you real? It's bad enough living together.'

'Why? We could make a good team, you and me.'

'Have you taken a bang to the head? Teams talk to each other. We don't. Anyway, I'll be fine. I'll kip at Mace's. Like you said, I have a good job. Hope you get yours. I need to go.'

Finn's dad leapt to his feet and slammed his fists on the table. 'What's wrong with you? We must stick together. That's what your mam wanted.'

'Was it? I think you're lying. Sure, she'd have wanted me to choose my own path, but you want me to be just like you. I've told you before. Why won't it sink in? I decide what's best for me from now on, not you.'

'You think life's a breeze, don't you? You've got it all planned. You don't know shit. If I get this job for us, it'll be the best opportunity you'll ever get in life.'

'How the fuck do you work that out? There's no way I'm ending up like you. Bed, biscuit factory, Labour Club, then back to bed. What kind of life's that? What kind of dad pushes *that* life on his only child? Sad is what it is.' Finn backed off, unbolting the front door. 'You died the same day Mam did. You just haven't realised it yet.'

'How dare you!' Finn's dad dragged him backwards, slammed the door shut and looked down on him as he tripped over his own feet, hitting his face on the banister upstand.

'Truth hurt, does it?' Finn wiped blood from his cheek. 'Now I get why she left.'

'Stop. No. It wasn't like that.' Finn's dad tried to help him up. 'Let me see what I've done. I'm so sorry. Son, I never meant to hurt you.'

'Get off, you prick.' Finn grappled with his dad, pushing

him away. Tempted to retaliate further, he grabbed a tissue off the mantlepiece and dabbed his wound before leaving.

'Son, wait,' his dad wailed. 'Come back. Don't leave like this. Said I'm sorry.'

Finn dived on the 192 up Stockport Road and dashed through Piccadilly, arriving at his destination just after eleven a.m. He smirked at the newly graffitied BJ's sign as well as dildos and gimp masks in neighbouring shop windows. Guzzling a can of Red Bull, he watched the shop assistant through the window twisting and twirling along the aisles to the sound of 'Kiss' by Prince before he pushed the door open, setting off the bell.

'Hi there. Anything in particular you are after? An ambulance, maybe?'

'It's not as bad as it looks. I fell.' Finn pointed to a large sign sprayed above the door which read *AUDITIONS*. 'What's their band like? Had many decent—?'

'No. No. Not happening,' an older bloke sneered with a proper attitude. He bowled over from the back door on crutches with a plaster cast, plucking at the neatly trimmed doughnut duster around his gob. 'What're you doing here?'

Finn bit his lip and pulled out his audition flyer, holding it up at arm's length.

'Keith give you that, did he? He must think I'm completely stupid. No offense, but auditions finished ten minutes ago. As soon as he gets back, I'll let him know you called.'

A lad nearer Finn's age rolled in wearing a *Planet of the Apes* T-shirt and a crazy multicoloured bucket hat. 'How much have you smoked, Bennett? Keith's in the back room, you lying bumboclaat. I'm Jake. You're the guy from the Church. Ignore my dickhead half brother. Bust his other foot if you want. He called you a midget.'

Bennett stormed into the back, barging past Jake. 'Oggy, we need a meeting ASAP. I'll pull the plug. Keith,' he yelled, 'you've got a lot of explaining to do.'

Jake steered Finn through the store away from Farooq's come-to-bed eyes and out back to the rehearsal room. 'This could get wild. Do you smoke skunk? Got some top shit.'

'Did someone shout me?' Keith's eyes lit up the moment Finn popped his head through the door. 'What happened to your face? Sorry, where are my manners? This is the boss, Oggy, on drums. Jake plays a variety of instruments, I think, and going off all the shouting, I guess you've met Bennett. Him and I are guitarists. He's on bass. I play lead.'

Bennett rolled a joint, grunting at Keith. Oggy leapt from behind his drums, banging his head on the light, and Finn checked out their cool instruments and overall band set-up before focusing on the artwork. 'This is mint. You do this? It's class.'

'Cheers, mate. You've gotta join us. You can't let me knock about with the piss-and-shit-your-pants brigade on my own. I need someone to have a buzz with.'

'This weekend's auditions are over,' Bennett barked. 'He's late. I'm having none of it. What happened to my conditions? We agreed.' He pointed at Keith. 'You planned this.'

'They hardly know each other,' Oggy howled. 'Calm down before you keel over. I dropped flyers off in loads of pubs as well as taxi wanks and takeaways in Levenshulme.'

'Can't beat a good taxi wank,' Jake replied, laughing and making Finn grin.

'Anyone listening to me? Auditions are over. Rehearsals are starting. Come back next week within the timeframe written on the flyer if you think you're good enough to perform with us. You can leave through the back like the rest.'

'Fine by me.'

'Finn, wait.' Keith rolled his eyes at Oggy, then him, before dashing through the door to the back yard. 'Stick the kettle on, Jake. Back in a mo.'

'You expect me to sing with that dick?' Finn yelled, pointing. 'What's his problem?'

'Take a breath. He'll come around. Oggy will be reprimanding him as we speak. I didn't know Bowden tried getting you to unblock the toilets because you were late.'

'The old bastard called me a boomtown rat as well, whatever that is.'

Keith sang 'I Don't Like Mondays' with real passion. 'Apologies. It's one of my favourites. Well done for standing up to him. We need someone who won't take off and quit if things become difficult. I have a few contacts. I can help you get a new job.'

'You show up at my door waving a flyer in my face when we've never even spoke on site, wanting me to join your band. You threaten to call the police on me. Now you want to help find me a job. Why?' Finn asked. 'Do I look like some deadbeat charity case?'

'Of course not. Please keep it down. I want you to join our band, but I'm willing to help you find a job whether you audition or not. I dug a giant hole with this competition, and I need help to find my way back out. Sorry if I crossed the line. I take it back.'

Finn rolled up his flyer, avoiding eye contact. 'This is well weird. I'm grateful. It's just I'm not used to people wanting to help. Listen, soz about the other week. What I said and that. I was angry; I'd had too much to drink. I'm shit scared of cars. I never get in 'em, especially with strangers.'

Keith leant against the drainpipe with a puzzled look on his face.

'I didn't mean it like that. Been thinking about what you said.' He crushed his empty can of Red Bull with his hand and launched it into the nearest bin bag, glaring at the tarmac. 'I'm no good at saying what I want to say. Thanks for stopping me doing something stupid. If it wasn't for you, I'd probably be in hospital now or in the pen. Been going through your stuff. I've looked after it, but my head's bursting with the rise and fall of the Magnesium Gurus and T. Rex. Soz about what happened to your best friend. You were right about me needing a change in direction. And cheers for what you said about my talent. The last thing I want is to let you down, but I need time to get my head around what happened to Mace and stuff that's going on at home,' he said, pointing to his cut cheek. 'That's why I'm late. Truth is, I don't think I was ready to audition today anyway. I might not be ready next week.'

'You got that at home? Do you live in a zoo?'

Finn shook his head. 'Me and my dad argued and it got out of hand. I fell. The last few years have been one great big car crash.'

'What did your mother have to say about you and your dad fighting?'

'She wasn't home.'

Keith paced the yard, scratching his chin, then the back of his neck, and didn't speak for a full minute. 'Our final auditions are next Saturday. We've moved it to the afternoon so we can rehearse more in the morning. I won't lie to you. I doubt we'll find someone with better vocals than you.' He rested his hands on Finn's shoulders, receiving a dirty look, then removed them right away. 'Sorry. If you audition and all goes well, it'll be hard going, but if you promise to be on your best behaviour – no arguing, no fighting and no being late – then I promise to help you work towards a better future. New surroundings might help take your mind off home and Mace's condition too. How is he, by the way?'

'Still in a coma.'

'Sorry to hear that. I'm sure he'll pull through.'

Finn received a text off his dad, apologising. 'Like I said, I need to sort stuff out. Do you mind if I ask where you went in '77? The papers said you just vanished.'

'Another time, maybe. It's complicated and very long winded,' Keith whispered, kicking the gravel. 'All I will say is this. One minute we had the world at our feet, and the next, we lost everything. Between you and me, before Daniel died, he told me he didn't belong. I don't want you to feel that way, but to be a part of something, you must first find enough self-confidence to give it a shot. Look, thanks for showing up and being honest. It's now down to you. My hands will be tied. Be here at half-past two on the dot one week today if you wish to live, or don't show up at all and therefore choose to exist.'

FIVE

Saturday, August 20th, 2011 - 11:00

Keith watched Finn vanish from his sights along Tib Street, unsure whether he'd done enough to convince him to return. Love Is the Drug would provide him, Oggy and Bennett with a second chance to put their shame to bed, but for Finn, the opportunity seemed more of an escape route from a life Keith knew nothing much about.

'Is he coming back?' Farooq asked, singing along to Dolly Parton's '9 to 5' with his rainbow-coloured wristbands on, having left Bennett's CDs neat and tidy. 'Earth to Keith.'

'Sorry. I certainly hope so.' Keith jammed his hands under his armpits and dug his elbows deep into the countertop, psyching himself up to give Bennett a piece of his mind.

'Well,' Oggy whispered, planting a bottle of water in front of him, 'why do you think hardly anyone showed up? I only sent a handful of flyers out. I assumed this was a done deal. Is he coming to audition next week, yes or no?'

'My gut instincts say he will.' Keith checked over his shoulder to make sure Bennett wasn't listening. 'Please, Oggy, back off a little. The poor kid's going through hell at the moment. His best friend is critical in hospital from a beating, he's just lost his job, and on top of that he has significant issues at home, which need addressing pronto.'

'Everyone has issues. Look at us lot. It's called life. I should've spoken to him myself. Why didn't he ask any questions?'

'He didn't exactly have time to speak with Bennett hounding him. Look, the last thing Finn needs right now are strangers breathing down his neck, trying to turn him into something he may not want to be. He knows where we are. We mustn't spook him.'

'Karaoke nights it is, then. What did you expect? We have no choice but to broaden our horizons. We can't start a band and enter a tribute competition with no vocalist. Does Finn know we want him to become Marc Bolan? Going off his face and baggage, there's a strong chance he's locked up next week or lying in a hospital bed beside his best pal.'

Keith necked most of his water. 'He knows, and I was hoping to have him sewn up before speaking to Charlotte. Can't we hold off for one more week, please? Don't do this.'

'Sorry, Keith. Bennett's going off his nut. One hurdle from three – or was it four? – simply isn't good enough. Plan B.' Oggy's jaw dropped when Bennett's bass shook the walls and windows during his rendition of 'Come Together' by the Beatles. 'Something to be cheerful for, I suppose. Can you feel that groove beneath your skin? Without a great bass player, there is no band. No roll in the rock, no rhythm in the blues, so do not mention Finn and antagonise him further. If he brings it up, stick to our story.' He took off, heading for the heart of Bennett's blatant tones.

'Bye, then.' Keith finished his bottle and had just stepped out back for some fresh air when Jake ambushed him, putting an end to his unfavourable thoughts about Finn's predicament.

'Bennett said he heard noises coming from Oggy's cellar the night of Daniel's reunion, and now Oggy just asked for details of my dating site.' Jake paced the yard in circles with just a pair of grubby tracksuit bottoms on, first clockwise, then counterclockwise. 'Last night I had gruesome nightmares. That kinky blurt stabbed my dates to death. All black women.'

'You're being ridiculous. How many times? Oggy isn't racist.'

'So he could be a murderer?'

Keith leant on the drainpipe, mystified by Jake's behaviour. 'Put some shoes on, you'll cut your feet. I need to set my rig up. I need a brew.' The thuds stopped. He popped his head in to find Bennett in a chirpier mood, fiddling with his amplifier, and waved him over.

'Can't you see I'm busy?' Bennett sighed and placed his inky Music Man Stingray electric bass guitar on its stand before hobbling over. 'Can't wait to hear you play after all these years. What've you done to him?' he asked, pointing at Jake.

'Oh no. This is your doing. When you slept at Oggy's the night of Daniel's reunion, did you hear noises in his cellar, yes or no? Jake reckons he's about to introduce a serial killer to his dating site.'

Jake parked his backside on the dustbin. 'What about the knife? Tell him, go on,' he said, blowing smoke in the air. 'We found a bloodstained knife in his dining room cupboard wrapped in a tea towel when we helped him have a clear-out two weeks ago. We think he—'

'No, no, no. Not we, *you*.'

'I think Rudy's decomposing under his floorboards. What if he threw his carpets and furniture out because they were caked in blood? We found a big black dildo as well. How can he say I'm numb? Why didn't that set alarm bells off with his mucky Mrs?'

'Please, Jake, no more now. This needs to stop. Sort yourself out and let's get on with it. I need to get some real riffs going. For the last time, Oggy isn't racist.'

'Who's racist?' Oggy towered above Keith and Bennett. 'We've got a lot to get through. Jake, grab your laptop. We need to download the relevant tabs. Follow Bennett's example. I want nothing less than hard graft and commitment. And put a top on; I've seen more meat on a butcher's pencil.' He helped Bennett inside.

The foul sofa went, along with heaps of junk, to the tip. Jake swept the outskirts of their new rehearsal area, mopping the more visible laminated floor, and stored his spray cans and dustsheets neatly in large crates. He crossed his legs on the meditation cushion behind his bongos and, as a band, they set up their equipment precisely where and how Oggy wanted it – Keith up top, Jake behind and slightly to his right, Bennett to his left, and Oggy to the rear, surrounded by his fiery Mapex Black Panther Velvetone drum kit.

'From now on, playtime is officially over. We don't yet have a vocalist, and regardless of what Bennett believes, Finn showing up earlier was nothing more than a coincidence. If he returns, he must audition like everybody else, and I'll hear no more about it. The rest of today is about us. If we put in a shit performance, we'll be a laughing stock and none of us will be able to show our faces in town again. You all know I'm firm but fair, and my job is to prepare this band for Love Is the Drug. Any issues with me running the show, speak now. Right, then. Bennett, are you happy with Keith and our new vocalist – if we find one – being out front soaking up every ounce of the crowd's attention?'

'Yes, boss. Cool with it. Just glad to play my part and bind our tribute band together. It's what us bass players do. All about the groove.'

Keith wanted to throw up. 'Out of curiosity, how are we judging the auditionees?'

'Why did only three turn up? Are you sure you posted the flyers?'

'Calling me a liar, Bennett? Didn't think so.' Oggy rummaged through his pockets, pulling out his notepad. 'We'll each fill in my tick list, then narrow it down. It's quite simple, really. White. Tick. Young. Tick. Slim build. Tick. Powerful voice. Tick. Done.'

'We can't use that,' Jake yelled, gesturing to Keith and Bennett. 'It's discrimination.'

Keith stuck up for him. 'Didn't sound the best, if I'm honest.'

'I don't get what all the fuss is about. Marc Bolan was white, young, he had a slim build until he hit the hard stuff. And he had a powerful voice.'

'I'm with Jake on this one,' Bennett added. 'You sound like David Duke before he set fire to large crosses and marched through the streets ranting against freedom and equality. Who's next on your hit list – women, LGBTQ, those with mental health issues?'

Oggy stood and tore up his piece of paper. 'Right. No tick lists. That okay? Glad to hear it. Hang on. Was it me you were talking about outside? Going forward, can I just make it abundantly clear I am not racist, nor am I a white supremacist in the Ku Klux Klan. Enough. We've heard Bennett play this morning, bringing much-needed pleasure to our ears, so Keith, let's kick off with one of your chosen favourites to see where you're at, and we'll join in. Don't worry if you're a bit rusty; take it nice and slow. Jake, easy on those instruments, and don't be afraid to chop and change. "Hotel California", here we go.'

Keith tripped over his amplifier cables and knocked his seat, sending his tabs flying. 'Apologies,' he said, gathering them together. 'Nearly there.'

'It's okay, we'll come back to you in a sec. Bennett, give us one of your favourites. Jake, join in on me. Keith, when you're ready.'

Bennett extinguished his joint and put on his red-and-white skull bandana. He set up his own microphone stand and performed 'Under Pressure' by David Bowie and Queen, giving Keith a cheeky wink. Oggy and Jake sat in awe, paying keen attention to Bennett's bass and surprisingly good vocals before entering the fray, whereas Keith neglected to chip in.

Farooq strolled in on his break, gobsmacked, impersonating a model from one of those fancy catwalks in Milan, and twirled on the spot, striking a confident pose. 'Benny, what a performance.'

'Wasn't it just?' Oggy high-fived him. 'We didn't know

you could sing. At this rate, you might end up playing and singing up top on your jack.'

Keith plugged in, raring to go, and struck the first chord on his Stratocaster, dying to put Bennett back in his box for the way he'd treated Finn. Nothing else in the world mattered. His bandmates joined in, but Keith's fingers weren't tough enough to generate sufficient electricity within him. The warm-hearted feeling they'd collectively bounced off one another in 1977 had gone astray. He froze, and his guitar didn't feel like it belonged to him. 'Sorry, Oggy. Still needs minor adjustments. The break knocked me sideways.'

Bennett had a childish smirk on his face.

'It's fine, Keith. Happens to us all. Degradation of small muscles and skills over time, that's all it is. Practice makes perfect. You might want to rehearse more at home, though, to get back in the swing of things. We sounded like four cats pissing in the same tin just then. Jake, ditch the bongos. From now on, you'll be mixing it up on shakers, cymbals and tambourine. If you listen, I promise to transform you into a fantastic percussionist.'

Keith struggled to master several songs that afternoon but refused to take a break.

'I hate seeing you like this,' Daniel said, lifting the hairs on Keith's arms. 'This ain't just a blip. My mam gave you a gift – throw that pesky guitar in the skip.'

Oggy checked his watch. 'Blimey. Doesn't time fly when you're having fun? Keith, don't forget to take your instrument home. Keith, are you listening? Finger exercises five times a day. And go back to basics. Save your favourite songs for future rehearsals once you're back up to speed.'

'If you need any extra schooling, Keith, call me,' Bennett said. 'Happy to help. Oggy, we done? Dirty dick has a date.'

Keith refused to bite.

'Another!' Oggy threw a navy wig from a box at Jake. 'What's her name?'

'Deborah.' Bennett wrapped his hands around his own throat behind Oggy's back, pretending to strangle himself, but Jake didn't find it amusing and flipped him the finger. 'Does she look like a zebra? Think I've seen a couple of her homemade movies. Debbie does Droylsden, Debbie does Didsbury. Don't be bringing her back here.'

'I won't be bringing anyone back,' Jake snapped, shaking his tambourine at Bennett. 'After arguing with Ronny on the phone last night, *he* had his fat hairy hands down his trolleys on the couch watching *Saturday Night Fever*.'

'Wait till this cast's off. Hope she's twenty stone with three heads and twelve kids.' Bennett gripped one of his crutches till his knuckles whitened and swung it at Jake, missing his chin by millimetres, before trudging to the kitchen in a huff.

'When do we get to meet Ronny? Hello? Okay, ignore me. Right, let's wrap it up there for today. You two, listen up. We obviously have a lot of work to do and can't rely on auditionees showing up, so we must scout a karaoke night or two this coming week. A boozer close by has karaoke on Wednesday night and we're all attending, no ifs, no buts.'

Keith grabbed his flat cap and coat. 'That's just great.'

'Problem? The only way we're going to progress further in this competition, guys, is if we stick together and keep pulling in the same direction. Capisce?'

***

The world passed Keith by at great speed through Oggy's car window. Unable to halt his thoughts from racing during his journey home, he pictured Daniel drifting away from Bournemouth beach alone, followed by Finn fleeing from BJ's, both doing their best to escape him.

'What's up?' Oggy asked, parking outside Keith's house. He pulled up his handbrake.

'Nothing,' Keith replied, unclipping his seatbelt. 'It's been a delightful day.'

Oggy sighed. 'I get you're frustrated, but you had a long break, Keith. You know yourself it's not like riding a bike. I'm sorry if this comes across as harsh, but you threw down the gauntlet to Clifford, so you need to get your head in the game if we're to compete in this competition. It doesn't matter how good you were in the past. You need to find your spark again and fast. It's in there somewhere. Daniel and Finn aren't here. We need you.'

'Is that right? Didn't exactly sound like that earlier. Don't for one minute think Bennett's offer to help was sincere. Did you see him winking and rubbing it in?'

'Look, we both know he can be a prat, but you've always ignored him before. What's so different this time? It's not just him, is it?'

Keith shook his head. 'It's Finn. Did I do enough? It's Daniel. We both know I didn't do enough, but I haven't jammed alongside another vocalist since … you know. It's Clifford. At this rate, his nephew's band will destroy us, but mainly it's Charlotte. We both know the first thing she's going to say when I come clean about what we're up to.'

'Stop overthinking things. Tell her the truth.' Oggy's eyes locked on to him. 'We have no control over Finn's choices, so it's pointless worrying about him at present. Didn't your shrink teach you that? Think I'll grab myself a spicy takeaway and a bottle of fresh orange on my way home. Maybe sit and chat to some wonderful women online.'

Keith knew he'd changed the subject on purpose, but he took the bait regardless and perked up, switching off the radio. 'Well done. Did Jake give you his dating site details?'

'He didn't, no. Something very odd about that lad. He kept asking why I wanted to go on there. Is he really that numb? I've been chatting to a gracious lady on a different site, and we're getting on really well, but I'm nervous about my speech impediment.'

'Have you spoken to her on the phone yet? Well, that's your next step. Exchange numbers. It won't be an issue.'

Oggy tapped his fingers on the steering wheel. 'I'm afraid of it going tits up.'

'Join the club. Could be worse. Did you hear the one about the schizophrenic bloke? A single lady asked if he was seeing anyone. He said, you mean like a therapist or hallucinations?' Keith climbed out, grabbed his guitar off the back seat and moseyed up the driveway, listening to Oggy chuckle. 'Oh, by the way, Jake thinks you murdered Judy.'

'That little— Listen, don't dwell on Finn or Daniel tonight, do you hear? And tell Charlotte. Sooner the better. What was it Daniel used to say? "If the light of love is meant to glow, the universe shall make it so." Have a good night.'

'Daddy, Daddy, there's a trip to Chester Zoo near Christmas. Can I go?' Helen asked, flying through the door. 'All my friends are going. I want to see the chimpanzees. Please, Daddy. Mummy said yes.'

'Dreams' by Fleetwood Mac was playing in the kitchen. 'No, I did not, you little fibber,' Charlotte shouted. 'The table's set. Tea's in about forty-five minutes.'

Keith closed the front door and placed his guitar in the cupboard under the stairs. 'Go play. I'll have a chat with your mum in a minute.'

'Thanks, Daddy.' Helen kissed him on the cheek and dashed upstairs, singing.

Keith followed her and popped his head around David's bedroom door. 'Homework?'

'All done.'

'Proud of you, son.' Keith rubbed his chin, thinking about Oggy's stern words, and grabbed the loft bar, unhooking the lock before pulling the stepladders down. 'Don't come out of your rooms, guys. The loft ladders are down. Won't be long.' He switched on the light and climbed up, scurrying to the far end. In the corner, gathering dust, lay Daniel's hard black guitar case from 1977. Wiping off the muck, he gripped the handle, slid it into the open space and knelt with his hands by his sides and his eyes fixed firmly on the latches.

'Your mind will soon be all over the place,' Daniel murmured. 'Take my advice, Keith. Open the case.'

Lacking courage, Keith darted to the hatch, sneezing, and made his way downstairs.

'Where have you been? I phoned you three times to see what time you'd be home.'

'Sorry, love. You wouldn't believe how much stuff Oggy had to throw away. What are we on tonight? Smells wonderful,' he said, about to lift the lid of the casserole dish.

'Beef stew. Dumplings.' Charlotte shooed him away with her oven mitten. 'Oggy?'

'Kind of coping. Too early to say. Just needs his friends for a while longer, I think.'

She stopped bopping while chopping carrots. 'Had some really sad news earlier. You remember Alf, who'd quietly watch the entire world pass him by through the window whenever you came to pick me up from work? He died this morning. Doris is grief stricken.'

'Don't know how you work there. You deserve a medal.'

'It's just the same—'

'As looking after us lot,' he said, completing her sentence. He opened the conservatory window to let some much-needed fresh air in and took a well-deserved rest in his wicker chair. Plucking polish and a clean cloth from the drawer, he cleaned Daniel's case.

'Would you like to tell me why you've snuck up to the loft and brought that filthy antique in here? We stored it out of sight for a specific reason, remember?'

Keith grimaced. 'I'll have you know, Daniel's vintage 1974 Gibson Les Paul Blue Sparkle cropped up in conversation earlier. I still haven't opened it since his mother gave it to me after his funeral.' He exhaled, unable to picture a positive outcome from the following discussion, but it had to begin, and he knew full well he had to word everything perfectly without hesitation. 'There's something I'd like to run by you.'

She dried her hands with the tea towel and sat opposite him, stirring the casserole sauce in a jug. 'Spit it out. You're worrying me.'

He crossed and uncrossed his arms. 'Remember that lad I mentioned the other week? Bowden sacked him for being late.'

'The boomtown rat,' she replied, giggling.

'Yes, him. He sang his little heart out at the Church the night of Daniel's reunion. His name's Finn, and he reminded me so much of Daniel on stage. Boy, does he transform. Breathtaking. You should've heard him, honey. He blew everybody away.'

'What does this have to do with Daniel's guitar?'

Keith stopped fidgeting with the handle on the case. 'Oggy, Bennett and Jake are forming a T. Rex tribute band in memory of Daniel for Sothis Media's upcoming Love Is the Drug competition. They've asked if I'd join and help convince Finn to join too. Crazy, right?'

She stopped stirring.

'I said I'd speak to you first, but they've invited me to attend a couple of karaoke nights in town to help search for a decent vocalist in case Finn doesn't join. Oggy's just covering all bases, putting together a small rota. What do you think?'

'You already know what I think,' she said, throwing her tea towel at him. 'Oggy's single and he wants his wingman to get plastered with. I wasn't born yesterday. Besides, last time you went out with him, he nearly got you killed.'

'Oggy's weaning himself off the drink and doing well. This isn't about him. It's about me. The moment I heard

Finn sing, this long-lost flame reignited inside, and it felt like I was back on stage at Rock Heaven. There's a lucrative recording contract up for grabs, and I'd love to get my hands on the purple heart trophy again.'

Charlotte placed her hands on his. 'You haven't played in years. Are you still able? You have responsibilities, and don't give me that "we need the money" nonsense.'

'There're uncertain times ahead before Christmas. Might even be sooner. We've got Helen's trip to pay for now. That wasn't planned for.'

'Don't even. We've been through far worse financially. I'm more concerned with what happens if *you* need professional help again. Where were Oggy and Bennett then, hey? They need to stop filling your head with magic. Wait till I see them.'

'Oggy was there when I needed him. Bennett *still* doesn't know. I'm getting old, and a large part of me wants to do something worthwhile in memory of Daniel.'

'Do you even know Finn? Is the Church his local? Is he a thug?'

Keith sighed. 'His mates seemed a little rough around the edges, but it goes to show, you should never judge a book by its cover. People are too afraid to take a chance on youth nowadays, and I refuse to be one of them. Finn has the potential to become a real superstar.'

'Sorry, Keith. You can't go through with this. You need to tell them no. You're nowhere near up to it. Finn isn't Daniel – no matter how alike they are. People are going to get hurt, and it's most likely going to be us – again.'

He shook his head. 'But—'

'I don't want to see you end up so full of life one night if it means you're so down in the dumps the next. It's not healthy. This is why we have set routines. They work. Have you had any audible or visual hallucinations lately?'

'What? No! Nothing. I'd tell you.'

'Would you? I knew Oggy's reunion would be a huge mistake. Leaving the Magnesium Gurus didn't cause Daniel to commit suicide. His death was a tragic accident. The coroner said so. Let it go. Enjoy the rest of your life.'

Keith groaned. 'I know. I'm trying, but it's not that simple, love. You didn't see him gazing down at me on the beach. You didn't hear him. He said he didn't belong. He spoke about the waves and being free. "Life is all about the tree." Bolan hit a tree.'

'Enough. It was nothing but a coincidence; your therapist said so. We're your family, not Oggy, not Bennett, not Jake and definitely *not* Finn. We love you, so please don't join this band. I've never felt so helpless, seeing you in that state. I couldn't explain it back then and I wouldn't be able to explain it now, but one thing I do know is our marriage would not survive if it were to happen all over again. Hang on. Have you stopped taking your meds?'

'No. Don't be daft.'

'Well, something isn't right. Are me and the kids not enough for you?'

'So not fair.' Keith couldn't help torturing himself over what he did or didn't do regarding Daniel's death. 'Knew you wouldn't entertain it.' Scurrying to the kitchen, he switched the kettle on and gazed out of the window, imagining his life in ten years' time.

‘I’m sorry,’ she said, creeping up behind him. ‘Anything to do with Daniel’s death frightens me still. Your therapist said stress is a major factor. I’m begging you, don’t do this. Please promise me. It’ll all end in tears – ours. Remember what we lost.’

Keith’s eyes welled up. ‘How can I ever forget? I think about them every day.’

‘But still can’t talk to me about them?’

‘I wasn’t there for my family, and I have to live with that.’ A warm sensation worked its way up Keith’s spine when she ran her hand under his thin cotton T-shirt, tickling his back. He finished stirring his tea and spun to face her. ‘You know I don’t blame you. Never have, never will. It took so much out of us to bring David and Helen into this world. I just want them to be proud of us when they grow up.’

‘You have nothing to prove. They’ll always be proud of us.’ She held his hands in hers. ‘You saved their mum from punk rockers in ’77 at the campsite in Rhyl.’

He sighed. ‘And look at me now. How can I tell our kids to focus on what they enjoy doing when I’ve spent my whole adult life working on construction sites as part of my routine? I don’t want us to end up like Alf and blooming Doris. When Daniel died, maybe my dreams died with him, but with our old band getting back together, I thought it could somehow keep my dreams alive. You’re right – it’s silly. We’ve had an amazing holiday and I’m sleeping fine. Daniel used to say, “Without music, life would be a mistake.” I just hope saying no doesn’t end up being my biggest mistake yet.’

She kissed him on his cheek. ‘I know for a fact giving you my blessing to join this tribute band would be mine.’

***

Although guilt-ridden about lying to Charlotte, Keith couldn't bring himself to quit the band after everything he'd promised Finn. He made numerous calls to his contacts in the construction industry, and a promising one led him to visit a nearby site hoping to find Finn a job right away. The vacancy had unfortunately been filled, but the rushing around caused Keith to show up fifteen minutes late to meet Oggy, Bennett and Jake outside BJ's on an overcast Wednesday evening for their first karaoke scouting mission. 'Sorry I'm late – couldn't be helped,' he said, sweating. He threw his rucksack in before Jake dragged the roller shutter down. 'Which pub are we starting at?'

'The Beehive,' Bennett snapped. 'You'd have known if you'd bothered to show up on time. Been on the blower to Finn, have you?'

Keith wasn't sure if Bennett was joking, but before he had a chance to ask, Jake tugged at his coat and yanked his arm. 'Need to speak to you about something personal.'

'If it's more nonsense about Oggy being a racist, misogynistic murderer, then no.' Keith speeded up, only to be hauled back. 'Get off.'

'It's not, I promise,' Jake whispered. 'It's Bennett. I saw Farooq giving him a chew.'

'What's wrong with that? Bennett loves sweets.'

'For someone who works on a building site, you're a bit slow. A chew!' He gestured.

Keith held Jake's arms, wrenched them down by his sides and dropped back further. 'Whatever programmes you're watching, stop. Farooq is far too young for Bennett; besides, he has a partner, doesn't he?'

'Yeah – Ronny. I've heard him on the phone with him, but it could be anyone. I've never met him. Have you? Has Oggy? I'm not shitting you, Keith. I got home from my hot session with Dungeon Debs and Bennett had his pants round his ankles with Farooq knelt in front of him. They were listening to the Bee Gees. He wouldn't answer his phone, and they locked the doors downstairs. I had to climb the drainpipe.' Jake lifted the bottoms of his jeans, showing off cuts and bruises on his shins. 'I fell in the bins.'

Keith shook his head. 'Your mind's playing tricks on you.'

'Is that right? If you saw Charlotte knelt in front of me and I had no pants on, what'd be going through your mind? See. Something's not right with him. He's hiding something.'

'Oh, see me later.' Keith ignored a text from Charlotte asking what time he'd be home from work and finally shrugged him off.

'Remember, guys, we're looking for a singer who not only sounds great but who looks the part too. We want to pull in a young, trendy audience.'

'Let's hope we can still get a good seat.' Bennett fired a dirty look at Keith, then smirked at Jake. 'Twenty quid says you can't pull a bird in here tonight.'

'Dick.' The Beehive wasn't far away, and when Jake spotted the bouncer, he stubbed his joint on the windowsill of a nearby café. 'You're on. Watch me go.'

Black-and-white pictures hung from the maroon paisley walls, offering outsiders a glimpse into Smithfield

Market in the '50s and '60s. It had huge welcoming antique fireplaces at either end, where cotton mill workers congregated, and it had something most long-standing pubs in Manchester had. It had soul, character and a powerful sense of place.

'Wait up.' Bennett commandeered one of three available tables with four stools and an excellent view of the karaoke area. It wasn't a stage exactly, but the staff did a wonderful job of cramming their equipment in.

'Here, gents.' Keith bought Oggy and himself a pint of Coke, a lager for Jake and a cider for Bennett before sitting down.

Oggy finished interrogating the barman and joined them. 'Cheers, fellas. Doesn't get busy in here till after eight,' he said. 'Perfect timing.'

'I need to be away for half nine. Sorry,' Keith announced. 'There's a group of lads coming in, though. Maybe they'll get up and sing.'

Bennett's face turned purple. 'We all know you've put all your eggs in one basket and don't want to be here. Surprised Charlotte let you come. Does she even know you're here?'

'Course she does,' Keith replied, shooting straight on the defensive. 'Charlotte isn't the monster you make her out to be.'

'Tell that to Daniel. He's the one who said it was only a matter of time before she made you leave the Magnesium Gurus.'

Keith sipped his drink, shifting to the next table, and noticed Oggy shaking his head.

'Work clobber on. Not drinking,' Bennett said,

splitting his sides laughing. 'If she finds out you're not at work, you're dead.'

'Pack it in, the pair of you. Remember why we're here.'

A smartly dressed blonde in her late thirties emerged behind the microphone. 'Welcome to the Beehive. I'm Jazz,' she said in a beautiful Irish accent. 'Before we begin, we want you to know this amazing venue will be one of many taking part in Sothis Media's upcoming Love Is the Drug '70s tribute competition. There's going to be many fantastic bands playing live, so please join us over the coming weeks. You won't want to miss this.'

Oggy whistled and applauded, inciting the punters to follow suit.

'Thank you. My wonderful friends are on their way round with song sheets and pencils, so please don't be shy. Hope to see a few of you up here shortly.' She got the night off to an absolute flyer, singing 'Son of a Preacher Man' by Dusty Springfield and 'Nutbush City Limits' by Tina Turner.

'Hey, she's not bad. Can't we ask her to join and we'll do some other '70s tribute?' Jake asked. 'What about Blondie?'

Keith scowled at his idea, then looked towards the entrance, noticing four attractive young women drift in off the street, chatting.

'Wow!' Jake said, ogling one of them. 'I'd marry her and let her have my kids.'

'You wouldn't know what to do with a fine-looking woman like that, and why the fuck would *she* want *your* kids? Told you, twenty quid.'

Keith watched the talent on show fast deteriorate while

keeping one eye on Bennett. Not one of them fared anywhere near as well as Jazz. Half the punters must've been tone deaf, crucifying great hits by Al Green, Frankie Valli, Eric Clapton and Ben E. King. Nipping to the bar, he scouted around to see if anyone fitted Oggy's controversial criteria, but nobody had Daniel's spark. 'Don't think we'll find Bolan in here tonight.'

'Give it a chance. Rome wasn't built in a day.'

'Next up from Glasgow, please welcome Jen.'

'She's the young lady Jake's asking out,' Oggy hollered with a big grin on his face.

Jen shone in her long black dress, waiting for her song to begin. Her friends cheered as her rendition of 'Love Will Tear Us Apart' gripped everyone. Jake dashed in, stoned, with a herd of other smokers, and his jaw dropped and stayed that way throughout her performance. The entire pub gave her a well-earned standing ovation.

'Bravo.' Keith unfastened the top button of his shirt and wafted his collar as more people squeezed through the door. Keeping clear of Bennett, he edged closer to Jake, wanting to hear his courting technique. 'Her name's Jen. Mint?' he said, holding them out.

'You need two, donkey breath. Watch and learn, coffin-dodgers.' Jake cleared a path through the crowd and positioned himself to one side of Jen, who had her back to him. Mid conversation, he tapped her on her shoulder. 'Hi. I'm Jake. Beautiful voice.'

She spun to face him, sipping her mojito. 'Ta.' Her friends attempted to block him off.

'You look amazing. I was wondering if I could get your number and take you for a meal or a few drinks?'

'That's sweet, bit a'm seeing someone, sorry.'

'No probs. Enjoy your night. I hope your boyfriend knows how lucky he is.'

Jen blushed, her friends chuckled and Jake made his way to the exit. Bennett and Oggy couldn't stop laughing, but Keith set his half-empty glass on the nearest table and respectfully wormed his way through the crowd to check on him outside. 'You okay? There aren't many guys with the guts to do that. I still remember how nerve-racking it was asking Charlotte out after watching her do the bump. Daniel used to say, "Asking girls out is like stepping on landmines. You either get lucky or end up blown to bits."'

Bennett chuckled alongside Oggy and whipped out his wallet. 'Unlucky, plant pot. Cough up. And Daniel never used to say that. Don't lie.'

'Yes, he did, and you know he did.' Keith hit back. 'What is your problem? You've had little pops at me all night. Why don't you grow up? It's not my fault Daniel didn't like you enough to have a genuine conversation.'

Bennett stood face to face with Keith, and Oggy hauled him back. 'Right, let's go inside and have one more drink.'

Keith put on his spectacles and read a text off Charlotte asking what time he'd be home. 'Sorry, Oggy. I've had enough for one night. Can I get my rucksack from the store?'

'Slumming it in real boozers too much for you?' Bennett snapped. 'You had it all as a teenager. Nice family, delightful house, lovely girlfriend. Daniel stuck up for you all the time. You were his talented little shadow who could do no wrong. That time's gone, Keith. We want loyalty and commitment, but you can't offer either. Run along to wifey.'

'Bennett, chill.' Jake threw his twenty-pound note at him. 'You're bang out of order.'

'He's right. Apologise now.'

'Why should I? He's not good enough to play lead, Oggy. You know it and I know it. It's only a matter of time before he buggers off again. That midget he's grooming doesn't cut it either. Finn isn't Daniel. He's nowhere near as talented. Daniel's dead.'

Keith lunged forward but Jake pulled him back by his coat. 'Finn isn't Daniel, I agree, but who are you to judge? Hearing him sing frightened you, didn't it? That's what's wrong with you. You're afraid he'll spurn your sexual advances like Daniel did. He told me you tried it on with him the night before his eighteenth. You were always jealous of us being together. Meeting Finn face to face brought it all back, didn't it? Don't blame *me* for *your* life choices and mistakes. If you want someone to blame, look in the mirror.'

'Tried it on. Very good. Piss off.' Bennett had to be restrained by Oggy, but it didn't stop him and Keith fast becoming embroiled in an eyeballing contest. 'You don't know what you're talking about. We're staying out to find a real singer. Might even find a half-decent guitarist knocking about. We don't need you or your hoodlum hobbit friend.'

'Bennett, go back inside. Jake, take Keith to get his gear. You're behaving like spoilt bleeding children.'

Keith held out his hand. 'Fifty quid says Finn not only shows up at the weekend but he blows away every ounce of competition you can muster.'

'Not good enough,' Bennett bawled, grabbing hold of Keith's hand. 'If Finn doesn't show, I take your cash and you leave the band.'

'Come on, let's go,' Jake yelled, tugging at Keith's jacket. 'You'll both have a stroke.'

Keith smirked, refusing to let go. 'Deal. See you Saturday.'

SIX

Saturday, August 27th, 2011 - 03:00

Finn opened his eyes and threw back his duvet to find himself wearing a bright yellow suit, a brownish waistcoat covered in shiny sequins and a pair of lemon ballet shoes. He dived out of bed and glanced in the mirror, running his short red wig through his fingers.

'Surprise, surprise. It's about time.' Two stools with microphone stands in front had been set up by his bedroom door. Marc sat on one of them barefooted with his legs crossed. Dressed in grey trousers and a jet-black top with silver patterns, he strummed his acoustic guitar with his clear crystal pick. 'Had a drink, have we? How many times? Go pee.'

Finn grabbed one of Keith's books, *The Lives and Death of Marc Bolan* by Lesley-Ann Jones, from his shelf. He held it open at page 263. 'Check it out: "We'd sit together with a bottle of Remy Martin and a gram of coke when Gloria was away."'

Marc grinned. 'Nobody likes a smarty-pants. I can't wait for him to come up and see me. Steve always made me smile. Now, go pee. You need a methodical mind.'

Finn took off to the bathroom, returning soon after. 'Happy now?'

'It doesn't take much pollution from the outside to stem the spirited tide on the inside.' Marc flicked through Finn's notebook. 'I see your mother's pen came in handy. Still a long way to go. This needs a title.'

Finn snatched it off him. 'Told you before. That's personal.'

'I know more about you than you know about yourself. For me, writing was like a worship. It never felt like *me* holding the pen. We are but instruments forged to play universal melodies for others, and in your case, you wish to impress Keith.'

'No, I don't. We chatted, that's it. Don't think Bennett's too keen on me auditioning.'

'More reason to show up this afternoon and blow them all away with your talent. Shall we? Come sing "Life's a Gas" with me.'

'Did you have to dress me up like Cilla Black?'

Marc shrugged and placed his hands on his hips. 'If you give up on your dreams, what's left?' He grinned and leapt from his stool. 'Sit and don't go all masculine on me again with that *real men* nonsense. Stop worrying about what others may think. If those around you cannot bring the best out of you, find those who will.'

Finn huffed and puffed but eventually sat on his stool.

'Let's see where you're at. I'll signal for your lines and nod when we sing together.'

'Okay.' Finn gripped his microphone with both hands, tapped his feet on the stool and sang precisely when Marc wanted him to.

'Sorry, but I wasn't feeling it. All you need is love, and mellow love is by far the sweetest. Inside out, *not* outside in. Girls just want to have fun. Learn what it is women want. Our love is their love, and their love is our love. In the '60s and '70s, we spoke freely about the miracle of love. Express yourself.'

'I'm not a girl. I'm not in love. And you were all tripping your tits off on LSD.'

'Not all of us. Fall in love with what makes you, you. Life isn't life without a smidge of femininity.'

'I don't know *who* I am or *what* I want.' Finn sniffed. 'Are you wearing perfume?'

'Drops of Jupiter from my wife, June, if you must know. She loves to pluck books from the shelves of our orbs' collective library, then snuggle up to me and read *The Lord of the Rings*. I was never the best reader, you see, but you'd be surprised how much truth there is in fiction. She read *The Hobbit* to me beneath the stars before travelling here. I love Tolkien. William Blake too. Splendid stories often start with a troubled beginning, but I love any writer who speaks to me like a friend. So intimate. Remember this when scrawling in your journal. Gets my rocks off, man. Pay attention.'

A metallic case filled with all kinds of makeup appeared on Finn's desk next to a photograph of David Bowie with a red lightning bolt across his right eye. 'I'm not wearing makeup. How is this preparing me for my audition?'

'You'd be surprised.' Marc rubbed his chin. 'Vulnerability is the birthplace of innovation, creativity and change. Makeup and costumes can help shield us from society's resentful and often hurtful negativity, protecting our orbs, maintaining a stable, healthy rhythm.

We all assume a persona at times in life, but we must not allow them to consume us, no matter how difficult our journeys become. Be courageous. Be spontaneous. I loved how David transformed into Ziggy Stardust, the rock star messenger for ETs. He and I were on the same wavelength when it came to what lurked within our minds, connecting us to what skulked beyond the stars, but if you wish to charge into battle with no armour, best of luck, my little cosmic dancer. On your head be it.'

Finn sighed, and the case vanished. 'Cool. Now what?'

'We concentrate on your vocal range. Grasp the words. Absorb the music. If you don't believe in yourself, nobody else will, so let's explore the sanguine segment of your mind, unlocking it with a fresh eighteen-minute warmup. We must go green. Night clubs and arenas are nothing like bedrooms, school halls and pub lounges. First, I shall prepare you for your audition. Second, I shall prepare you for Love Is the Drug, where the final is a full makeup and costume event – just saying. And finally I shall prepare you for your next nine-year cycle. If vocalists can't be bothered to warm up, you'll find they never completely show up. Your mother taught excellent vocal skills and exercises for children, but adult vocalists are very much like athletes, Finn. We must warm up your muscles with more robust techniques. The more routines, the healthier your voice becomes. Are you ready?'

Finn sulked, tapping his feet against the chest of drawers.

'Stand up straight, arms by your sides. Spread your feet in line with your shoulders. Look left, look right, chin up, chin down. Rotate shoulders forward and backwards, squeeze upwards, release. Big yawn. Pretend we're lions. Place your tongue between your teeth and lips. Rotate clockwise around your mush and anti-clockwise. Repeat nine times, then six, then three. Try touching your chin with the tip of your tongue; open and close your mouth eighteen times to free your jaw, then full body stretches. Release all unwanted tension so as not to constrict your breathing muscles. Well done. Hips even, chest lifted, neck above shoulders and gaze forward. Sleep pattern improved. No distractions. Posture perfect. I'm impressed.'

'You finished? What's wrong with my mam's vocal exercises?' Finn sneered, slumping on his bed, propping his head up with his fist. 'Her methods warm me up faster.'

Marc raised his voice. 'Apologies for being blunt, but it's time you stopped clinging to your mother's underside, playing piggyback and suckling on her mammary gland. We must move on from her methods. This isn't one of your school competitions where you just stand there in your naff shorts and pullover with your socks pulled up to your knees, singing lullabies. This is about overall performance. Believe in me and you'll believe in yourself. Stand up. Come on. I don't want to hear what you're not. Show me what you've got.'

Finn stripped, hurling his wig at Marc, and warmed his vocal cords using his mam's techniques. Humming minor and major pentatonic scales, he sang melodies via lip trills, making the loudest sirens possible, and sang his way through the vowels, exhaling on a hiss.

'I see I've upset you, but there's no way you could understand the following as a child. Stop moping and think energy – frequency – vibration. Fluctuations of your vocal cords, which are caused by renewable air being driven from your lungs, generate sound. Inhaling expands your chest, contracting your diaphragm, and exhaling contracts your chest, relaxing your diaphragm. I get this is new, but give it a go before saying no.'

Finn shrugged. 'Do I have to?'

'If you wish to succeed, yes. You won't master this first time, so don't fret. Forget your surroundings. Become one with the universe. Exhale, discharging leftover vessel tension, and close your eyes. Step one. Inhale through your nose, fill your lungs to twenty-five per cent capacity. Hold for nine seconds, do not release. Step two. Inhale through your nose, fill your lungs to fifty per cent capacity. Hold for another nine seconds, do not release. Step three. Again, through your nose, fill your lungs to seventy-five per cent capacity and hold for—'

'Hang on.' Finn couldn't hold his breath any longer. He spluttered and hunched over, guzzling water from his bottle. 'I can't do it. My mam's techniques are well better.'

'You mean easier. It's just new. Focus. The only difference between success and a lack of is the time and space it takes to learn.' Marc patted Finn on the back. 'Once you master one hundred per cent lung capacity, spirit and matter merge into one, preserving the health of stem cells whilst promoting brain tissue regeneration. You must be at peace with yourself and your surroundings to achieve this thus catching a glimpse of the real you, where you come from and where you'll return to in the future. Powerful waves must flow freely to your major organs instead of crashing into them like rocks, then fill your mind's tiny cup till it tips, showering you with the wonders of our universe. Have you watched *The Sound of Music*?'

Finn wiped his mouth and shook his head. 'Why would I?'

'Why would you not?' Marc saluted. 'Captain von Trapp at your service. Let's begin with the cosmic solfège. The magical middle C. Deep breath. Do-Re-Mi-Fa-Sol-La-Ti-Do.'

Finn coughed once more and put his hand to his mouth.

'Take your time. Changing our pitch stretches our muscles. So, on me when you're ready. Do-Ti-La-Sol-Fa-Mi-Re-Do. Repeat nine times. Up, then down, drink more water and deep breaths in between. Now, inhale, counting to three, and as you exhale, make that hissing sound you did while counting to nine. It's grown on me. Repeat six times. Now, I'll be myself, you pretend to be Gloria and let's dive straight in with "To Know You Is to Love You". On me once more. That's more like it. We have green, and I see a sneaky tinge of blue slithering towards your larynx. Woo-hoo! Super groovy, huh? That, I felt. My heart's all aflutter. Have another sip of water. Lubrication helps maintain a healthy vibration.' Marc clapped his hands. 'There are certain chords with magic mists within them. When I used to play a C major, I heard like twenty-five melodies and symphonies up in here. I had to pull one out.' Marc lowered his head, deep in thought.

'Are you okay?'

'Our duet brought back many wonderful memories.' Marc blinked three times, and him, his kit and the costumes vanished. Popping his head through the glass minutes later, he had red, puffed-up eyes and wore the same tight-fitting shiny white suit he had first shown up in. He pulled his zip down, revealing a red-and-black Chuck Berry T-shirt, and wrapped his purplish feather boa around Finn's neck. 'It's been an absolute pleasure, but my work here is done.'

'What? That's it? One rehearsal? You must be joking.'

Marc dived onto Finn's bed with the greatest of grins. 'We guide, we do not spoon-feed. I've helped put some colour back in your cheeks. All you need now is a band to accommodate your tremendous vocals. Stand your ground and shift through the gears. The only person stopping you from being you is you. I can't believe it's nearly thirty-four years. My weary vessel would've been sixty-four soon.'

'I should've realised.'

'It's all right.' Marc slipped his lemon ballet shoes on and glided towards the open window, pointing to the clear night sky. 'We all knew we weren't from here. We felt it beneath our flesh and in our minds. We couldn't ignore it. You mustn't either. You either exist or you evolve before returning home in a cosy, minute neuromodulate sphere. I've been a minstrel, a cavalier, an empress of the blues and a glam rock superstar.'

Finn panicked. 'But we've only just got going. I can't do this alone.'

'You're never alone. When journeys end, our flames extinguish. When journeys begin, our flames reignite.' Marc wiped away his tear and looked Finn in the eye. 'You weren't to blame for your mother's passing, and you mustn't be afraid of sharing your feelings.' He ran his fingers through his corkscrew curls. 'Speed, alcohol, the fence, the sycamore tree. None were to blame for my passing, and neither was Gloria. A voice within advised me to put my seatbelt on when we left Morton's, but my malevolent primitive ego and its insatiable affiliation with matter had already doused my fire. I witnessed a huge white flash before escaping a darkness which seeks to suppress benevolence in all beings.'

'You can't just leave like everyone else. I have questions. I need answers. Please stay.'

'I shan't be too far away. Commit to a spot of light humming to cool your vocal cords down.' Marc hugged Finn and kissed him on the top of the head. 'Allow yourself to grow. Become an integral part of this show. Live your best life by trusting the wonderful soul in your suit, and I promise, the colourful lights shall guide you home when the time comes.'

Finn dropped to his knees when a bright violet light shone through his mirror, attaching itself to Marc's body. 'Don't go. Please, not yet. How did you know you'd crash into a tree? How did you know you'd die before you reached thirty?'

'The wizard never arrived from my past. Never look back or take things for granted. Always have fun and look to the future. Best of luck.' Marc winked. 'Don't dream it's over, and don't be afraid to follow the pink cuckoo. I'll be seeing you.'

***

Finn shot off the bus in Piccadilly around quarter past two with his rucksack filled with bottles of water, desperate to become a part of the show. Having finally made his mind up which T. Rex hit to sing, he arrived at BJ's music store in jeans and a T-shirt and loitered at the door before pushing it open, setting off the bell. 'Hi, Farooq. You good?'

'All the better for seeing you,' he whispered. 'I hear Keith has his heart set on a cute little white boy from the hood auditioning today. How sweet and sexual is that?'

Bennett bowled in from the back room without his crutches and plaster cast, growling at Finn, putting a stop to their conversation. 'Look what the cat dragged in,' he said with a right narky attitude.

'I'm here to audition this time,' Finn replied, wiping sweat from his forehead.

'Don't bother.' Bennett handed him a new audition flyer. 'You need to sing one of the listed T. Rex songs. I doubt you've heard of any. Tons of cracking vocalists are due shortly. Oggy and Keith nipped out. Best you leave now to save yourself further embarrassment.'

The song Finn had chosen to sing wasn't on Bennett's list. 'I'll wait, thanks. Jake in?'

'Upstairs watching National Geographic. He's at one with the animal kingdom. If you ask me, Bolan was right. We all live in a zoo.'

Jake thundered in, flipping Bennett the finger, wearing a psychedelic T-shirt which read: *If Jesus comes back, capitalists will kill him again.* 'Ignore that bitter, angry ape. You just lost him his bet with Keith. If you didn't show, Keith had to leave. Don't know what his problem is, but we better get bog roll for when Keith shows up. He'll cream his pants when he sees you.'

The bell above the door rang out once more, and Keith and Oggy had million-pound-lottery-winning expressions on their faces. 'Am I happy to see you? Stick the kettle on, please, Jake. Did you sort things out at home?' Keith whispered. 'Mace out of the woods?'

Finn nodded.

'So, you know, I've been struggling to find you a job. It's grim out there at the minute. I won't stop enquiring, though. You have my word.'

'Lads, listen up.' Bennett whistled to the auditionees. 'Come through, take a seat at the side and fill in the forms with your addresses and phone numbers. You're first.'

'I haven't warmed up,' Finn snapped.

'Tough. If you're as good as everyone thinks, you shouldn't need a warmup. Lads, have you heard him? This diva needs a warmup. Do you? Didn't think so.'

They burst out laughing, but Finn took a deep breath, wanting to punch Bennett in the gob. His attitude unsettled him enough to make him hold up Bennett's revised flyer.

Keith took it from him. 'You've gone too far. You're purposely aiming to manipulate the auditions.' He handed it to Oggy. 'Look.'

'Great to have you back, Finn,' Oggy said, shaking his head at Bennett's flyer. 'In case you're wondering, we haven't chosen a band name yet. Not very professional, I know. We're going to be jotting down names in the coming weeks: a bit of a brainstorm once the song choices are finalised. Any questions or concerns? Probably best we know what your intentions are and how serious you are about becoming our vocalist and winning this competition right from the outset.'

'Think you're best off asking *him* that question.' Finn pointed at Bennett. 'If this is a proper band, whoever's in charge needs to sort his attitude out. Told him I need time to warm up and he gobs off, turning these muppets against me.'

A lad at the front of the line stood up. 'Who you calling a muppet? Hurry the fuck up, shorty. I've got somewhere I need to be.'

Finn flexed his fingers and stuck out his hand, protecting his personal space. 'Sit down, big man, before I put you down.'

The others joined in, mouthing off as Jake split them up, but Bennett wouldn't give in. 'Knew this'd happen, Oggy. Told you. He's a thug. He has to go.'

'Warming up is an important part of my audition, you whopper,' Finn yelled, looking to escape. He made his way towards the exit to a chorus of boos and shrugged at Keith, hoping for backup. 'You either want me to audition or you don't.'

Keith glanced at Oggy with raised eyebrows, and he nodded. 'Wait. How long do you need, Finn?'

'Eighteen minutes.'

Bennett dived into the centre of the room, waving his arms in the air as if landing a small plane. 'Chill your fucking jets, everyone. What's with the preferential treatment? And what's this precise warmup time bullshit?'

'I'm more interested in why you're dead against Finn joining our band. Is there something you'd like to get off your chest? If so, now's the time. Nothing. Vocalists who warm up take their singing very serious, and that for me is a huge tick in the box. If auditions drag on, so be it.

Anyone else wish to warm up?' Oggy scanned the room, but there weren't any takers. 'What about you, gobby bollocks?' he asked, pointing at the lad Finn had argued with.

'You lot are fuckin' amateur. You won't win shit.'

Oggy belted his drums. 'Is that right? Think you'll find your most fundamental chromosomes were fired across your mam's back and mopped up with your dad's sock, but hello, I'm the fuckin' retard. Out! The sugar butty bus is waiting. One less audition.'

Bennett handed out lyrics with a wounded look on his face, Keith threw off his jacket, fiddling with his guitar, and Jake shook his shakers, chuckling at Oggy's outburst.

'Finn, I agree that guy was a tool and Bennett's behaviour towards you has been dreadful, but if you want a future with this band – and your body language tells me you do – then you mustn't chuck your toys out of the pram. You must, however, listen and learn to keep your emotions in check. Do you think you could manage that from now on?'

Finn nodded, not knowing where to look.

'Glad we're on the same page, kid. Do what you need to do out back. If more auditionees show up while you're doing your thing, I'm afraid you'll need to go to the back of the line in dogshit alley. There's no room in here or the shop.'

Finn left them to it, closing the back door, then made his way to the far end of the yard, getting straight down to business with his warmup. He still couldn't get past seventy-five per cent lung capacity, which resulted in a bout of coughing, but he drank enough water from the bottles in his rucksack, tooted his inhaler and nailed his solfège, exhaling on a hiss. The music in his mind stopped, and he opened his eyes to find Keith, Oggy, Jake and the other auditionees staring at him through the kitchen windows and door. He closed the gate and joined the back of the queue, unable to keep still as it poured with rain, but Farooq brought him his jacket and made cups of tea for those who stayed.

'Ready, Finn?' Keith said, handing him a bath towel a good hour and forty-five minutes later. 'Apologies for the wait. Bennett got a rollicking, by the way. Dry off, head straight for the microphone and just be yourself.'

Finn took one last mouthful of tea, spat it out on his way inside and ploughed through the auditionees who had made the cut, adjusting the microphone stand to suit his height.

'Get ready, guys.' Oggy dived into position, ushering Keith and Jake to theirs. He snatched the massive joint dangling from Jake's mouth. 'Playtime's over,' he roared. 'You can have it when we're done. Would you mind telling us a bit about yourself, Finn?'

'Nowt to tell. I'd just like to sing "Teenage Dream".'

'That's not on my list,' Bennett screamed.

'Zip it, you. Finn, what do you hope to gain from entering Love Is the Drug?'

The room fell silent, and Finn swilled his water, looking directly at Oggy. 'Not sure, really, but if you give up on your dreams, what's left?'

Oggy smiled. '"Teenage Dream" it is, kid. We'll start low and take it slow. Feel free to join us when you're comfortable enough to audition.' He got them off to a flyer, urging Keith and Bennett to join in, then hit Jake on the head with his drumstick for pulling faces. 'Stop showing off, you prick.'

Finn took a deep breath, listening carefully to the beat, and tapped the microphone three times, closing his eyes. As he searched for the soul in his suit, a strange warmth rose from the base of his spine and spread from his groin to his stomach and throat. The words leapt from his lips, and for those three or four minutes, he lost all sense of time and place. Convinced his mam stood beside him in BJ's, spurring him on, he sang his last word, the music faded, and he opened his eyes more than confident he had nailed it. Keith, Oggy, Jake and the auditionees showed their appreciation with a round of applause, but Bennett stood gobsmacked.

Farooq dashed in from the store with his hands over his mouth. 'Oh my God,' he shrieked, jumping up and down on the spot. 'Everyone in the shop literally just froze listening to you. You have the voice of an angel.'

'That was breathtakingly awesome.' Oggy added. 'Auditionees, off you trot. Thank you for coming. We'll give you a call later today. Finn, do you mind having a wander around the store for a few minutes while we have a chinwag about your audition?'

'Stand there in the corner. You can hear everything,' Farooq whispered, leading him into the shop before heading to the till. 'There is a crack in the wall halfway up. With a bit of luck, you might see them if they are near the kitchen.'

Finn hummed a little to cool down his vocal cords, then pressed his eyelashes against the broken plaster, earwigging.

'Pretty certain there aren't any objections to Finn joining our band from us three, so off you go, Bennett. The stage is yours. Why would you not want Finn to join our band based on what we all just witnessed? Am I missing something?'

Bennett grabbed a handful of ten-pound notes from his jar and counted them out on the kitchen worktop. 'Here. You didn't have to sink so low.'

'Guess I missed something too. What are you talking about?' Keith asked.

'You know.' Bennett couldn't keep still. 'Giving up on his dreams. Daniel said that.'

'Did he?' Keith asked, smirking. 'That's a new one.'

'It was part of *our* genuine conversations! Look at the goose pimples on my arms. Only Daniel could do that with his voice. You all felt it, right – the electricity Daniel generated? Wasn't as strong, but fuck me, did I feel it.'

'Likewise.' Oggy grabbed Bennett a glass of water and sat him down. 'You've gone really pale. Drink it and breathe before you keel over. In all my years, I've only ever come across two vocalists as talented as Finn. Did you see him outside? He's had some form of training. Surely we *all* agree on that. It's like watching Bolan, Daniel and the entire von Trapp family rolled into one. How does a young lad like him from the local council estate sing like that? His timing, his control, his range and the way he worked his way through the gears was phenomenal. How the pissing hell did he memorise our lyrics so quick?'

'Run that bit past me again,' Bennett asked. 'What lyrics? When?'

'Relax,' Keith replied. 'I gave him some to familiarise

himself with last time he was here. There's more to him than meets the eye. I sensed it when he sang in the Church. This lad is gifted. He has what it takes to become a superstar. Clifford won't know what's hit him.'

'So we're all in agreement. We offer Finn the role of Marc Bolan and enter Love Is the Drug? Hands, let's see them. Unanimous. Hallelujah! Finn,' Oggy shouted. 'Come back in, please.'

Finn entered with his hands in his pockets, pretending to look surprised.

'Congratulations. We'd like you to join our band and become Marc Bolan as from now. You up for it?' Oggy shook hands with him.

'All of you?' Finn asked, eyeballing Bennett.

Keith and Jake shook Finn's hand, then Bennett approached, holding out his. 'I'm sorry for being a helmet and calling you a midget. Won't happen again.'

'Cool. I just want to sing. I'm in.'

Jake cheered, and Farooq raced in. 'Benny, I have locked the shop. Finn, congratulations,' he said, hugging him. 'That was marvellous.'

'Great audition.' Oggy puffed on his cigar and brought a crate of lager in from the kitchen, handing out cans, which Finn kindly refused. 'The hard work begins now. The competition opens in under three weeks and the full costume final's only two months away.'

Farooq butted in with his hand in the air. 'Did you say costumes? I can get them really cheap, can't I, Benny? My good friend Rhonda has a stall in Affleck's. Effeminatus on the first floor.' He placed his hands on his hips. 'Her friend Sadie is a cosmetologist too.'

Bennett wouldn't look at him. He scurried to the kitchen, where he washed up the cups.

'Sothis will pick up the bill for all finalists' costumes and makeup, but let's not get ahead of ourselves by worrying about that now. We need to qualify first.'

'I can ask her to call in one day if you prefer?' Farooq rolled his eyes at Bennett and checked his watch. 'Is that the time, moody? Must dash! Shame on you.'

'Hang on before you all sod off,' Bennett said, blocking the doorway. 'Paula asked if we could perform at her promotional gig out front for Candy Pink Cavern across the way next weekend. Just a couple of songs to help flog a load of gift sets.'

'The prostitute?'

'Stop saying it like that; you make it sound disgusting.'

'Isn't it? Sorry. A live audience is just what we need to get in the groove. Tell her we're in. Oh, now our tribute band is formed, we need a name, so thinking caps on and keep practising. That goes for you too, Bolan. See you here nine a.m. sharp next Saturday.'

***

Finn dropped leaflets in shop doorways and stuck flyers to billboards and construction site hoardings. He pinned plywood to the tops of pallets raised on cinder blocks in the street beneath the dark clouds, providing a makeshift stage for Paula's promotional gig. She sent him out wearing a Candy Pink Cavern T-shirt, armed with a thick metallic dildo along with revised lyrics for 'Tell It Like It Is' by Aaron Neville. Thankfully, Oggy handed him a lavender wig and white spectacles to hide his identity.

Finn took a deep breath and marched towards his mic, waving his dildo at the pests, then thrust it in front of his crotch without making eye contact with anyone. Keith and Oggy shied away at the back. Jake found it hilarious, but Bennett seemed more interested in chucking cider down his throat. Once their revamped soul classic had ended, he unplugged his guitar and darted into BJ's with no explanation. They performed 'Children of the Revolution' without him.

'Have you spoken to your contacts?' Finn asked, following Keith and Oggy inside.

'Sorry. It's been hectic. I'll do it this week, I promise.'

'I hope Mata Hari leaves us alone now. Where'd Bennett bugger off to?'

Jake dashed in, jumping around at the window, blowing kisses at a vicar, and once he'd attracted his attention, he sucked his middle finger, ran it around his nipple and stuck it up at him. 'Priest means beast,' he chanted, before he was distracted by two female escorts in white leather miniskirts and Candy Pink Cavern T-shirts. They rushed by carrying an old decorator's pasting table, shunted it against the nearest wall in the rehearsal room and stacked paper plates and multicoloured plastic cups on top.

'Prostitutes are doing the catering?' Oggy spun round to find Judy gawping at him. 'Oh look, numbnuts; reincarnation is real after all. Please, not now. Not here. Rehearsals are about to begin.'

Judy pulled one of Paula's flyers from her handbag and threw it in his face. 'I came to the house God knows how many times. Stop ignoring my calls. I want the rest of my stuff.'

'So glad to see you, Rudy,' Jake said, reaching for a hug. 'I mean Judy.'

She gave him the finger. 'Get stuffed, weasel. And the least you can do is give me my personal items back, since I persuaded Rupert not to press charges for his broken nose.'

'Wupert.' Oggy laughed. 'Fucking Wupert! What did you expect me to do, slap him on his arse cheeks and tell him great job? I loved that bed.'

'Just not the woman you shared it with. Rupert is a highly respected restaurant owner.'

'Gold digger,' Bennett muttered, trying to disguise his words with a cough.

Jake scrolled through the tracks on his CD player, cranked up the volume and gripped a cowboy hat from one of the boxes. Jamming his thumbs into his jeans pockets, he hopped and heel-tapped to 'Boot Scootin' Boogie' by Brooks and Dunn. 'Five, six, seven, eight.'

Judy threw a microphone at Oggy, which just missed Finn, and took off, stealing a box full of sex toys on her way out. 'I want a divorce, you fat, useless spastic.'

Farooq appeared again, this time with a bloke in a fancy suit with funny eyes, whom Finn recognised from Keith's newspaper articles. 'Ladies, please: back to your house of ill repute.'

Bennett resurfaced, necking another can of cider. 'Cheers, girls. Really appreciate it. They're wonderful, aren't they? Close the shop, please, Farooq. Call Rhonda.'

'No need. I'll be off soon enough. Be sure to pass on my regards. Judy looks well, Oggy. Did you know Becky's back in town? I'm Clifford, everyone, CEO at Dual Ventures and Manchester's number one music mogul. Do you have a name?'

'Finn.'

'Well, Finn, the minute you realise you're wasting your time with these foolish fantasists, call me. I'll introduce you to a real band managed by my sister. She'll change your entire life, won't she, Oggy?' He shook Finn's hand, passing him his business card, then smirked at Bennett. 'Are you going to tell them or shall I?'

'You're not welcome,' Keith roared. 'Leave and take your false promises with you.'

'Now, now. As landlord of this property and across the way, I'd say I'm more than welcome. Still no leash for him, Oggy. Hard to believe this was my very first studio. A breathtaking energy once waltzed through those very doors. I can still feel her presence.'

'Oi! Tell us what? Spit it out, Clifford, then crawl back under your rock.'

'As of now, Bennett has three months to vacate BJ's and Candy's. He's behind on his rent, and let's just say Candy's hasn't exactly met or fulfilled our lease obligations. I'm guessing everyone here knows he's a pimp.' Clifford put his hand over his mouth. 'Oops.'

'Piss off!' Jake yelled, turning his attention to Bennett. 'Don't just sit there. Tell the bog-eyed turd to lick your hoop.'

'If only Daniel could see us now. I'm not sure if he'd laugh or cry. Finn, you can do so much better. My new state-of-the-art studio is just up the road.'

'Out.' Keith had to be held back by Oggy.

'Apologies. Daniel's death must've been absolutely

heart-wrenching, but more so for Bennett, I'd say. After all, he was Daniel's lover. Guess you weren't that close after all, Keith. Goodbye. See you at the competition, or maybe not. Finn, I look forward to your call.' Clifford bolted, leaving everybody in shock.

Bennett, white as a ghost, slumped in his seat with his head down. Oggy dotted stools about the room, Finn and Jake raided Paula's buffet, grabbing small paper plates with piled-up triangular sandwiches, and Keith sat directly in front of Bennett, glaring at him. The stupid bell rang, and in waltzed Farooq with Paula and a six-foot drag queen.

'Jake, we can excuse you and Finn. You don't need to be here for this.'

'We're staying, Oggy. Popcorn, anyone?' Jake asked, shaking his box.

'Hi. I'm Rhonda.' She had long black eyelashes, uneven makeup and a red photo album tucked under her enormous arms. 'Great to see some of you again after all these years. Feels like I've been purposely tucked away,' she said, kissing everyone on both cheeks.

Bennett stood to greet them. 'I fucked up. Guys, you remember Rhonda from '77. Back then she was Ronny, lead singer of Heaton Mourning.'

Keith and Oggy reintroduced themselves and Finn shook their hands, keen to learn more about his bandmates and his new surroundings, but Jake just froze.

'Farooq filled us in. I've missed you and Beryl so much.' Rhonda kissed Bennett on the lips and ran one of her huge hands down the side of his face. She lugged a stool next to him and opened her album while Farooq and Paula squeezed in. 'I'll pass it round.'

'Today's been fantastic,' Bennett said, coughing and trembling. 'Thanks guys. It means a lot to Paula and me. This tribute band happened so fast.'

'What you're all doing is astonishing. Just shows you're never too old to accomplish your desires,' Rhonda said. 'I spent many a teenage year dreaming of Bolan's pocket rocket.'

Jake shoved his hardly touched plate of food onto the floor. 'You're Ronny? You don't look like you play much snooker.'

Bennett groaned, then necked more of his cider. 'Keith, Oggy, what Clifford said about Daniel and me was true. We were having an intimate relationship for nine months leading up to his death. I'm sorry. I wanted to tell you.'

Keith laughed it off. 'You and Daniel – lovers? In one of your sordid dreams, maybe. Daniel wasn't a homosexual.'

'He was curious. And for the record, *he* tried it on with me. *Not* the other way round.'

'Why didn't you tell us you're a pimp?' Jake asked. 'Pretty sure that's the first thing you start with when inviting family to stay.'

Bennett focused on the filthy floor beneath his feet, and Rhonda and Farooq budged up closer to support him. 'Jake, I'm sorry. You've met the girls. I couldn't stand back and watch them work those brutal streets any longer. I had to do something.'

Keith drank his lager at a much faster rate. 'What did Clifford mean? Explain.'

'He called after you and Oggy went to see him at his apartment. I'd never heard him so incensed. He told me you'd already found a singer and asked me to play along.

Unsettle Keith, stop any decent vocalists from joining and he'd wipe my debts clean. Finn, I'm so sorry. I ignored his calls after your audition blew me away. I refused to give him your name.'

Finn stopped munching his sandwich and listened, trying his best to take it all in, hoping Clifford's hand grenade wouldn't blow up his band's future.

'That's what today was about. Introductions to get us on side.' Keith jammed his hands under his armpits, ready to erupt. 'Once you heard Finn audition, you thought wow – cash cow. Fame and fortune. Admit it. *Did* Daniel take his own life? Did you write that nasty note to him? If not, it's fair to say it was referring to your relationship?'

Bennett raised his voice. 'So you know, I dumped Daniel the night before Rock Heaven. I didn't need to write him a note. I told him to go fuck himself. You're no saint. You had no time for him once you met Charlotte.' He stood up, pointing. 'Daniel planned to tell you about us on your camping trip to Rhyl, but you left him alone by the campfire.'

'You!' Keith jumped to his feet, barking at Bennett. 'How dare you lay the blame at my feet after all the grief you've aimed at me the past few weeks!'

Oggy dived between them, keeping their fingers out of each other's faces. 'That's enough. Everybody relax. Let's all take it down a notch. Finn's vocals frightened Clifford. Don't you see? This is precisely what he wants. You're both playing into his hands.'

'He's lied to us all these years, and on top of that, he's just tried ruining Finn's career before it begun. How can *we* trust *him*? I don't see how this can work, Oggy.'

'We were in love, but today isn't about Daniel. If we don't win Love Is the Drug, Jake and I will lose our home, Farooq will lose his job and our girls will be back on the streets. I had no choice. Today's event was vital. I knew the consequences of my actions.'

Jake flicked through Rhonda's photo album and every few seconds, he shook his head. 'That's you – *Beryl*?' he asked, pointing to Bennett performing on stage at the Birdcage. 'Is that how you did your foot in? Am I related to a transvestite, a cross-dresser or a gay pimp?'

'*We're* drag queens. *And* we're in a relationship. We gear up for fun, but Ronny dresses up for her stall works.' Bennett rolled his eyes at her. 'I prefer the buzz on stage.'

Jake shot from his seat. 'Where do you fit into this, Farooq? It's just, I saw you knelt in front of Bennett with his pants round his ankles ready for a game of naked leapfrog.'

Finn kept quiet and kicked his plate of party sausages under his chair, watching Bennett lean forward, placing his head in his hands. 'When you caught me with my hand down my shorts, I wasn't beating off to Travolta. I found a lump on my nads. With Farooq being a medical student before he danced, I asked him to take a look. My GP's confident it's a group of veins bunched together, but I'm getting a second opinion at the MRI.'

Keith shook his head in Jake's direction. 'That's all well and good. I'm glad it's nothing serious, but can we please get back on topic?'

'Shit with Daniel *just happened*. You know what he was like. He had to try everything life offered. Daniel said if we stuck together, we could take on the entire world.'

'Bennett, Beryl, whatever, we're your friends. Our take on you and Daniel will take a bit of time to come to terms with, but it's nothing we can't overcome. Nothing's changed.'

'Everything's changed. I'm sorry. I can't think straight.' Keith grabbed his guitar, made his way to the door, and spun to face Bennett. 'For the record, I didn't leave Daniel alone at the campsite. He was with Charlotte's sister, Millie.'

'Daniel isn't here, Keith. We are. We need your help. Please, stop running away. How can you stand there and say I can't be trusted when you're about to abandon Finn the same way you abandoned us? Shame on you.'

Keith blanked Bennett and struggled to look Finn in the eye. 'I'm so sorry, guys. I'll be in touch once I've had time to process.'

'You can't just leave.' Finn shot up after Keith to change his mind, but both his worlds collided when his dad blocked him off at the door, drunk and piss wet through, clutching his journal.

'When were you going tell me you'd been sacked? What happened to Mace? Get your things.'

'Oi. You are?' Bennett yelled. 'Haven't you heard of knocking?'

Finn snatched his journal from his dad's hands, and his legs turned to jelly. 'Going through my things now? Nice one. Why do you have to ruin everything for me?'

'I've hardly seen you, son. Knew you were in trouble. You don't belong here. These none-hit wonders are using you for your talents. They'll do anything to exploit you. You should be ashamed of yourselves – you're nothing but vultures. I've come across your sort before. Fuckers like you killed her. I've been here before. Is she here? Where is she?'

'Now hang on a minute, pal. We've had a very unpleasant afternoon. Who killed who?' Oggy asked. 'Finn, what's your dad talking about? Let's calm down and put the kettle on. Have we met? You look familiar.'

'Keep your mucky hands off my son, you freaks of nature. Finn's having nothing to do with a bunch of has-beens. I'm taking him as far away as possible. You hear? His mam would wipe the floor with all of you, God bless her soul,' he cried. 'She was so special.'

Oggy, Bennett, Jake, Farooq, Rhonda and Paula never said another word, but Finn pushed his dad towards the exit, about to burst into tears. 'It's okay, everyone. We're leaving. Sorry about this, Oggy. I'll call you. Dad, we need to go. Please, Dad. Now!'

SEVEN

Saturday, September 3rd, 2011 - 18:45

Keith switched off his phone the minute he left BJ's and walked all the way home to an empty house, drenched and subdued. He found a note from Charlotte on the coffee table stapled to a Candy Pink Cavern flyer, stating one of her friends had attended their promotional event, therefore she needed a break from her lying husband. 'Enough!' Pacing up and down the lounge, then storming to the kitchen, grabbing two cans of lager from his fridge, he emptied his medication into the sink, then stomped upstairs, knocking back a handful of paracetamol. He switched on his radio and ran himself a hot bath, pouring in half a bottle of lavender Radox with a handful of Epsom salts.

Off came his soaking wet clothes, which he launched across the tiled floor before pulling the toilet seat down to rest his cans on. He flung his underpants into the washing basket, dived into his stress-blocking bubbles, lay back, cracked open a can and racked his brains for any dead giveaway signs verifying Bennett's relationship with Daniel. 'Cat got your tongue, Danny boy?' he muttered. '"Love Is the Drug is a fantastic idea." Why did I listen to you?'

'My fault? Your suppressive ego has you trapped in its somatic vault.'

Keith sighed. 'Blah. Blah. Blah. Clifford showed up today and blurted out *you* and *Bennett* were in a homosexual relationship leading up to your death. *Lovers.* Is that even the correct term? Don't get jealous, but Bennett introduced us to his new squeeze: it's only Ronny from Heaton *bloody* Mourning. Remember him - *her*?'

'Course. Fuzzy, firm ass. Ronny and I were like two wild apes mating in the grass.'

Keith sat up, searching for him. 'Are you joking? Show yourself.'

'Why would I be joking? I learnt so much about myself from those I'd been poking. I slept with men. I slept with women. Who decides what's right? After all, we are apes with primitive carnal appetites.'

'Is there anyone you haven't slept with?' Keith clenched his bubbly fists, splashed down hard in the water and slid along the bath till his knees rose. 'Anyhow, I quit the stupid band. I knew I couldn't do it without *you*. Finn's so much better off without *me*. Truth is, they can all see I'm struggling,' he sobbed. 'I used to be somebody. Now I'm nobody. Everything I once was has upped and left. Charlotte and my kids are gone too.'

'If you give up on your dreams, what's left?'

'Ooh whoopee doo. Your boyfriend told the truth for once.'

Daniel raised his voice. 'Stop. The more you drink, the further you'll sink.'

'Worked for you. If you refuse to show yourself, guess I'll see if Rock Heaven truly does exist.' Keith downed a full can, singing along to 'Everybody Hurts' by REM, then closed his eyes, listening to 'Sound of Silence' by Simon and Garfunkel. He drifted back and forth until he slid right under, seeing how long he could hold his breath, and after a substantial amount of time, he opened his eyes to a blurry bathroom. A dark shadow arched over him, centimetres above the water, and grabbed his arm, yanking it forward. Surfacing from beneath the bubbles at great speed, gasping and spluttering, he found a blotchy red handprint fading from his wrist and slowed his breathing down as somebody hummed the tune to 'Spaceball Ricochet' by T. Rex. Shifting to his knees, he watched the door close by itself, then stood and rinsed his face, taking deep breaths as he found himself wearing the same skin-tight orange T-shirt and baggy corduroy shorts he had been wearing on Bournemouth beach. 'Daniel.'

'Are you coming out to play, or are you too unsettled by the thought I was gay?' The outline of Daniel's body became visible in the mirror when a radiant light from above shone through an abundance of dust particles. 'I travelled beneath the skyway from a desolate place to see my best friend and his chunky rounded face.' Daniel wore the bright yellow T-shirt and black-and-white striped shorts from the morning he had drowned, and his silver locket on its old black shoelace hung from his neck.

'You haven't aged a single bit.'

'*You* have. You still look like my mam's favourite gnome but with a grey complexion, and Charlotte's quaint flowery décor reminds me of home.' Daniel smiled. 'It was always you she wanted, but she ain't no Aunt Millie. You mustn't take her for granted.'

'I haven't. I wouldn't. She's the mother of my children.'

Daniel sniggered. 'Daddy's little heroes. You named them after prominent collective beings, Bowie and Shapiro. I'm deeply sorry for your initial conception woes and the part my death played in your nervous breakdown. Charlotte wasn't to blame – no mother is.'

'Can I come with you? Am I at death's door? Is this Rock Heaven?'

'Here's hoping its more of a universal dress rehearsal.' Daniel waltzed up and down behind the glass. 'Listen carefully to my voice. You mustn't be here. You have a choice. Stop blaming others. Stop blaming yourself. You must for the sake of your mental health. I surfed the ocean waves yet fell. You remember "The Dove"? You recited it so well.'

Keith came close to tears, recalling how much his body had trembled the last time he'd read Daniel's poem out loud, overlooking his grave at his funeral. '*Someday soon, I shall find my wings – take off to the skies above. To a peaceful place, where I dance and sing – unafraid to show my love. I know in time, I shall return, as yet I know not when. There's so much more about life to learn, before savouring this world again.*'

'Lovers *is* correct.' Daniel clicked his fingers; the bathroom door flew open, and Keith's landing transformed into their beach encampment on that dreadful morning.

'Wow. How did you do that?' Keith warmed his cheeks, poked their glowing fire with a stick and wiggled his toes, running his bare feet through the smooth, warm sand. 'Bennett said you wanted to tell me the truth. He said I left you on your own by our tent in Rhyl. Did I hurt your feelings by going off with Charlotte? Is it true?'

Daniel shrugged it off. 'I felt a little put out before Millie showed. She still doesn't do underwear. *Commando.*'

'How lovely. Thanks.'

Daniel stopped connecting the stars with his fingers, shot up off his sleeping bag and vanished in a cloud of smoke and specks of ash. Returning right away with his guitar case, he handed it to Keith. 'Your vessel is an instrument: neurons and hormones are the keys. Let us generate beautiful music from the stems and root bark of life's tree.'

Keith rested Daniel's guitar case on his lap. 'Was your passing an accident? Did you top yourself because I told you I was leaving the band? Tell me the truth. I need to know.'

'I made my choice. Now you must choose. Open the case or walk in my shoes.'

Keith unclipped the latches but stopped, placing Daniel's guitar case on the sand. 'I can't do it,' he squealed. 'Just tell me. Was it my fault?'

Daniel shook his head. 'Pipe down. Long before the tide came in, I had drowned.'

'You should've told me about you and Bennett. I'd have understood. *Times* were different. *Laws* were different. Hell, *men* were different. Please stop with your rhyming slang. Talk to me. Properly. Let's have the conversation we never had. I'm all ears.'

Daniel munched a pink marshmallow from the end of his stick and folded his arms. 'I cried myself to sleep most nights, afraid I'd lose those I loved because I was different. Marc Bolan showed the world that was okay. He embraced his vibrant beauty within from an early age, which reflected outwards, manifesting exquisitely in his appearance and performance. I strived to be him, but hearing his death filter through Oggy's enormous silver ghetto blaster on the bonnet of his bright orange Mini broke the camel's back. Drained of my charm, charisma and magnetism, I lost all faith in my ability to recharge my vessel's electrical current. Nobody should have to sail their ship alone. Ending my journey ruined my friends' and family's journeys too. For that, I'll never forgive myself.'

'You didn't. We loved you being different,' Keith replied, wiping tears from his face. 'I needed educating. I should've tried harder. Who are the sailors of the skyway?'

Daniel sat beside his guitar with his legs crossed. 'Primitive vessels cannot travel far. Quintessential life forces can and do their best to stop spirited journeys ending prematurely by uniting our bloodlines with universal ley lines, bursting with positive energy. Some of us see the crescent. Some of us see the whole of the moon. I'd often perform with Eddie Cochran in my dreams, but their main man visited me once in a forest filled with white gardenias and pink cuckoos for story time wearing a black pointed hat and cloak. He told me when Marc would die and how. I couldn't hack it. After a while, my orb jammed like yours, making it impossible for my sailors to break through. I became caught in a trap, struggling to interpret their voices and visions, but having been here so long, trying to reach you, I've had time to reflect. Once bonded with human receptors, animated quintessence from our orb seeks to displace neighbouring primitive neurotransmitters and resonate at 72 Hz within a healthy vessel.'

The three pointed sand structures Daniel had built in 1977 materialised beside him. 'The Pyramids of Giza are a replica of this, mirroring the outer condition as well as three inner stages of consciousness. A vessel will always perish through age, but firmitas, utilitas and venustas, the feminine fundamentals our universe thrives on, withstand the test of time, craving excitation. Universal cycles, the speed at which sailors travel in a neuromodulated vacuum and love's golden frequency all add up, leading home to the land of love, but I didn't make it. I escaped the ape, believing I would. Having forfeited my journey, I became a lonely castaway in the murky land of nothingness, hoping for a splash of colour or a trickle of music from Tesla's fleet of love liners. You must try your hardest to remember who you performed with in your dreams.' Daniel smiled, handing Keith his guitar case once more. 'You called in the morning before camping in Rhyl. A white origami swan lay on my sill. You looked so happy, tapping its beak. You grabbed my journal, dying to peek.'

Keith frowned. 'That, I remember. You shouted at me and snatched it before I could read it. Was your relationship with Bennett the reason?'

Daniel scoffed. 'Whenever we performed, we always tuned our instruments together. We played what our souls wanted to hear, then Oggy and Bennett joined in. *We* set the tempo. Before I passed, I tuned my guitar to the same frequency Bolan did, attaching a capo.'

'Bennett calls that cheating.'

Daniel chuckled. 'Ignore him. That bonobo threatened to pee on my chin. Remember, open mind, open chords. Accommodate your vocalist. Some say Bolan's lead playing was often hit and miss. They poked fun at him for having a limited knowledge of music, but his tunes were no fluke. He played what his soul wanted to hear too and used his talent to share his experiences.'

'I'm truly sorry I rolled over back then and went to sleep.'

'Hey, it's difficult to realise you're drowning when you're everyone else's anchor. I failed to understand that a life lived for others is a life worthwhile. Sadly, now we're in the same boat. Your inner spectrum is deteriorating, meaning your orb will soon disconnect from its tiny cup, separating spirit from matter. You don't belong here. We must turn the tide. Let's perform "Lady Stardust" and push you back on through to the other side.'

Keith finally opened the case and lifted Daniel's snug Blue Sparkle and capo from its resting place. Noticing a homemade accessory compartment built into the plush cerulean lining, he flipped it open, revealing Daniel's journal with the Great Sphinx and the Pyramids of Giza sketched on the front, along with his white origami swan. 'They've been here all along!'

Daniel beamed. 'I stopped writing once I became lost. Winning Rock Heaven was never about our recording contract. It was all about what the purple heart trophy represented. You'll see. Energy, frequency and vibration allow journeys to continue by keeping primitive neurotransmitters stable. This guarantees a healthy vessel. Start us off.'

Keith shifted his capo up and down the neck, playing standard open shapes, causing Daniel's Blue Sparkle to sound more like a mandolin, and as soon as Daniel sang the first line of 'Lady Stardust', Keith's knees juddered, and he sat in awe, absorbing every universal sound his teenage surroundings offered. 'You were amazing.'

'*We* were amazing. Well done.' Daniel placed his hand on Keith's heart, then his forehead. 'Everything you are, ever was and ever will be is stored in here. Knowledge, creativity and love. Protect and reflect. It's a shame we must sink to the dark depths of our inner ocean before salvaging enough of ourselves to rise again. We hide our identities. We lose our identities. Some of us never even find our true identities.'

'What happens now?'

'For you, stop existing and start living. For me, hopefully a new life awaits if collected and permitted to enter the core gemstone gates.' Daniel hugged Keith, and colourful beams of light replenished his spirit. His clothes disappeared, he boogied on the spot beneath purple rain to a cover version of 'We Are Family' by Sister Sledge, and psychedelic sparks surged from his soul. 'Don't feel ashamed. Those who are seen dancing are thought to be insane by those who cannot hear the music. You were never ill. Just chemically imbalanced.'

Floral scents filled Keith's nostrils, and he reached out his palm, catching dewdrops. He dabbed them with his finger before popping them into his mouth. 'Salty.'

'I've waited so long for my second chance. First stop,

Club Copernicus for a dance. Please steer clear of my penitent path. Don't end this particular journey in the bath. Embrace your newfound strings. You're still my everything. Love is the only drug we need. We'll always be together, Keith. Forever in electric dreams.'

'Breathe,' Charlotte screamed. 'Breathe.'

Darkness ensued before an almighty flash of light presented Keith with a bird's-eye view of Charlotte administering chest compressions to his naked body on their bathroom floor. The emergency services operator tried keeping her calm on loudspeaker, then, counting to thirty, she tilted his head back, lifted his chin with two fingers and pinched his nose. Sealing her lips over his, she blew into his mouth, watching his chest rise. On her third cycle, Keith spurted salty water from his mouth, coughing as she laid him in the recovery position, slapping him and screaming. Daniel's guitar, capo, swan and journal lay beside him as he screamed, 'Django. I awake!'

***

Keith spent most of Sunday at Daniel's grave and called in sick Monday and Tuesday, visiting special places they'd go together as teenagers before returning to work on Wednesday. He made himself a cup of tea, hoping to fade into the background at the far end of the brew cabin, and flicked through the first few pages of Daniel's journal on his quick break. Leonardo da Vinci's *Vitruvian Man* had been sketched on page 3, Michelangelo's *Sistine Chapel* on page 6 and Georges de La Tour's *Penitent Magdalen* on page 9. Each had *Hidden in Plain Sight* written in bold letters and underlined beneath. 'Oh sugar.' He switched on his phone from his rucksack and *ping*, a message from Oggy popped up first. It read: *URGENT! Finn's dad showed up at BJ's when you left, causing a scene. There's something important we need to discuss. CALL ME ASAP!*

Keith tucked Daniel's journal safely back in his rucksack, slung it over his shoulder and rinsed out his cup, heading to the compound for a better signal. He ducked down at the back of the cabin away from the commotion at the main gates and checked his voicemail messages, listening to his last remaining contact confirming he had no job vacancies for Finn. Bennett had texted, calling Keith a coward, Jake begged him not to leave their band, Finn asked if he was okay, and Charlotte wanted to know what time he'd be home. Guilt-ridden for leaving Finn, Keith took a deep breath, knowing Bowden would be less volatile once his meeting with sub-contractors had finished. He hovered by the office door, listening to him laughing and joking with two electrical engineers.

'Come in if you're coming,' Bowden screeched. 'Jesus, Keith, you're pale as fuck. Have you eaten? You sure you should be back at work? It's not contagious, is it?'

'No. No,' he replied, unsure what to do with his hands. 'What's going on at the gates?'

'Some snotty-nosed reporter and mental health charity, Inner Vibrations, are quizzing folk. Mental health is a myth dreamt up by lazy bastards who can't be arsed putting a shift in. Nobody's allowed to speak to them. Do you understand? Now, what is it you want?'

'I'm after getting somebody a start,' Keith said with his arms by his sides.

Bowden leant back in his chair and locked his fingers together. 'Are you mad? The agencies are pecking my head every day. Now there's all this talk of pipe fitters' wages being cut, expenses being halved and planned strikes with Unite, who are on their way as we speak.'

'I know. I'm fully aware. Do you remember Finn?' he asked, avoiding eye contact. Stepping to one side in silence, he accidentally knocked over a fire extinguisher.

'Eh? Look at me.' Bowden removed his specs, and with no hint or warning, he erupted like a volcano, slamming his safety folder on the desk. 'Do I remember Finn? The bleeding boomtown rat. That lowlife caused ructions for me on his last day.'

'Nobody's happy when they get sacked. He needs a job.'

'I'm sure he does.' Bowden opened his site diary. 'Fifth of August – comments made by Finn to me. "You can't have me cleaning other people's shit. It's not right. I'm not doing it. I refuse, you fuckin' bully." This is what he said to Trevor: "Clean your own shitters. You couldn't run a bath, never mind a construction site. Tell Bowden he's a noncey old age pensioner who stinks of piss." How the hell have you got mixed up with that foul-mouthed little urchin?'

'He's changed,' Keith replied, wincing. 'Can't we give him a trial? Say till Christmas. I'll need a hand. If he's bucked his ideas up, which I know he has, we could put him back on the cards. Work would've picked up by then, surely?'

Bowden folded his arms and stretched his long legs

out in front of him. 'You're asking too much. Sorry. I've turned lads away with real potential. That scrote's not coming back.'

Keith nodded. 'Well, I hereby give you one week's verbal notice. I'm resigning. Don't worry, I'll put it in writing, and so you all know, I've been struggling with my mental health for most of my life. Did you get that? You want me to write it down or shall I go see Inner Vibrations and the reporter at the gates about this so-called bloody myth?'

Bowden leapt from his chair, knocking the first aid box off the filing cabinet. 'You duck-eggs out, and don't breathe a word of what you just heard. *You* need to get your emotions under control,' he screeched, booting a box full of copper fittings across the office.

'I'm emotional, am I? Don't think I'm picking them up,' Keith yelled. 'Finn's right. You're nothing but a bully. Your playground tactics won't wash with me.'

'Now listen here,' Bowden snarled. 'Trevor wanted Finn blacklisted from every site in Manchester. That nasty little midget was pissed up, off his head on God knows what, puking in the hoist. He called Gibbo a bellend and Trevor a waste of oxygen.'

Keith shrugged and sighed, determined to stick up for Finn no matter what. 'That doesn't sound like the lad I know. I'm sorry, Bowden, but Gibbo is the one who deserves to be jobless, not Finn. Nobody likes him, and I'm pretty sure Trevor exaggerated.'

'You didn't see him spitting feathers. Now, you're in charge of half this pissing building site, so you can shove your resignation up your arse. How's about those apples? Think of your family. You're going to throw all that away on a shit-stain? Has he kidnapped them? Do I need to call the police?' Bowden collapsed in his chair with his head in his hands.

'I'm not the only one with mental health issues on this site or any other site, I can assure you. What's the real reason Inner Vibrations are here?'

Bowden rubbed his face, then linked his fingers together, resting them on his stomach. 'Trevor hung himself. Debt related. His poor wife found him. It's touch and go.'

'Blimey.' Keith gathered up the copper fittings and put them neatly into their boxes.

'I'll make sure what you divulged earlier about having a tough time stays within these four walls. I'm trying to help you. If the guys out there under your command find out, they won't understand. They'll think you're weak like Trevor. You'll lose all respect.'

'Is that right? What about Finn?'

'We've been through this. Not happening.' Bowden passed Keith a folder. 'Get a brew. There's a new mental health toolbox talk to run through. I can speak to HR and get you some paid leave. We'll dress it up as a bad back. Off you go. We'll talk later.'

'Unbelievable. Let's just brush it all under the carpet. I don't think so.' Keith slammed the office door, barged past the electrical engineers and made a beeline for a young woman with a microphone at the gates. 'Is this live?'

'On radio, yes. It'll be on Granada Reports this evening also. I'm Elaine. You are?'

'Keith.' He approached the bloke from Inner Vibrations. 'Can I grab a T-shirt, please?'

'Most definitely. I'm Lucas. We focus on positive

thinking with music in mind. We have a place on Swan Street. We used to be all about awareness, but we're now looking to understand the root causes of mental health by listening and sharing our good or bad experiences from our diaries and journals. Expressing ourselves creatively is key.'

'Keep up the great work.' Keith stripped to his waist, exposing his pot belly to an encore of wolf whistles, and put on his new T-shirt, which showed the human brain with colourful musical notes floating by.

'Ready?' Elaine asked. 'I'm here with Keith in Piccadilly Gardens outside a building site where one man has tried taking his own life at a time when construction workers have the highest male occupation mortality rates from suicide. Are you surprised by these statistics?'

'No, Elaine, I'm not. We are but numbers. Every single human life should be treated as priceless, but we're valued only by how well we keep economic wheels in motion. I know what it's like to live with mental health issues, and my heart goes out to this man's family and everyone affected.' Keith pointed to his T-shirt. 'I wish charities like this existed when I was ill. Truth is, I spent a lot of time alone in a mental institution, suffering when my best friend died. Everyone thought I'd run away. On the inside, part of me had. I lost my friends, I nearly lost my wife, we lost our unborn children, and I lost my love for music all due to excessive amounts of stress. Every individual is unique, you see, when it comes to how much trauma our bodies can withstand. There is no one size fits all, and we all need time and space to recover. Recently I had a relapse, and I'd like to apologise to my wife, Charlotte, who I love dearly, as well as my friends and family, for not being honest about that. You've probably heard of Sothis Media's upcoming tribute competition, Love Is the Drug. Well, my bandmates Oggy, Bennett, Jake and I have entered with an extremely talented young vocalist named Finn, and we'd love to help Inner Vibrations get their message out there by wearing these T-shirts throughout, if that's okay?'

'We'd be honoured.'

'I think I know who you are,' Elaine said. 'You're from—'

'The Magnesium Gurus, AKA the none-hit wonders. Rest in electromagnetic power, Daniel Saunders. And Clifford of Dual Ventures, if you're watching, you failed to split us up. We're back, and we're coming for what's rightfully ours. Finn, our gifted vocalist, was sacked from his job here on this very site because he stood up for himself against bullies in that office there.' Keith pointed to Bowden and his engineers at the office door. 'Men, young or old, have feelings. We have emotions, and if we continue to hide them, especially in predominantly male surroundings like construction sites, then those statistics you mentioned, Elaine, will continue to climb at an alarming rate. I want everyone to know I just resigned from my position on this site simply because I don't want to work for men like these anymore. We need change. We need support and understanding to replace shame and stigma.'

'It's great to catch up, Keith. Huge fan. Do you have a new job lined up?'

Keith exhaled, knowing Charlotte would kill him. 'Not yet. Finn and my bandmates need me,' he said. 'We're going to win Love Is the Drug for everyone who struggles to be themselves in a world where folk get rich off other people's pain and suffering. Everybody in Manchester in need of a feel-good vibe is more than welcome to come cheer us on in the coming weeks. Once our performance timetable is agreed, we'll let you know when and where. Thank you.'

Lucas hugged Keith. 'God bless you.'

'Yes. Thanks, Keith, for speaking up. Our deepest condolences to you and your family too.' Elaine spun to face the camera. 'Wow! Those who have never heard of the Magnesium Gurus, believe me, you're in for the ride of your life. True winners of Sothis Media's Rock Heaven back in '77 and now in collaboration with Inner Vibrations. I can't wait for Love Is the Drug. It just got mega exciting. Back to the studio.'

***

Keith spent the rest of his day surrounded by nature at Debdale Park, delving deeper into Daniel's journal and feeding white swans with a tremendous weight lifted from his shoulders. He flicked through sketched geometric shapes and stopped at a section filled with numbers. *Earth's natural frequency is 7.83hz. 7 + 8 + 3 = 18. 1 + 8 = 9. Sailors of the skyway bang a gong at three distinct stages of the birth cycle to make certain mother and child's minds stay synchronised. 12 weeks: 1 + 2 multiplied by three tiers of consciousness equates to 9 years of childhood. 24 weeks: 2 + 4 multiplied by three tiers of consciousness equates to eighteen years: 1 + 8 = 9 years of adolescence.*

36 weeks: 3 + 6 multiplied by three tiers of consciousness equates to twenty-seven years: 2 + 7 = 9 years of adulthood. A protective stream of melatonin is introduced after the first trimester reducing oxidative stress therefore paving the way for a compatible quintessential being to steer the primitive vessel once the orb is fully formed at 720 days: 7 + 2 = 9. With his mind blown to bits, he skimmed further. Daniel's feelings for Bennett were evidently clear, but his mum found them in bed together and threatened to disown him. He responded by sneaking away with Bennett to Reading Festival on August 27th, 1977, where they both ended up intoxicated and Daniel cheated on him with an unnamed teenager.

Realising he had to face the music, Keith arrived home with his rucksack over his shoulder around teatime, in the most stress-free of moods, and whipped out his sandwich box, rinsing it under the hot tap. He washed the pots, put out the bins, locked the door and dried his hands with a tea towel, then nearly jumped out of his skin when he spun to find Charlotte glaring at him. 'Jesus! Everything okay?'

'You tell me,' she said, leaning against the fridge with her hands behind her back. 'You avoided me all Sunday. You're up and out the door early in the mornings, tucked up in bed early at night, hoping this conversation would never happen, then I hear you on the radio, having resigned from the job you've had for decades, talking about your past mental health issues. You weren't meant to go in. Don't you think we should've discussed this together, especially a topic as personal and painful as our miscarriages?'

'Spur of the moment,' he replied, rubbing his chin. 'I'm on TV later. Good, hey?'

She shook her head. 'Keith, your mental health issues aren't in the past, they're in the present. The decision you made to resign was manic and irrational. You missed your appointment with the crisis team, so I booked you another.'

'Pardon? Why would you do a crazy thing like that?' he asked with his arms out wide. 'You just had a go at me for not including you in my decisions.'

'You haven't taken your replacement meds,' she replied, raising her voice. 'We need to sort out your CBT sessions, and you were grinding your teeth again in the early hours. It's got louder over the past few weeks. Your mouth guard is in the bathroom cabinet. Use it.'

Keith filled the kettle and plonked two cups on the side, dropping tea bags in both. 'Brew?' he said, hoping the discussion would end there.

'Tea won't solve this. We can't afford the mortgage and bills on my wage alone. Phone Bowden and tell him you made a huge mistake due to illness.'

'I can't go back. I won't. I'm weaning off my meds.' He grabbed a teaspoon from the cutlery drawer, opened the top cupboard and clutched the biscuit tin. 'Chocolate bourbon?'

'Stop. Keith, look at me. You need to see the crisis team. I'll drive you to A&E.'

'I can assure you, I'm fine. I have everything under control, I promise. I'm not five. I'm not going. This is the first time I've felt prepared to move on with my life and put Daniel's death behind me once and for all. Not happening, love.'

'You hide your emotions at work and hide your emotions at home.'

'How am I hiding? I just blurted it out for all to hear,' he yelled, pointing to the radio. 'I told Bowden and the whole of Greater Manchester; I am not ashamed anymore.'

'So you're a celebrity now, that it? Your groupies haven't seen you at your worst. They haven't had to resuscitate you on our bathroom floor. That's your problem – you used to keep it all in. Now you're being selective. You tried to kill yourself.'

'Err. No, I didn't,' he said, sweating. 'I nodded off in the bath. We've all done it.'

'The pills. Stop lying. You lied about working overtime. You lied about being involved in the band, and what you did earlier was reckless. If I didn't have first aid training through work, we wouldn't be having this conversation. David and Helen would have lost their dad forever.' She stood deep in thought with her hands on her hips. 'Okay. Let's be honest. Stop stirring and talk me through precisely what happened to you in the bathroom *that* night. I want to know everything you experienced, and I'll tell you what stage we're at. Please let me in.'

He strolled into the conservatory with two cups of tea and made himself comfortable in his wicker chair. She sat facing him with her legs crossed, listening to him talk first about Bennett's revelations and everything that had gone on with Clifford at BJ's. He spoke fondly of his duet with Daniel on the beach and showed her his journal, telling her where he had found it, but she wouldn't even look at it. When he had finished speaking, he smiled, waiting for her response, but her facial expression gave nothing away whatsoever.

'So your body was in the bath, but your spirit was in Bournemouth?'

Keith glanced around the room before answering. 'We

might've gone back in time, I'm not entirely sure. I heard jazz music. There were multicoloured flashing lights all around me. I felt so alive. The entire experience seemed so real, from the smooth sand between my toes to the alluring scent of flowers.'

'So you didn't accidentally nod off and you didn't try topping yourself. You heard Daniel's voice, after all this time, but he ignored you, so you pretended to drown just so he'd show himself and – what, save you?'

'Pretty much. Do you get it now?'

She shot from her seat like a rocket. 'So Daniel saved you, not me? Have you heard yourself? Is he here now? No. These audible and visible hallucinations are precisely what you promised to tell me about. Next time you're being interviewed for TV and radio, lead with that story. See what happens.' She stamped her feet, threw a cushion at him and stormed off to the kitchen with clenched fists, banging cups and saucers.

'That hurt.' He rubbed his eyebrow to check whether the zip had drawn blood, but thankfully it hadn't. Praying she'd simmer down, he kept quiet, misjudging the situation entirely.

She appeared with a bright red face, swinging her arms like a blooming windmill, and threw a basket of dirty washing at him, which tipped onto the carpet. 'You promised me.'

'Stop!' He had no option but to duck out of the way when she whipped her high heels off and threw them at him one after the other. One missed his head by a matter of centimetres. 'Calm down. You're like a woman possessed. Maybe *you* should have CBT?'

'If you think this is some sort of joke, get out. Pack your things together and go stay at Oggy's. Get him to wash up after you. Can't you see what's going on? You found out Daniel was bisexual, and the trauma triggered homosexual dreams.'

'Pardon! I am *not* having homosexual dreams.'

'Heterosexual men do not say "You're my everything" to other heterosexual men.'

'That's just how Daniel is – *was*. You know how he loved to tease me. It was his mum's favourite song by Andy Gibb, remember?'

'Funny how Finn reminds you so much of Daniel. We hadn't had sex in six months before that night you told me about him in the Church. Should I invite him over to sing for you? He's the only one around here who seems to float your fucking boat.'

Keith's jaw dropped. 'Too far. You're being ridiculous. Daniel removed all my self-pity in a matter of minutes on Saturday night. Isn't that what you wanted? Seeing *is* believing. I know what I saw, I know what I heard, I know what I smelt, I know what I tasted, and I know for a fact how I felt.' He received a text from Oggy and read it out, wiping tears from his face. '*Finn texted to say he's sorry, but he's left the band. He's moving to Glasgow with his dad in the morning. WE NEED YOU NOW! I'm on my way to pick you up.*'

Charlotte burst out laughing. 'So, what's it this time, fight or flight? Finn and your stupid band or your family? You can't have both. Your head will explode. Who's Django?'

'Think maybe I dreamt about him when I was younger.

Not like that. Look, all I know is Daniel wanted everyone around him to be happy. So do I. I used to love performing. I used to love the electricity. I love you and our kids, but I'm sorry. Not knowing where he went and not being there for the people I care about has crippled me with regret for decades. I refuse to make the same mistake with Finn.' Keith grabbed his house keys off the mantelpiece.

'You don't get it, do you?' Charlotte sobbed. 'Grandiose delusions. Sound familiar? This is how it started last time. Believing Daniel's hype. Seeing him dance on the wall or on the bus, hearing his pathetic poetry in your head. Now he's trying to get you into bed. You're living in a dream world. You. Are. Having. A. Relapse. Finn is not Daniel. Daniel is *dead*! We both know precisely where he went. He's six feet under in Southern Cemetery.'

Keith tried hugging Charlotte, but she pushed him away. 'So why did it feel as if I was the one who died? I need a better routine if I'm to spend my twilight years with a smile on my face. You used to love hearing me play. You used to love singing along. What if Daniel's right? What if love is the only drug we all need? It must've been this overwhelming feeling of love I experienced inside what seemed like an intergalactic pod or a spiritual foetus that brought me back. Look, it's difficult to explain right now.' Gathering a few essentials in a carrier bag, he grabbed his coat, rucksack and cap from the cloakroom, gripped Daniel's guitar case with his journal inside and left with a large lump in his throat. His phone bleeped the moment he closed the front gate. Charlotte's text message read: *Told you this would end in tears. You need help. CALL THE SAMARITANS NOW!*

Oggy pulled up by the kerb and dived out of his Jeepster with his beer belly hanging over his jeans, his flies undone and a big fat cigar in his mouth. He grinned, looking genuinely pleased to see Keith in one piece. 'Your amazing PR stunt got you bin-bagged,' hey? I'm sorry, mate. That was brave what you did. She'll come around. Is that Daniel's Blue Sparkle?'

Keith shrugged. 'His mum gave it me after his funeral. It's been in my loft for years.'

'Any more secrets?' Oggy gave Keith a blank look. 'Stick your stuff in the boot. You can stop with me as long as you like. Plenty of room.'

Keith homed in on the sweet sounds of Beethoven's Ninth Symphony from Oggy's speakers. 'Did you go Reading Festival in '77 – a few weeks before Bournemouth?'

Oggy shook his head and drove away. 'Bournemouth was the biggie. Why you ask?'

'Been thinking about the rivalry between us, the Narcissists and Heaton Mourning back then. Did Daniel or Bennett ever mention going? What about Clifford?'

'Clifford was pissed he couldn't afford to go,' Oggy said, chuckling. 'I seem to remember his band going, but they refused to lend him the money. What's this about?'

'Curious how Clifford knew more about Daniel and Bennett's relationship than us.'

Oggy braked hard and pulled over at the nearest bus stop. 'Think it's best you let sleeping dogs lie. You need to focus on your own relationship right now. How would you feel if you really lost Charlotte, hey? When we lost Daniel, we lost our best friend, and boy, did it hurt. We now know Bennett lost so much more. Love is love, Keith.

Don't rock the boat. I gallivanted around the country for Clifford so much over the years, I didn't pay Judy enough attention. She said she didn't feel wanted anymore, and the cruel thing about this world is there's always some shithouse lined up waiting to park their car in your drive once you've left for work. You need each other. Have you had your tea?'

'Nope. I'm not hungry.'

'I've got a wack of wibs in the fweezer for when we get back.' Oggy grabbed a newspaper off the back seat and dropped it on Keith's lap. 'First, we need to deal with this.'

The front page showed a sky-blue Vauxhall Astra wrapped around a tree near Cringle Fields. 'You've told me this tragic story. Her unique and soulful voice would've been very much at home during the Harlem Renaissance.'

Oggy nodded. 'The Judy Garland lookalike in the photographs above Clifford's mantlepiece, yes. She necked a cocktail of pills and booze just like Daniel and took off. Nobody understood why. Some say she couldn't handle the fame; some say she suffered with severe anxiety and depression. Well, that's her husband with their nine-year-old son.'

'You've lost me.'

'Remember when I said in all my years, I've only ever come across two vocalists as talented as Finn. One was Daniel and the other was her. Keith, her name was Josie Finnegan,' Oggy said, pointing to the photo. 'And that's the guy who caused a scene at BJ's after you stormed out. Has it registered yet? That's right. It's Finn's dad!'

EIGHT

Wednesday, September 7th, 2011 - 19:45

Finn shoved *The Wizard's Gown – Rewoven: Beneath the Glitter of Marc Bolan* by Tony Stringfellow into Keith's rucksack before zipping it up. He lay on his bed in his tracksuit bottoms and switched on his laptop. Typing in *pink cuckoo*, tonnes of images popped up of April wildflowers, which he knew nothing about. He tapped in *what women want*, instead bringing up films women his age mostly enjoyed, then scrolled through the first list he came to. The top three were *The Notebook*, *The Sweetest Feeling* and *Dirty Dancing*. Choosing *The Notebook*, he downloaded it, blanking Keith's texts.

'Bags are packed,' his dad said, pushing Finn's bedroom door open. 'Set your alarm for half five. What you watching?'

'Nowt much.' He put on his headphones the minute his dad left, made himself comfortable and pressed play, watching a man in a boat row along an enormous lake with swans and geese, taking off to the sound of music. His dad barged in, panicking, seconds later, wanting him to follow him. Pausing his film, Finn whipped off his headphones and rushed to his dad's room to find him peering through the net curtains.

'Who's in that fancy car, staring at the house? What if it's to do with Mace? They'll get what's coming to them if they think they're putting you in hospital.'

'Stop being paranoid. Told you I wasn't involved. Shift, let me have a look. It's Keith and Oggy,' he said, pushing past him.

Finn's dad slumped on the edge of his bed with his head in his hands.

'Chill. I'll get rid.' Finn grabbed Keith's rucksack and shot downstairs, leaving it by the front door, and stuck on his trainers from beside the gas meter cupboard. He headed outside with his hoody on, approaching the kerb. 'Not nice being ignored, is it? You're so full of shit! What happened to not taking off and quitting if things became difficult?'

Oggy stuck the top half of his body out of his car window further along the street and gave Finn a big thumbs-up. 'I'll give you two a few moments to yourselves. Breathe, kid.'

'I'm truly sorry.' Keith leant against a lamppost with his arms folded.

'Are you?' Finn stuck his hood up to keep his ears warm and shoved his hands into his front pocket. 'I just messaged to see if you were okay. Now I know. Bye,' he said before turning his back on him.

Bennett's van came flying around the corner with him in the passenger seat and Jake at the wheel. Oggy dived out of his Jeepster, waving them down.

'Finn, wait, please.'

'Why should I? You left me the same way you left them.'

'At least allow me to explain, then you can punch me in the face. Daniel's death rocked me. I blamed myself, had a nervous breakdown and ended up in hospital until it was safe for me to function properly again. By the time I returned to some form of normality many months later, Charlotte had had our first miscarriage. After two more, we were told we couldn't have children by natural methods. I'd lost these guys their recording contract and the ability to do something I truly loved. Life was never the same again for us. We lost everything apart from each other.'

Bennett sat on his neighbour's wall, smoking a joint with Oggy, and Jake nudged up close, drinking tea from a flask. Finn turned to face Keith and checked his neighbours weren't listening. 'Soz for your loss. I get it. You actually lost your marbles, though?'

'Afraid so. I've been on and off medication ever since.' Keith stepped forward and squeezed the tops of Finn's arms. 'I needed time away back then. I thought I did again, but I just needed a little space to find myself. I'm not leaving. Not now, not ever.'

'Keep your voice down.' Finn brushed Keith's hands away, spotting his downstairs curtains twitching. 'Don't want my dad kicking off in the street.'

Keith stepped back. 'Shall we sit here by the kerb?'

Finn sat on the cold paving but kept his distance, flicking stones into the hole left by the stolen grid. 'You do know I'm not Daniel, right?'

'Of course. You sound like my wife.' Keith joined in,

lobbing stones. 'My sleep patterns went haywire; I didn't know what was real. Sometimes it was like living in a nightmare, sometimes it was like living in a dream. It was as if my entire life drained from my head to my toes and I just existed. I'd see frightening things, beautiful things, and hear voices, which made little sense. The more I heard, the more I listened, eventually realising the faintest one belonged to Daniel, but my meds shut the rest down. Oggy filled me in with what happened after I left BJ's. I get now why you struggled to sit still in my car that night to Khan's. I'm so sorry to hear about your mother. We all are.'

'Shit happens, right?'

'But it shouldn't. Not to anyone. Must've been so difficult for both you and your dad.'

'His work transferred him. We're off for a new start. Mace is over the worst. He's moving away too. Stop looking at me like that. You said I needed a change of scenery.'

'I never meant so far away. Great news about Mace, though.'

'Look, my bags are packed. I don't own much.' Finn stood. 'We're leaving early, but I hope you and the guys find someone decent. I need to go. I'll be cheering you on.'

Keith sprang up and brushed his backside. 'Listen. I'm sorry I let you down.'

'You believed in me more than anyone else in the past nine years. I felt wanted and on the verge of belonging, but I can't help feeling like everyone I get close to rejects me. I wanted everything to work out. I honestly did, but my dad needs me more than you guys. He can't handle rejection right now. He's been through enough. I'm sure you can understand that. Forgot.' Finn grabbed Keith's rucksack from behind the door. 'It's all there. Check.'

'No need.' Keith scribbled his address down on an old receipt from his pocket. 'If you ever want to talk, you know where I am, and if you ever want to come back and see us, I can come get you. It's no problem. On the train, obviously.'

Finn shook his head. 'You're definitely nuts.'

Keith laughed. 'One last question before you begin your new adventure. Daniel seemed to go someplace in his mind when he sang. When I witnessed your performance in the Church, you seemed to do the same. Where did you go? How did you feel?'

'That's two questions.'

'If I know you as well as I think I do, one answer kind of covers both.'

Finn bowed his head, finding it difficult to speak, then looked Keith in the eye. 'Closer and closer to my mam's energy every time. Look, thanks for giving a shit. Meant a lot.'

'My pleasure. Write or call anytime. I promise I'll never ignore you again.' Keith waved Oggy, Bennett and Jake over. 'Truly sorry, guys, but his mind's made up.'

A big silver 4 × 4 cruised along the street and parked next to Bennett's van, blocking the street. Out climbed Rhonda with Farooq, and she placed her pink feather boa around Finn's neck. 'Please don't go. I've been so looking forward to measuring you up for your costume.'

Finn burst out laughing. 'I need to grab a shower.'

'Is that you that honks?' Jake asked. 'Thought it was that smelly retard again.'

Moon-Head's window flew open. 'Do you lot know what time it is? Shut the fuck up or I'm calling the police. Who've you come dressed as, Cruella de Vil?'

'Listen here, twenty-bob-cabbage-head,' Rhonda shouted. 'Shut your pie hole and close your window unless you want a stiletto sticking out of that monstrous cranium.'

Moon-Head slammed her window shut. They all roared with laughter and Finn received hugs, handshakes and offers of condolence before waving them off. His dad sat watching TV with his specs near the end of his nose, pretending he hadn't heard a thing. 'I'm gonna chill,' Finn said, wrapping Rhonda's feather boa around his dad's neck. 'See you in the morning.'

'Night, son.'

Finn had a shower, listened to T. Rex on his phone for a good half hour, then shoved on his T-shirt and shorts and updated his journal before making himself comfortable on his bed ready to watch *The Notebook*.

'There's a brew here if you want one,' his dad shouted. 'Come down a sec. I'd like you to see something on TV. Quick.'

Finn nipped downstairs and sat at the dinner table. 'I'm shattered. What is it?'

'Please, just watch. Turn the volume up a bit.'

Finn did as his dad asked and watched Keith being interviewed by a reporter outside his old construction site. The minute it finished, Finn leapt out of his seat. 'What a whopper. He's got no job now because of me. He has a family. Is he real? Dad, I need to call him.'

'Hold your horses. I meant to give you this on your birthday, but you didn't come home, and I struggled to find it.' Finn's dad passed him an old, creased envelope. 'It's time I stopped running from my past and time you started running towards a brighter future.'

Finn unfolded a note from inside, paying attention to every single word: *Hello, my dear, excuse the pun, but as you know, my mind has been like a box of broken biscuits for some time now. I know you'll blame yourself, but you mustn't. You were my lighthouse. I've been so tired and torn between who I've been, who I am and who I'm expected to be. I simply needed to be free. I love you both with all my heart, but like an anchor, I sunk a little deeper each day into the darkness. I didn't belong here anymore. If truth be told, I don't believe I ever did. I know how difficult this will be to read, my love, but I couldn't have left our son in better hands. You'll no doubt want to wrap him in cotton wool, but you mustn't let the end of my journey stand in the way of him beginning his. One day there will be a knock at the door from a group of gentlemen, wanting to help. Let them in. They're not the vultures you and I have come to know. They have what it takes to put some colour back into this dark and dingy world, saving many more from drowning. Let our son go his own way and I promise I will be with him every step. Lots of universal love, my darlings. I'll be seeing you xxx.*

Finn folded his mam's note up with tears streaming down his face and gave his dad a massive hug. 'Mam was really suffering, wasn't she? Sorry I blamed you.'

'I'm the one who should be sorry. I was selfish. I couldn't bear the thought of losing you too. If being with the Magnesium Gurus is where you belong, then you need to stay. I'm sorry I never made you feel wanted after we lost your wonderful mam. I have and always will be proud of you. Believe me, I tried everything to save her.'

'I believe you. How did she know Keith and the guys would show up?'

'Think she just expected it, given your talent, son. Any idiot can see how much the Magnesium Gurus have your best interests at heart. I was wrong to think they were taking advantage. I'm sorry I failed her, and I'm so sorry I failed you. I didn't know how to speak to you about her. Still don't. I miss her so much. You were right. My shitty routine never helped either of us. That's why I need a new start. I asked your friends to wait. Told them the decision to stay and continue in their band and competition was yours to make. Oggy offered to put you up. Dry your eyes with that kitchen roll first,' he said, with his hand on the door lock. 'You wanted to make your own choices. So what's it to be, son?'

***

Oggy handed out bacon butties and sat behind his drums, troughing, the following Saturday morning. He wiped his greasy hands on his jumper and took a large gulp of his tea. 'Now, listen up. Our first live performance in this competition is less than a week away. I demand nothing but hard work and commitment from everyone. I'm supplying all fizzy pop and sandwiches for the day, even the alcohol at the end. I've told Farooq no interruptions whatsoever. No partners or ex-partners, no media pricks, no prostitutes and no disgruntled parents.' He wiped brown sauce from his face and threw his napkin in the bin. 'Before we run through names for our band, I'd like to give you a taste of what's coming.'

Keith dimmed the lights and placed a CD in Bennett's laptop, which he'd connected to a giant screen on the brick wall, showing performances from bands they'd soon be up against.

'Next up is Physical Graffiti at local venues over the past year. These guys are the ones to beat, so pay close attention while finishing your breakfast.'

Finn dragged his stool forward and rested his chin on his hands, unable to look away. The lead singer belted out his notes with ace vocal control, and each member of the band knew their job, playing like they trusted each other with their lives on a smoke-filled stage in some fancy warehouse studio. Clifford appeared from the shadows, grinning.

'Ignore that smug bastard and focus. What do you make of our rivals?'

Jake threw his hands in the air. 'They've got better equipment; they look and sound ace and they're going to take a massive shit all over us.'

'Can you be any more negative?'

'Oggy, he's right,' Finn added, clocking Keith and Bennett's blank expressions.

'Okay, so they're good. To be the best, we must beat the best. What do they have that we don't? They have a theme with their dark clothes and eyeshadow. They have that togetherness on stage. We need to create our own lasting impression.'

'Why not wear makeup throughout the competition?' Bennett asked, pulling their Inner Vibrations T-shirts from a large cardboard box. 'We could match the colours with these, showing our commitment to a cause, like the suffragettes, and have Candy Pink Cavern on the back. Sex workers have mental health issues. They're discriminated against all the time.'

Jake shook his head. 'Are you real? Let's all wear daft helmets too and call ourselves the Vagina Miners or Space Dockers. Can someone tell Larry Flynt here brothels are illegal?'

'We don't do mucky mags. It's a massage parlour.'

'Where you massage sausages, melons and muffins.'

Oggy switched off the video and folded his arms. 'Sorry, Bennett, Jake's right. Paula's not on the same page when it comes to "Inner Vibrations". We can't promote prostitution. Let's keep it clean and vote on wearing makeup throughout the competition.'

'Guys, we'll be judged on our performance,' Finn said, 'not what we wear. If we went up against Physical Graffiti today, we'd get slaughtered. We need to rehearse.' He watched Jake's hand shoot up with Bennett's, but Keith and Oggy agreed with him. 'Did you ever meet my mam?'

The room fell silent before Oggy leant forward, nodding his head. 'I met her once at the Academy. She kept herself to herself, but you'd never have thought it, the way she lit up the stage. Her performance reminded me of a family-friendly fountain firework. Pretty, not too loud, yet so colourful. It was as if someone lit the blue touch paper and stood back with everyone in the crowd, waiting patiently, wondering whether she was a dud. Boy, did she surprise me. The moment her words left her lips, people whistled and cheered as she projected her colourful shower of sparks spanning from floor to ceiling, grabbing their attention. Her routine was so intense. When it seemed like she was about to fade and splutter in the darkness, she had that extra spark, keeping her audience on tenterhooks right till the very end. The last time I felt so magnetically drawn into a performance like hers was when I stood beside Keith in the Church watching you.'

Finn's bottom lip quivered. He couldn't look Oggy in the eye in case he cried. 'Thanks. Did she have many dealings with Clifford? My dad said she auditioned here once.'

Oggy left his seat and approached Finn, resting his hand on his shoulder. 'Nowhere near as many as he'd have liked. He begged to manage her, but she told him all he cared about was power, not people. To him, your mum was the one consummate professional who got away. Make him feel that way about you and we have a fighting chance. We need to be a team like them on that video, which means sticking together. I know it'll be difficult, but Clifford will be seething after Keith provoked him via his beloved media, so I need all of you to promise to keep your emotions in check. And by that, I mean we can't lash out at Clifford or anyone else if things aren't going our way.'

Keith, Bennett and Jake shrugged and nodded at each other before promising, then Farooq ducked under the screen, interrupting. 'Just grabbing some tissue. I know him,' he said, pointing to Clifford's nephew. 'That is Antoine Decker AKA the pecker wrecker. He went to my college. Thought he was something special. Not a nice person.'

'Runs in the family, then,' Keith said. 'What's a pecker wrecker?'

'He wore dental braces and preferred men.'

Oggy looked deep in thought. 'You learn something new every day. I dated his mum, Becky. Clifford's twin sister. That's right, Jake, a wonderful *black* woman. We even discussed starting a family.'

'You banged Webecca Decker, whose son's a pecker wecker,' he replied. 'Nice.'

Everyone sniggered except Oggy, who frowned. 'Just wasn't meant to be, I suppose. Shame, really.' He threw his drumstick at Jake. 'Names for the band, numbnuts.'

Finn knew it was going to be a long day and didn't want to go first in case he made himself sound like a proper nugget. He slumped in his seat with his hands stuffed in the front pocket of his hoody, doing his best to hide.

'Diplodocus,' Jake screeched.

Finn chuckled, Keith and Bennett blanked him and Oggy looked straight through him. 'Bennett, your turn.'

'What's up? Diplodocus, T. Rex. They're both dinosaurs. Doh!' Jake opened the back door to let some fresh air in and lounged on the floor in the corner. He dragged his tin of tobacco and block of weed from under his chair and licked his papers, sulking.

'Tran-Rex?' Bennett added, handing out cups of tea.

Finn and Keith couldn't stop grinning, but Oggy belted his drums, taking everyone by surprise. 'Am I the only one taking this competition serious? We need a highly recognisable name before we can enter the competition. Focus, please. Keith, your turn.'

'We could call ourselves Magnesium Gurus again. Still has a catchy sound to it.'

Jake glanced at Finn, Keith and Bennett, then glared

at Oggy. 'Not when he says it. No way you're introducing us in pubs round here. Welcome, we're the pissing Goo Woos.'

'Juniper Suction,' Finn said, still laughing at Jake. 'Marc loved plants, trees and nature. You probably know it's the title of one of his songs, but thought it sounded cool.'

'Let's vote once more. The Magnesium *Gurus* or Juniper Suction?'

'How come *you* haven't chosen one?' Jake asked.

'If I must. Thunderwings. Again, after one of Marc's songs.'

'Sounds like a pack of sanitary towels.'

Finn smirked and voted for Magnesium Gurus, but Keith, Jake, Oggy and Bennett voted for Juniper Suction, making him feel like a valued member of the team.

'Juniper Suction it is,' Oggy announced. 'Congratulations. Finish your cuppas and nip to the bog. Finn, do your freaky eighteen-minute drill. Anyone who's made alternative plans and wants to leave early is sacked. Yes, I'm serious. Our first live gig is at the Ship. Five casual men firing on all cylinders, performing T. Rex songs.'

'Jesus, Oggy. I know the landlady, Maureen.' Bennett threw a strange look in Keith's direction. 'Jake and I won't be able to show our faces in there again if we screw up.'

'Look, the punters won't give a shit. They probably won't even realise we're there. Hand out the set list. Chop chop.'

Bennett gave out sheets of paper, Jake made sure they had bottles of water and plenty of weed within reach and Finn left them to it, stepping out back to warm up his vocals. Keith tapped him on the shoulder.

'Two things. First, I've got us both a job on the agency starting Monday – if you don't mind working with me, that is.'

'Are you mad? That's mint,' he said, hugging him. 'What's the second thing?'

'I need your help. I have Daniel's Blue Sparkle and I need to play it, otherwise we'll most definitely get slaughtered by those other bands. Daniel's mum gave it me shortly after his funeral, but Bennett doesn't know I have it. He'll hit the roof.'

'Does Oggy know you have it?'

Keith nodded. 'Did you see the way Bennett looked at me? He reckons I'm the weakest link. We can't afford to enter this competition with one hand tied behind our back.'

'Calm down. Let me do my warmup. I'll think of something.' Finn completed his preparations and made his way to his microphone. 'Oggy, if it's okay, Keith would like to try something new. Do you have any blindfolds?'

'Next door do,' Jake replied, sniggering. 'You want handcuffs and whips as well?' He shot off and returned with a handful of pink fluffy blindfolds, handing them out.

Finn rested his on his head. Oggy, Bennett and Jake put theirs on and Keith swiped Oggy's keys for his Jeepster and left. He reappeared with an old black guitar case, opened it on the kitchen worktop and rigged it up, diving into position.

'Do you mind if Keith and I perform "Life's a Gas"?'

Oggy folded his arms. 'Once you've promised to keep your emotions in check like the rest of us. I don't miss much, me, you know. Well?'

'I promise to keep my emotions in check. There. We good?' Finn tapped his microphone three times and as soon as Keith struck the first chord, he closed his eyes, listening carefully to the sounds. The energy within him flowed, causing his insides to vibrate, but once he'd sung the last word, he opened his eyes to find Bennett had stormed off, leaving his blindfold on the floor.

'That was the best I've heard you play, Keith,' Jake said, adding, 'Good job as well. Oggy was giving Bennett the lead if you hadn't improved by the end of the day.'

Oggy clipped Jake round the back of the head. 'You'd start World War III in an empty room, you. Nothing personal, my good friend. Bennett craved a reaction from you, and boy, did he get one. That's the Keith we all remember. Clifford's going to cack his trousers. Knew you still had it in you. I'll check on Bennett in case he thumps you one.'

'I'll go,' Finn said, stepping forward. 'It was my idea.'

Bennett was leaning against his van, smoking a joint. 'Did you all plan that sat around Oggy's dining table last night?'

'It wasn't like that. Keith knew it might upset you, but you know how much he's been struggling. Sorry, Bennett. This one's on me. I wasn't taking sides. We all have our reasons for wanting to win Love Is the Drug. We now know we need to be at our best to pull it off.'

Bennett blew out a huge cloud of smoke and nodded. 'Watching you two reminded me of when Keith and Daniel used to perform together. They were the talk of every town. I'd get jealous and worked up over how close they were, but that in there just then, that was even better.

It's taken me years to be as good as Keith. Whatever you do, don't tell him he inspired me. Oggy and I used to cling on to any attention we could get in the '70s. When Daniel died and Keith left, we simply weren't good enough to continue at that level, that's the truth. Year upon year we faced rejection. I never knew Keith was sick. Why didn't he tell me him and Charlotte struggled to conceive? It's all they ever wanted.'

'You should have this conversation with him. You know that, right?'

Bennett sighed. His hands wouldn't stop shaking. 'Daniel told me his Blue Sparkle was a gift from the gods. His mam said she gave it to the rag and bone man, which I always struggled to believe. I remember calling him a cheating bastard for using a capo. He'd just laugh. "Keep an open mind with open chords and do everything in your power to accommodate the vocalist. All that matters is that our collective performance connects with our audience." Maybe I didn't know him that well after all. One minute he was kind, affectionate and everything ran along nicely, then he turned so cold. It was as if someone flicked a switch and I lost him.'

Finn folded his arms. 'Maybe Daniel was sick too, like my mam and Keith.'

'If he was, he did a brilliant job hiding it. Does Keith have anything else of Daniel's?'

'Again, you'll have to ask him. Do you know how many times I've dreamt of performing in a proper band? Physical Graffiti will kick our arse if we don't rehearse soon.'

Bennett rolled his eyes, then threw his stub on the ground and stood on it before wrapping his arm around

Finn's shoulder. 'Come on, Bolan. Let's add some catchy riffs and stomping bass to those sublime vocals. You did the right thing promising not to let your emotions get the better of you. Don't end up bitter and twisted like me. Life's a bit like you – too short.'

***

Juniper Suction arrived at the Ship the following Friday evening to perform live for the first time in Love Is the Drug. Keith, Oggy, Bennett and Jake set their gear up, but Finn hunched over the bar after completing his warmups in the empty beer garden.

'What's all this?' Keith asked, glaring at the pint Finn had just finished as well as the full one in front of him. 'This isn't part of your preparations. Barman, a pint of water, please.'

Finn necked a shot. 'Sixteenth of September. For Marc and Daniel. Rest in peace. Is it just me who finds it weird the competition's starting on this exact date?'

'Definitely not. I usually prefer to focus on the day Daniel entered this world rather than the day he exited it, but today felt special. Thanks for coming to Southern Cemetery this morning. We haven't been to Daniel's grave together for years. Grief can be a strange thing. Now drink, then go pee.'

Finn gulped his water. 'Still can't believe how fast it's come round. Keep asking myself the same question. How did I end up here? Every time, the answer's the same – *you*.'

'Don't mention it. Glad to be of service.'

'I wasn't thanking you,' Finn said with a raised voice.

'I'm bricking it. This means so much to you guys. What if I fuck it up?'

Keith sat close beside him. 'You won't. Elaine's coming with friends from her work, Lucas is coming with his Inner Vibrations chums to cheer us on, and we don't have a clue if any judges are showing up. Could be him. Could be her. Have you seen the queue outside? At least some good came from my media stunt.'

Finn glared at him. 'Not helping.'

'Give over. Rehearsals went well. Like Oggy said, tonight's all about valuable experience.'

'Fuck. Look.' Finn pointed to Gibbo and a gang of lads from their construction site shuffling to the front of the audience. 'This night's getting worse. I need more time. I'm gonna chuck my ring up.'

'Don't you dare let your old life interfere with the new. Ignore them at all costs. Here, borrow my shades. I'll grab something to wear on your head. Once you get into the first song, you'll be fine, trust me. We're in this together.'

'Problems?' Oggy said, interrupting.

'He's nervous,' Keith replied, 'but I've told him he's not alone. Tell him, Oggy.'

'That's right. If you're crap, we're all crap. Bennett's friend Maureen says we can start whenever we want, so no added pressure.'

More and more people piled in off the street and Finn plonked his elbows on the bar. 'Won't get busy, *you said*. The punters won't give a shit, *you said*. I won't be able to move in a minute. Them at the front are off our site. If that cock says one word, he's getting it.'

'You made us all a promise, remember. Keith doesn't

seem bothered; why should you? Keep calm, kid. Copy me. In and out, breathe slowly. There you go. You'd be surprised how many people don't know how to breathe properly. Now, how do you feel?'

'Like Michael fucking Bublé. I wanna go home.'

Oggy chuckled. 'Drink up, freshen up and throw water over your face. Works for me. Bennett's shouting. Keith, let's go. One, two. One, two.' He tapped Finn's microphone, making sure it worked.

'Have faith. Remember the Church. You can do this,' Keith said, passing him Jake's bucket hat. 'There. Incognito.'

Bennett did his last-minute checks, Keith followed suit, Oggy dived into position behind his drums, and Jake winked at every woman who came through the door.

'Hi, evewyone. First, we'd like to welcome you to the Ship. We are Juniper Suction, and with your support, we're hoping to weach the final of Love Is the Dwug. Hope you have a twemendous night. Feel fwee to join in with the lywics.'

Gibbo and his gang sneered at Oggy's speech impediment, but most of the punters focused on the microphone, waiting for *you know who* to appear. Finn's chest tightened, and he used his inhaler on his way to the stage, refusing to make eye contact with anyone before Oggy kicked the night off with 'Jeepster'. Finn's timing was way off, his hands wouldn't stop shaking and he dropped his microphone twice, but on the plus side, nobody recognised him.

'It's fine, kid. Deep breaths. "Telegram Sam",' Oggy said, giving him some much-needed encouragement. 'Take your time. Tap your feet to the beat if you need to.'

Finn did as Oggy suggested but missed his cue completely. Keith gave him the thumbs up, Jake went cock-eyed and Bennett winked. Finn's heart pounded. He sounded like his balls had been trapped in a vice, and once the song finished, he fully expected a rollicking from Oggy for destroying one of his all-time favourites.

'Can't get any worse,' Bennett said.

'Can only get better,' Keith added.

'Chin up, kid. If you've never failed, you've never tried. Fingers crossed no judges have shown up yet.'

'Thank fuck I'm in disguise.' Jake lowered his head. 'That was wank.'

Gibbo and his gang pointed and booed Keith even though he hadn't put a foot wrong, then started on Finn. 'Oi, mate. I'm talking to you. You need to invest in singing lessons, pal. Your guitarist should be locked up. He's a nutjob.'

'Prick!' Finn spun to confront them but tripped and tumbled to the floor with his arms spread out. His bucket hat fell off and his shades slid to the end of his nose.

'I remember you,' Gibbo yelled. 'You used to clean our shithouses. *Boo! Boo!*'

Keith helped Finn up and brushed him down. 'Stop stressing. Do *not* retaliate. I don't need your protection. We'll handle it. Get some fresh air. Go.'

Finn clenched his fists, ready to charge at Gibbo, but hesitated when, through the baying crowd, he caught sight of a pink cuckoo flower on the wrist of a beautiful blonde with big blue eyes. Wearing a sexy white vest top, smart black blazer and skinny jeans, she answered her phone, then vanished. Finn stuck his hat and shades back on without saying a word and shot to his feet, barging past the unimpressed bar staff, but he couldn't find her. Diving into the gents to cool off, he placed his dry mouth over the water fountain nozzle and guzzled as much as he could, desperate to flush out the alcohol he'd drunk. After peeing for ages, he washed his hands, banged his fists on the vanity unit, booted the panels and rinsed his face in a sink full of cold water, watching it trickle down his red puffy cheeks in the mirror. 'Marc, where are you? I can't do this. Marc, please. Help me.'

Two lads staggered in and shot into the same cubicle, snorting coke. 'That band's toss,' one of them said.

'Nah, the band's sick. They just need a new singer. He's dogshit. You see that fit blonde with the pink tattoo out back? Well worth a punch in the pants. I'm getting her number.'

Splashing his face one last time, Finn realised help wasn't coming and slammed the door on his way out, hoping the floor would somehow swallow him up. He glanced at his band huddled together, pleading with Maureen and the bouncers to give them a second chance, when the blonde with the pink cuckoo flew through the beer garden door, spilling most of her drink down his Inner Vibrations T-shirt.

'I'm reyt sorry. My fault,' she said, covering her mouth with one hand. 'I wasn't watching where I was going.'

'I'd have seen you if I wasn't in such a rush to leave.' Finn grabbed a handful of napkins from the far side of the bar and wiped himself down. 'Let me get you another. You're not from round here, are you?'

'Sheffield.' She smiled, dipping into her crossover bag to get her purse.

‘Love your tattoo,’ Finn said, fidgeting. ‘Is it a pink cuckoo, by any chance?’

‘What? How do you even know that?’

‘Let me guess, your birthday’s in April and you’re a bit crazy.’

‘Mine’s a vodka lemon and lime,’ she replied, puzzled. ‘Look, I really need to go pee, but I’ll be back in a sec. Don’t leave.’ She dashed into the ladies toilet, and a few minutes later Finn waved to get her attention, then moved to the opposite side of the bar out of the way, passing her a drink.

‘So, why in such a hurry to escape? I missed the first vocalist. Heard he was awful.’

Finn bit his lip, then changed the subject. ‘Have you ever had the feeling you don’t belong? By the way, I’m Finn.’

‘Niamh. Your reyt deep for the start of a night,’ she said, fiddling with her silver bangles. ‘I’m a woman. We’re supposed to look and behave a certain way from the minute we step out of bed to the second we climb back in. As a teenager, when I didn’t belong, I’d wear my mum’s makeup and pretend to be someone else. Still do, especially if it’s time of the month. I get to hide in plain sight, looking good on the outside when feeling like shit on the inside. That make sense? Not sure why I told you all that.’

Finn smiled. ‘Never thought of it like that. So, if I needed to be someone else right this second, what advice would you give me?’

Niamh’s eyes lit up. ‘Never look back or take things for granted. Always have fun and look to the future. Come with.’ She finished her drink, grabbed Finn’s hand and dragged him through the crowd into the ladies toilets. Pulling her bag over her shoulder, she laid out her makeup on the vanity unit. 'You trust me?'

Finn nodded.

'Rinse your face, then close your eyes and keep still. Don't open 'em till I say. We have peachy-pink blush and blue eyeliner for starters.' She wouldn't stop giggling, and every time she touched him, tingly sensations fired through his body. 'Now for your mascara and rosy matte lipstick. There. Reyt, open 'em.'

Finn did as she asked and glanced in the mirror. 'Wow! What did you do? I look amazing. I even feel different.'

'That's because you're now someone else.' She kissed him on the cheek, placed her makeup back in her bag and swung it over her shoulder. 'Hopefully your amazing T-shirt dries off soon. I need to get back to my mates or they'll think I've been spiked. Maybe see you in a bit. My round. Come say hi. Don't be shy.'

'Thanks, Niamh.' Finn watched the door close behind her and took one last look in the mirror. 'Let's do this.'

A middle-aged woman charged through the door. 'Oi, are you listening to women have a piss, you scruffy twat? You want locking up.'

Finn shot past her and located Niamh with her mates near the bar, dancing to 'Super Bass' by Nicki Minaj, before making his way to the stage.

'Where've you been hiding? Who did that to your face?' Jake asked, handing him a bottle of water. 'Look. We're that shit, they've switched the jukebox back on. Reporters are here, Inner Vibrations arrived, and it's like naked nans night now the goo-woo groupies have turned up. Just been sick in my mouth. Her with no teeth and big cow's udders keeps blowing kisses at Oggy.'

'Much prefer her with silver hoop earrings.' Finn pointed to Niamh and positioned himself behind his microphone.

'Sexy-arse riding boots. I'd let her tap dance on my todge in them. Bit tall for you?'

Oggy interrupted. 'Seem to remember someone being dead against makeup. Funny how things turn out. Pop your eyes back in your head and show her what you're made of.'

'You've fucked it now,' Jake said. 'They've got boyfriends, look.'

'Them two! Dogshit, am I?' Weird rushes of energy whooshed from Finn's back and stomach to his groin. This time they swirled close to his heart, then vibrated in his throat. He necked a gob full of water. 'Oggy, let's show them coked-up clowns what we're made of.'

'That's the spirit.'

Finn tapped his microphone three times. The jukebox cut out and the chatter stopped. 'Sorry about earlier, everyone. Lost my sense of direction a bit. That guy out there was spiking people's drinks,' he said, giving Gibbo the finger through the window. 'Anyway, I'm back and I'd like to dedicate our next song to someone who threw her drink over me not so long ago. Let's just say it woke me up.'

Niamh stepped into Finn's line of sight, sipping her vodka lemon and lime. Moving her glass away from her lips, she smiled with bright red cheeks and shook her head. Instead of smiling back, he kicked his leg out and winked, handing Keith and Bennett the perfect opportunity to get the crowd going with 'Hot Love.' Finn tapped his feet, clicked his fingers and sensed the beat working its way through his body. Off came his microphone; he launched the stand to one side like a proper rock star and moved around, cocky and smug, glancing in her direction. Stopping on the spot, he sang his heart out with his eyes closed, and when he opened them, Juniper Suction had attracted the attention of the entire pub. Wolf whistles echoed throughout, everybody clapped, even the two clowns, and when the song ended, Keith scratched his head, Oggy slouched on his drums, Bennett ruffled his doughnut duster and Jake didn't move a muscle. A delighted member of Maureen's staff wandered across with a tray full of drinks, but Finn stayed on water.

'Shall I go first?' Bennett asked. 'What the fuck just happened?'

'Great, kid. That was like performing with Bolan himself.' Oggy patted Finn down. 'You sure he's not in there somewhere?'

'You found something to focus on – or should I say *someone*? She's talking to her friends about you. They're moving closer for our next song. She has Bette Davis eyes.'

'Keith, you're so weird.' Jake held his arms out. 'But thank fuck. I'm too young to live on a park bench. You gave me goose pimples, you electric pube.'

'Honestly, I'm buzzing my tits off. Come on. Let's do "Jeepster" and "Telegram Sam". This time properly.' Finn grabbed his stand and attached his microphone, diving straight in. He'd found so much energy and self-belief, he didn't want his transformation to end. His admirers bopped and jived, which gave him an added incentive to swing his hips some more. His confidence in his ability shone through, and he wanted to share it with as many people as possible. A sizeable crowd bowled through the doors the moment Finn finished singing, and the place filled up as more and more people squeezed in to glimpse what Oggy believed to be the start of a '70s glam rock revival. The bouncers stopped letting people in. 'Thanks, everyone. Back in a sec.' Finn tossed his microphone to Jake and leapt off the stage, searching for the pink cuckoo.

'We've got another two songs to do,' Oggy snapped. 'You can't just bugger off and drop everything for a bird. No offence.'

'None taken,' Keith replied, chuckling. 'Let him go.'

Jake gripped the mic. 'Finnie's little heartbeat's running away.'

'Knob.' Finn dashed to the bar with electricity flowing through his veins. 'Maureen, have you seen Niamh? You served us both over there before.'

'You just missed her. She looked in a real hurry.'

Juniper Suction played '20th Century Boy' and Finn boogied either side of Thomas Street, wanting to thank her again for her help. Stomping to the corner, he froze on the kerb when he spotted her climbing into the back of a flashy chauffeur-driven Hummer with Sothis Media advertisements plastered all over it.

NINE

Wednesday, September 21st, 2011 - 17:30

Keith had planned to collect David and Helen from school and take them for their tea before heading to BJ's to meet Sadie, the cosmetologist, but Charlotte cancelled on him at short notice without giving him an explanation. 'I can't do this,' he yelled, throwing his hands in the air.

'Take a chill pill. She'll come around.' Finn finished the Big Mac Keith had treated him to after work and wiped the sauce from his cheek, licking the residue running down his fingers. He tapped on the window to get Farooq's attention. 'How come you're still here?'

'Going for a meal with Benny and Rhonda. Would you like to come?' he asked, fiddling with the charity boxes on the counter.

'FaceTiming my dad tonight, otherwise I would,' Finn said, yawning.

Keith scratched the back of his neck. His mind wandered. 'Another time, maybe.'

'No problem. It is Benny's big comeback at the Birdcage in a few weeks. Do you think you could make it? Here is the flyer. It is amazing. No offence, Keith, but you do not look well. Here is a constructive tip. Love is all about the electricity – not the plumbing.'

Finn wrapped his arm around Keith and guided him to the back room. 'Chin up, mate.'

Oggy was typing away on his laptop, Jake was flicking through an animal magazine and Bennett lay rolling a joint. They'd lined tubs of sweets up on the kitchen worktop, and Keith dived straight for his favourite flying saucers, grabbing a handful of lollipops. 'I could really do with being someplace else, Oggy. Can I please give this a miss? My head isn't in it.'

'Sadie's on her way. Rhonda too. Makeup worked wonders with Finn. It's important we get it sorted for our upcoming gigs. I'll drop you off to see Charlotte and the kids straight after they've been, I promise.' Oggy rubbed his hands together. 'Now cheer up.'

Keith pulled childish faces behind Oggy's back, swiping the evening newspaper, then dragged his chair to the window and slumped into it.

'You know I've got eyes in the back of my head, right? Finn, if you saw that pretty young blonde again from the Ship, where would you take her on a first date?'

'Nice restaurant, few bars after. Somewhere you can chat and get to know each other.'

'Chat?' Jake yelped in complete disagreement. 'You want a dark corner in case she wants you to tickle the tiny man in her boat under the table.'

Finn blanked him. 'Can't see me ever getting her number now. One, she's a judge, and two, she couldn't wait to get away in Sothis Media's Hummer.'

'Nonsense. Never put yourself down,' Keith said.

'What if she had a schedule to keep to? They're referred to as Sheffielders or Dee-dahs and they call everyone duck, I think.'

'Finn's got a sticky dick over a duck. Quack, quack.'

'Freak. Holy—! Sothis just updated their website. You can't half pick 'em, kid. If she was a judge, she ain't now. She's their new event manager and she's in overall charge of the entire competition, so please tread lightly, Casanova, till we exit the competition.'

'Oggy's right,' Keith added. 'Last thing we need is any allegations of favouritism or cheating. Clifford will be onto it like a flash. He's that malicious. The best things come to those who wait. Remember that.'

Jake sniggered. 'That's a right kick in the dick, but this'll cheer you up. Going back to wildlife. You know I love monkeys and apes. Well, I got chatting to this bird, Sasha, online, and we clicked, so I took her to Chester Zoo.'

'On a first date?' Keith asked, unable to keep his nose out. He threw his depressing newspaper onto the floor and whipped his spectacles off to give them a good wipe.

'We got near the chimpanzee enclosure, and I pulled a box of chocolate fingers from my rucksack. The thing was, I kinda forgot you weren't allowed to feed the animals.'

'There are signs everywhere,' Keith told him, emptying sherbet into his mouth.

'I slipped *one* chocolate finger through the mesh. The chimp snatched it from my hand, swung up on a thick branch, frigged its shit-box with it, *then* ate it.'

Keith rolled his eyes and frowned at sewer mouth, struggling to swallow. He spun his chair to face the wall and for a split second, cancelling his daughter's trip crossed his mind.

'They fought, bit each other and shagged each other's brains out. One of them had a proper big dongle. He yanked at it, swinging his hips left to right, and did the windmill.'

'What?' Keith asked. 'Never mind. Got it. Knew I shouldn't have come.'

'Sasha snatched my chocolate fingers and hauled me away before the attendant collared us. *I* didn't tell it to ram it up its poo-chute. She dumped me the next day for her ex, Richard.' Jake's shoulders sagged. He looked genuinely upset. 'It was rough. The worst I've felt since Peter, but I only had myself to blame. Deep down, I always knew she loved Dick.'

Oggy, Bennett and Finn split their sides laughing, but Keith popped his spectacles on and stuffed his bag of sweets into his pocket for later.

'See how similar we are to apes. Remember the punters at Paula's party.'

'Women with wampant wabbits are nothing like masturbating monkeys.'

'It's no secret. We're 98.8 per cent chimp, but people just won't accept it, especially rich white mandrills. Primates are black, brown and white. They exhibit high levels of male-to-female aggression too – violence, sexual abuse, rape and murder. Don't you think it's weird how other animals have fur and armour to survive bad weather, but we need clothes for winter and suntan lotion in summer? What if we descend from ape-fucking Martians? What if that was the only way their species could survive?'

Bennett shook his head. 'I was about to say words like *primates* and *descend* made you sound educated and more mature. You could've gone with *experiments*, but no: you shot straight for the gutter with ape-fucking. What's life on Mars actually like?'

Oggy added his thoughts to the mix. 'If aliens are real, why not land and say hello?'

'Would you take a chick in Thomas Cook and ask for an all-inclusive holiday for two to Helmand Province?' Jake asked, smirking. 'If benevolent extra-terrestrials came to help us all, capitalists would call them malevolent communists. They'd never be welcome.'

'Rhonda's here,' Farooq shouted, lifting Keith's spirits.

'Great timing. Now shut your thesaurus, Jake, get your head out of the clouds and no more rubbish about extra-terrestrial interbreeding, you hear?'

Bennett dived off the stairs, a tad giddy, and Rhonda waltzed in, dolled up in a long white fleece coat. She had her hair bunched up and rings on each finger and was emitting an alluring fruity fragrance. Oggy and Finn greeted her with a kiss and a hug, Jake half-heartedly shook her hand and Keith smiled, dying to know more about her and Daniel's shenanigans.

'Sadie's running late, but apart from Finn, jot down your idols you wish to look like.'

'Three Little Birds' by Bob Marley played on Bennett's laptop, and he relaxed on his own with a giant cone. Keith tottered to the kitchen, washed a cup and poured himself a glass of water, checking his phone for a reply from Charlotte.

'Here we have Bennett,' Jake said, impersonating David

Attenborough. 'The great white baboon has dragged his knuckles to the corner of the room with a distinctive look of low self-esteem. Increasingly withdrawn, he's opted to be antisocial in his natural habitat.'

'Please leave me alone.' Keith cringed. 'If he sticks a flying saucer up his backside and eats it, I'm off. This time I won't come back.' Hearing someone tap on the store window, he left Jake and Finn in fits of laughter and went to see who it was, opening the door to a young, smartly dressed woman with a cute panda rucksack on her back.

'I'm Sadie,' she said in a Geordie accent. 'Lovely to meet you. Is Rhonda here?'

'She is. What's this?' Keith asked, pointing to a pink-and-white badge on her jacket.

'ADDER. Action for Dystonia. It's a charity close to my heart, like. It affects different body parts and can be anything from cramps to muscle spasms, causing severe pain and discomfort. Awareness is key. That's the staff of Hermes, which represents healing. The serpent represents wisdom, and the laurel wreath represents enfolding the whole of humanity: bit deep mind. I'm doing a charity run in Liverpool next year, raising money for further studies into the pineal gland malfunction and cerebrospinal fluid circulation. You can sponsor me if you like?'

'I'd love to. Please, go through.' Keith locked the door, and after Sadie had introduced herself to Juniper Suction, he handed her photos of their idols before storming off to the back yard, beckoning Finn. 'I know Niamh will be swirling around in your mind at great speed, but I need your advice. I'm going nuts. Say you found answers to certain questions you and your friends had been asking all your adult lives but sharing them could destroy everything you'd worked hard for. Would you tell them?'

Finn sat on Bennett's wheelie bin with his arms folded and gazed at the floor. 'It's taken nine years for me and my dad to have a proper conversation about my mam. Thirty-four years have passed and you three *still* haven't had one about Daniel. No matter how good or bad the truth is, knowing's better than not knowing, but if you think Oggy and Bennett's dreams will be shattered a second time, promise me you'll wait till this competition's over. I have to wait to get Niamh's number, so the least you can do is keep whatever it is to yourself till then.'

Keith ran the dates through his mind. 'You're right. I'm sorry. I promise I won't do anything to jeopardise our band's dreams. You have my word.'

'Finn, Sadie wants you,' Jake said, puffing on a joint. 'Keith, you look miserable, man. Does Oggy's house still stink of shit? Has Charlotte traded you in already?'

'Please, give it a rest. What've you got in that?' Keith asked, pointing to Jake's glass pipes and grip-seal sample bags in a tin, exploring an alternative method of escaping.

'Super-strength skunk. You want a toot? It'll help you relax. Watch. Your turn.'

Keith filled his lungs and exhaled an immense cloud of white smoke. 'Is that it? Don't feel a thing.' He took another two hits in quick succession and dropped Jake's pipe, touching his face. 'Oh my. I hear my guitar humming. I love you. You're so beautiful. Why are your cheeks different colours? Daniel's a dandy in the underworld. I see Finn. He's a child star: a star child, even. You're baby strange. I'm right, aren't I? We need to spread this love.'

'Shit. Wrong pipe. You blew the last of my snowflakes, you moody muppet.'

Warm, colourful beams of light shone outwards from Keith's skin. He hugged Jake. 'This feels so good. It's exactly the same as my near-death experience.'

'What? Oi. Too far. Your hand just brushed my todge. It'll wear off in a sec. Keith, don't be a dick, let go and breathe. Sit down. Tell me about your NDE. Oggy and Bennett will kill me if they see you like this.'

'Apeman' by the Kinks played. Keith launched Jake aside and he dashed inside and cranked up the volume. He grabbed Finn's microphone, beating his chest with one hand. 'Join in with the words, beautiful people. Dance with me.'

Farooq, Rhonda and Sadie clapped, egging him on. Oggy joined in, tickling his armpits, and Bennett's jaw dropped. Keith, however, got right into the swing of things and took it a step further. He whipped off his shirt, making wild chimp noises, and kissed Bennett on the lips, swiping his cone. Knuckle-walking around the room, then jiving with his pot belly out, he took a drag and waved his fists in the air with his back to them when the music stopped. 'L'amour est la drogue. Yo, Ronny with your fuzzy, firm ass, we be like two wild apes mating in the grass.'

'Enjoying yourself?' Charlotte asked, standing beside Farooq with her arms folded.

Everybody fell about laughing apart from Rhonda and Bennett.

'It's not mine,' Keith said, popping it in the ashtray. His colourful trail-backs and humming sounds ceased. 'What happened? Why are you here? Where's David and Helen?'

'At my parents. Sorry to interrupt, Oggy. I can see how much this means to you all. I wondered if my husband would like to join me for something to eat.'

'Please, take him away. He's turned my house into a pigsty and corrupted the youngsters with his crazy antics.' Oggy gave Charlotte an enormous squeeze. 'Meet Bennett's partner, Rhonda. Farooq you've met. This is Sadie. Have you met Finn?'

Charlotte shook Finn's hand and leant forward before he could speak. 'Finally, a face to the name. You've caused quite a stir in my home.'

'This is Bennett's pain-in-the-arse half brother, Jake.'

'Nice to meet you all. It's been a while, Bennett,' Charlotte said, pulling him close, giving him a massive cuddle. She rubbed his back, kissed him on his cheek and muttered something in his ear.

Keith's eyes filled a little as he rushed about, searching for his coat. 'Get your wotsit off my stuff, Jake. You gave me hallucinogens. I trusted you,' he babbled. 'Finn, I'll call you later. Bye, everyone.' He heard the door lock behind them, and loud cheers followed.

Charlotte smiled and nudged Keith beneath the flickering lamppost outside Candy Pink Cavern. 'Hope you haven't been getting preferential treatment in there,' she said, peering in the window.

'Wouldn't dream of it.' He linked his arm with hers, free from fear and negativity. 'I know you think I'm crazy, but with Finn's voice and our experience, we can all have a brighter future. What did you say to Bennett?'

'Something you both should've said to each other a

long time ago.' Charlotte exhaled. 'I'm sorry I broke our school routine. We want you to come home.'

'I'd love to, but I can't – not yet. I think it's best we overcome this performance routine first, don't you? The next three weeks will be tough. Please come watch us.' The blinds in BJ's were closed. The outdoor speakers played Charlotte's favourite hit, 'Sweet Nothin's' by Brenda Lee, and they held hands, swinging their hips to the upbeat tempo till her song finished. He glanced at the cobbles beneath his feet for a second, brushed her fringe from her face and kissed her, tasting his favourite cherry lipstick. 'I promise not to lie to you ever again, and I promise to see my crisis team to discuss what's best going forward.'

'I'll be by your side every single step of the way. Besides, when did you learn to speak French? That undoubtedly floats my boat.'

***

Juniper Suction performed at the Castle Hotel, the Deaf Institute, the Bay Horse, Night and Day Café and the Band on the Wall, leaving Keith shattered, but to find out whether their hard work had paid off, he and his bandmates met at the Printworks to hear the live announcement of the finalists for Love Is the Drug.

'I need a drink to settle my nerves,' Keith said, showing Oggy his trembling hands.

'Don't be soft.' Oggy paid for their taxi and climbed out on Shudehill, leading Keith along Dantzic Street. Finn and Jake waited for them opposite the Arndale, having selfies with fans. 'Trendy shirts, smart trousers and cool shoes. Who've you two mugged?'

'We're celebrities now,' Jake screeched. 'We didn't pay for a single drink.'

'Introduce any of your new friends to the delightful world of DMT?' Keith asked.

'You make it sound like I forced you to smoke it, you juicy little jive bomb. We need to have a good chat about that, you and me.'

'Moving on.' Oggy rubbed his hands together. 'The finalists aren't being announced till nine, so we can have a few jars elsewhere.'

'Are you deaf? We're loved in there. The atmosphere's wild. Come see.'

'Where's Bennett?' Keith asked.

Oggy planted his giant hands on Keith and Jake's shoulders. 'Guys, guys. We're all precisely where we need to be, and that's together. Isn't that right, Finn?' He high-fived him, then glanced at the Birdcage sign on Withy Grove, lit up in gigantic neon yellow letters. 'It's Beryl's comeback night. Cabaret. Drag queens having fun. Look at it as added research for our own performance. Two birds, one stone.'

'One of them birds is our Bennett, you bell-sniff. *It's too soon.*'

'Mate, come on,' Finn said. 'Bennett thinks we're meeting later.'

'In here – half-naked women. Over there – half-naked men. Not a tough choice.'

Keith stuck his coat on and zipped it up, folding his arms. 'Jake, Finn's right.'

'Not listening to a man who touched my todge and snogged Bennett after tooting the last of my snowflakes. I have to live with him. Once I see him in drag, I can't unsee it. No.'

'Guys, focus. We need to get our act together,' Oggy said. 'Rhonda's on her way.'

Jake glared at each of them, ranting. 'That in there might make you all hard, but not me. Lick my hoop.' He stomped off past the taxis and perched on a window ledge behind other smokers, swapping his fag for a joint just as Rhonda crossed the road.

'When you're ready, give big Cecil a nudge on the door. He'll get you all stamped up and Farooq will escort you to VIP. I'll get a message to Sothis so they know you're just over the road. See you in there. Can't wait.' Rhonda smiled, kissed Keith on the cheek and whispered, 'You and I need to have a little heart-to-heart later, dear. There was only ever one guy who said I had a fuzzy firm ass before mating with me in the grass.'

Keith's heart pounded and fluttered. He kept his distance with his head spinning, praying he hadn't ruined everything by opening his big mouth, and Finn plonked himself down on a black security bollard beside Jake. 'The last three weeks have been a right buzz, admit it. I haven't felt so alive since my mam died. We're like family. Brothers.'

'I get it.' Jake squirmed. 'But tonight, Bennett's our sister. He's wearing knickers.'

'It's two hours, tops. Instead of thinking about *yourself*, think about how much it would mean to him-her to see us walk through them doors as a team.' Finn took a deep breath, fist-bumped Jake and ducked back into the bar with Oggy in tow.

Keith took Finn's spot and waited for Jake to look at him. 'I know its new and it's awkward, but it's just life. Now it's sunk in, I'm not over the moon about going in myself, but sometimes we need to put other people's feelings first. I've loved jamming with all of you these past few weeks, but it's not about Bennett, you, me, Oggy or Finn as individuals. We're connected now. Let's cross this finish line together. Come on. We might all be dead soon.'

Jake stubbed his joint out and headed to the bar with Keith, resting his head on Finn's shoulder and sticking out his bottom lip. 'If it's too weird or there's too much meat and two veg on show, we're coming straight back here and you're paying.'

Hordes of rowdy women elbowed their way up the line outside the Birdcage, begging Finn and Jake to sign their breasts. Oggy nipped inside the doorway, chatting to Cecil; he stamped the backs of their hands with a purple heart and Keith dragged his feet.

'Me and Finn'll stick with hen parties,' Jake yelled. 'Keith, you and Oggy are on six-packs and trouser snakes.'

'Best behaviour, you hear me?' Oggy said, guiding them through the lobby. 'Follow Cecil, and no backchat.'

Keith couldn't see more than three feet in front of him due to vast machines blasting smoke and fog. He kept hold of Oggy's shirt till he made it to the UV lights at the bar, hoping Rhonda wouldn't jump out and interrogate him. 'Three pints of lager, please, and an orange juice. What's on tonight?' he asked a member of staff.

'Vegas Showgirls, Dreamboys and the Rebels.'

'Your kid is too old and far too ugly to be a dream boy.'

'Shut your grid.' Jake turned to Finn. 'Our Bennett might be a showgirl.'

'Don't you mean Beryl?' he said, blowing him a kiss.

Farooq sprang out, clapping his hands. 'I get you are all nervous, but Keith, you are sweating buckets. We have a tab,' he screeched. 'Come. Show the bouncers your stamps. The Rebels are up next.' He boogied to 'Funkytown' by Lipps Inc. on his way to the comfy settees, introduced them to his friends, then grinned, targeting Jake with the lyrics.

'We won't see much if Lurch is at the front,' he said, grinning.

Farooq's jaw dropped. 'Take that back, you nasty pasty. "You gotta move on."'

Spotlights lit up the perimeter of the stage, and the DJ leapt in front of the curtain. 'Before we continue, please, everyone, show your appreciation for Beryl from the Rebels, who had a lengthy spell on the sidelines because of injury. We love you and we missed you.' The venue erupted with admiration. 'Some of you may not know this, but Beryl is a bit of a moonlighter. She's also a member of an amazing local band whose name is currently on everybody's lips, and they're here tonight to support her comeback. Please give a warm welcome to a group who at nine p.m. tonight will find out on our big screen whether they've made the final of Love Is the Drug. It's only Juniper Suction. Give it up.'

The audience went ballistic, cheering and applauding, so Keith, Oggy, Finn and Jake responded by waving and bowing to their fans. Beryl blew them kisses before 'New

York, New York' bellowed from huge speakers and the Rebels lined up in pink-and-black shuttlecock outfits, kicking their legs and hiding their faces behind silver glittery masks.

'You will love this,' Farooq said. 'I choreographed the entire routine myself.'

'Honestly!' Finn said. 'You need to show me some moves.'

Farooq's face lit up, but Keith cringed when Rhonda slapped her backside in his direction before two half-naked male dancers manhandled her. She launched her mask into the deafening audience and joined Beryl doing the splits, showing their pink frilly knickers. Jake covered his face with his hands. Oggy encouraged Keith to dive into the swing of things, whooping and clapping, Rhonda belted out her words, and Beryl strutted her stuff, kicking her legs higher than anyone else in her group. Finn hauled Jake from his seat. Farooq and Oggy boogied at the table, Rhonda smooched Beryl centre stage, and once 'I Want to Be a Rockette' finished, they headed across.

'Electrifying. Is there anything you can't do?' Oggy asked, giving Beryl a bear hug. He ruffled her wig. 'Unbelievable.'

'It's great to feel free. This, my friends, is the real me,' she said in a feminine voice, dabbing her eyes with a hanky. 'I sounded like Daniel then. Not long now. I'm shitting it. I was nowhere near as nervous for Rock Heaven. Thanks, all of you, for coming.'

'Behave, Beryl. We wouldn't have missed this for the world, would we, guys?'

'Brilliant. Really enjoyable.' Keith shook Beryl's hand

and checked his watch, keeping an eye out for Rhonda. After dancing the Macarena, he snuck off to the toilets.

'Need a hand?' Rhonda's look of excitement turned to seriousness. She put her drinks down on the nearest table and placed her hands on her hips.

'Smashing performance,' Keith said, avoiding eye contact.

'Don't give me that. You know about Reading Festival. It was forever ago. Nobody cares.' She grabbed her drinks and stepped closer. 'It was just sex. Daniel and I mated everywhere, dear. On the sand, in the sea and up against a sycamore tree, until Clifford's sister Becky caught us bang at it, then took off. Oggy and Clifford arrived in the early hours to collect her. Heard she was in a right state. End of story.'

Keith downed what he had left in his glass to cure his dry mouth. 'That can't be right. You're mistaken. Oggy and Clifford weren't there. Why would Oggy lie?'

Rhonda stood toe to toe with Keith. 'I've watched you play Daniel's Blue Sparkle. I also know he used to hide his journal in there. So if you're thinking of hurting Bennett by dragging me into your war of words with him over who loved Daniel the most, ram it. I am but one raunchy orangutan in a long list of carnal conquests.'

Keith leapt in front of her to stop her walking away. 'I don't want this to get out either. It'd ruin us. Did Becky tell Clifford and Oggy what she saw?'

Rhonda shrugged. 'If she did, you'd think it would've all come out.' Purple curtains at the back of the stage parted to reveal an enormous projector screen. 'Showtime. You know, Daniel had a supersensitive soul. Just a crying shame he felt the need to hide from those closest to him. Best of luck reaching the final.'

Keith had eyes on him from opposite ends of the bar. One set belonged to Bennett and the other to Oggy. He necked his pint, knowing he'd made Finn a promise. If Juniper Suction didn't make the final, would he see Finn ever again? Would Oggy return to his old drinking habits? Where would Bennett and Jake live? What would happen to Farooq, Paula and her escorts? Raising his glass to both Oggy and Bennett, Keith resurrected his groove beside Finn and Jake, waiting for the verdict. He refused to spoil everyone's future this time around.

Rhonda glided across the stage, tapping her microphone. The screen lit up live from Sothis Media's set-up on the cobbles of the Printworks, and smartly dressed men in suits spoke, but the volume had been muted. 'Nearly nine, wonderful people. Can I please have your undivided attention? Where are you? Juniper Suction, please make your way up here.'

Keith took deep breaths as he wormed his way through the enthusiastic crowd. Rhonda ramped up the volume. Oggy and Bennett made it on stage before him, then Finn and Jake joined them in a line beside the screen, holding hands. 'I can't stop shaking.'

'Hello, Manchester,' Niamh said, shuffling three magical rainbow invitations.

Finn squeezed Keith's hand with far too much excitement. 'It's her. Shit, sorry.'

'Ask her out tonight if we make it through,' Jake said, giggling. 'Are you sure she didn't see you crawling about on your hands and knees, licking the Ship's floor?'

'Shush. She's about to speak.'

'My colleagues have spoken at length about what Love Is the Drug means to us, so I'm going to dive reyt in. I am delighted to announce in no particular order the first of our three phenomenal Love Is the Drug finalists … *Physical Graffiti*.'

'Close your eyes,' Jake shouted, impersonating Oggy. 'The cwingey bull fwog's dancing with Webecca Decker and the pecker wecker cwew.'

'Not helping.' Keith peeked to find Niamh opening her next envelope. 'The second band through to the final is … *the Wall*.'

'This is dragging like a seal's arse. You should've dived on the Hummer's bonnet, Finnie boy. She's making us sweat.'

The Wall congratulated each other on screen. Cheers and applause filled the Birdcage, and Keith, on tenterhooks throughout, couldn't stop quaking. He kept his eyes open, but Oggy, Bennett, Finn and Jake had theirs closed and their heads bowed.

Niamh reached for her last envelope. 'Who will be joining them?' She dropped her head, reading the magical rainbow invitation, and tried to hide the excitement on her face with her hand. 'Competing with Physical Graffiti and the Wall on Bonfire Night at GAZE for our prestigious recording contract and the purple heart trophy is … *Juniper Suction*.'

The Birdcage erupted. Keith dropped to his knees with his head in his hands. Oggy and Bennett dived on him, and Finn and Jake jumped about screaming.

'Wow! Huge congratulations, guys. Fully deserved.'

Rhonda handed them Inner Vibrations T-shirts and threw bags full to the crowd. 'Stick them on everyone. Let's show our support for Juniper Suction by marching with them to collect their magical rainbow invitation. On me, beautiful people. Printworks, here we come.'

***

Sothis Media's white stretch limousine came to a standstill on a smoggy car park in Manchester's Gay Village, and Juniper Suction climbed out wearing Inner Vibrations jumpers, prepped with facial moisturiser, primer and concealer. Rockets soared through the sky, discharging a vast array of colours, before Keith shifted his attention to the flashing green GAZE sign. 'Wow!'

Jake hooked his thumbs in his pockets. 'Back door for the riffraff, is it?'

'We are not wiffwaff. It's the staff entrance, numbnuts.' Oggy dashed at a flock of pigeons, scaring them away. 'Sodding vermin.'

'Oi, they're living creatures,' Jake yelled, throwing crisps from his pocket, luring them back. 'They eat, drink, piss, shit, fuck, carry diseases and live amongst their dead just like us, you loon. Can you fly? Didn't think so.'

Oggy didn't reply. He gave their names to the doormen and each of them received a pass, which they hung around their necks.

Keith stood in front of the *Love Is the Drug, Guy Fawkes Sextravaganza* banner on the brickwork, which had *Guy Fawkes* replaced with an offensive homophobic slur. Thankfully Sothis Media's event staff showed up before Bennett saw it and led Juniper Suction through a maze of rainbow-coloured corridors to the sweet sound of jazz music.

'Focus. We still have work to do.' Oggy flung open the doors of a spacious room with brown leather sofas, widescreen TVs and full-length mirrors. It even had its own bar.

Ronny sprung out in a trendy tangerine suit with a white handkerchief poking from his top pocket. He wore expensive silver shoes and had his hair trimmed short and dyed to match. 'Tons of celebrities have arrived, receiving the rainbow carpet treatment. Tried getting on TV. It's manic out there, yet in here it's so relaxed. Wait till you step foot on stage. OMG, the sets are amazing. Here on rails are your suits. Finn, you have some additions for later, which Bennett and I conjured up. Cubicles across the way. Quick, try them on.'

Keith made a beeline for a modish cardinal-red all-in-one suit with his name tag on, white stars stitched to its lapels and thin white stripes down the sides. Oggy had an emerald suit, Bennett had a midnight blue one, Jake's was mustard, and Finn had an indigo one. Each had coloured blazers flecked with glittery Inner Vibrations motifs on the chest and back, matching knee-high boots and labelled-up wigs and headwear.

'Absolutely terrific. Aren't they, guys? Thanks, Ronny. They're fantastic.'

'Hands together.' Keith clapped, encouraging his bandmates to show their gratitude, then ran the thin silky satin material through his fingers, fiddling with his shiny cuffs. He whipped off his T-shirt behind the curtain, changed into his suit and emerged in front of a full-length mirror, zipping up his trousers. 'Thank you so much.'

'You're all welcome. Now hurry.' Ronny clapped his enormous hands. 'Shuffle about; let me know if they fit. There's still time to make slight adjustments.'

'Mine's tight round the crown jewels,' Bennett said.

'You want me to nip to the chemist and grab you some Vagisil?' Jake asked, teasing.

'Don't bite.' Ronny gave Bennett's trousers a slight tug here and a little shunt there. 'Is everything okay? You've been silent this morning.'

'I'm fine,' he replied, raising his voice. 'Somebody wouldn't stop talking in their sleep last night. Anything you'd like to share, my dear orangutan? Something about Daniel's journal or Reading Festival, maybe?' He smirked at Keith, placing his hands on his hips.

'You sure you didn't get us mixed up with Showaddywaddy?' Jake asked, sulking in the mirror. 'I look like you've fired me from someone's hoop after a curry.'

Ronny stuck his long finger in Jake's face. 'For the record, I chose your colour especially,' he snapped before storming out of the dressing room close to tears.

'I was only saying. Tell me I don't look like a man turd.'

Farooq chased after Ronny, and Sadie seated Juniper Suction in their illuminated bays, getting straight down to business, laying on a thick foundation. She applied waterproof makeup, ensuring the colours of their eyeshadow and lipstick were identical to their suits, and by adding a yellow tartan scarf and blond spiky wig, she transformed Keith into Rod Stewart. Oggy impersonated 'The Catman' Eric Singer, Bennett had his face fully whitened and wore a short black and navy-blue wig, mimicking Gary Numan, and although Ronny begged Jake to be Phil Lynott from Thin Lizzy, he loved Ray Dorset from Mungo Jerry.

'I'll check everything's fine with our equipment. Sothis has it all set up on a huge rotating stage platform. Won't be long. Everybody behave.' Oggy left their dressing room, and Sadie dashed off to find Ronny and Farooq.

'What're we having from the bar?' Jake asked, pouting his canary-coloured lips.

'You heard Oggy. Let's keep our minds clear and focus.'

'Who put you in charge?' Bennett gave Keith a right snidey look. 'Pint of cider and a Jack Daniels and Coke for me. Pint of lager and JD and Coke for Finn.'

'Just water for me,' Finn said. 'I'll be over here warming up.'

'I'll have his. Bennett's pissed,' Jake whispered. 'You steal his Hello Sailor book?'

Oggy ploughed through the door. 'This place is phenomenal. Gather round, quickly. I want to say a few words before we head out. Barman, can you line the drinks up? Cheers. As you know, we're up against two fantastic tribute bands tonight, Physical Graffiti and the Wall. Remember, only three of us have experienced this kind of atmosphere, so Keith, Bennett, we need to help Finn and Jake. There are two songs per tribute act in the knockout stage. We must engage with our audience. Interact. We're up first, so we need to leave a lasting impression. This is what we've worked hard for. Together, we're the best T. Rex tribute band in Manchester. And together we can win this competition.'

'Juniper Suction.' They raised their drinks. Sadie and Farooq returned without Ronny, and Sothis Media's event staff gave them their five-minute call. Oggy fist-bumped each of them. 'In line – let's go. Finn, on you.'

'We just saw Niamh,' Farooq announced. 'She is the most beautiful girl in the world.'

'Lead us out, Casanova,' Keith added, punching the air. 'Time to shine.'

Bennett barged past him. 'You just couldn't leave the past alone, could you?'

Keith ignored him, dismissing all negative thoughts; the music faded, smoke fired from large cannons at either end of the stage, and the DJ bawled, 'Trick *or* treat. Kicking off this glorious Love Is the Drug Guy Fawkes Sextravaganza, a tribute to '70s glam rock superstars T. Rex … give it up, guys, girls and all in between for … Juniper Suction.'

'Love Is the Drug' by Roxy Music thundered from the speakers. The floor bounced beneath Keith's feet, and as the doors swung open, sounds of rockets and bangers filled the club. Sparkling red, gold and silver confetti showered Juniper Suction from above. Oggy belted his drums, giving Finn that all-important nod, Keith kept well away from Bennett, and they dived straight in with 'I Love to Boogie'. Finn had the audience eating from the palm of his hand with his mouth-watering jigging and jiving from one end of the stage to the other. They applauded with their hands held high above their heads. Some tried grabbing his legs, and the roar generated when the song finished had Keith's hands tingling.

Finn shifted his microphone stand, kissed Oggy on

the head and addressed their fans. 'What a welcome. Thank you. Have you got enough energy to keep up? Okay then. Guys, let's show them what we've got. Join in. "Thunderwing."'

Parts of Keith's body moved in ways he never knew possible, giving him an almighty buzz. He had whopping great damp patches under his arms to prove it, strutting back and forth during his solo stint. He winked at Charlotte on the front row, filming him on her phone, and Bennett invaded his space, strong-arming him into a head-cutting duel. Keith came out on top, receiving the most cheers. Juniper Suction gave their all collectively, and once their set had ended, they held hands, blew kisses to their fans and bowed their heads.

'What an opening! Please show your appreciation for Juniper Suction,' the DJ roared. 'Will they return for the final round? Guess we'll find out. Next up, Physical Graffiti.'

Juniper Suction left the stage to rapturous applause, but Finn didn't stick around. He darted to their dressing room before Keith could congratulate him on his mesmerising performance, and Bennett followed, looking miffed. Oggy and Jake stayed behind to get a look at Physical Graffiti, and by the time Keith arrived in their dressing room, Finn had thrown off his coat, whipped off his wig and was sitting upright in front of his mirror.

'Did you see Niamh? Where's Sadie? I need her to fix me up.' Dabbing himself with wipes, Finn made himself more presentable, adding a touch more eyeliner and lipstick.

'Relax. It's just a girl. Say hello and ask her if she wants a drink. Now, keep still.' Bennett tidied up Finn's lips. 'Deodorant. I'll grab one of your gifts from Ronny and me.'

Keith offered his own advice. 'Fantastic performance. You brought the best out of us all, and Bennett's right. Woo her. And stay out of trouble.'

'Ignore *him*,' Bennett snapped. 'He married the first woman brave enough to put her hands down his pants and doesn't know what century it is. Here, try this on for size.' Resting a leopard-skin stovepipe hat on the dressing table, he thrust a pair of black boots with enormous tongues near Finn's feet and unravelled a blue sheet to reveal black leather pants, a long thin leopard-skin overcoat and a vibrant pink Raleigh Strika T-shirt. 'Since you move about more than us, Ronny and I made you a backup suit. Stand up. Let's have a gander.'

Finn jumped to his feet, looking smug, and held his new clobber in front of the mirror. 'Don't know what to say.' Off went his sweaty satin suit and on came his new-fangled outfit.

'Here.' Bennett pinned Finn's stovepipe hat to his wig, wrapped his pink feather boa around his neck and gave him one final touch-up. 'Now I'm stumped for words.'

Posing and pouting in the mirror, dressed to impress, Finn spun. 'How do I look?'

'Like a glam rock superstar.' Oggy said, appearing out of nowhere. 'A Crazy Little Thing Called Love' by Queen was playing at the bar, and he shuffled his feet, clicking his fingers. 'She'd be crazy not to fancy you. And stay out of—'

'He knows,' Keith said, adding, 'Don't be afraid to tell her how you feel.'

Finn swiped his money and phone from his jeans and

took off. Oggy headed to his bay to check social media, and Bennett summoned Keith to the bar. He ordered them both a brandy and Coke, and Keith necked his in one. 'Felt great sharing a genuine stage with you again after all these years. The camaraderie was there for all to see.'

Bennett tapped his fingers on the bar. 'Daniel's mam told everyone she gave his belongings to the rag and bone man. Then his Blue Sparkle miraculously shows up in your possession. So, do you have Daniel's journal, yes or no? Ronny seems to think so.'

'Don't do this. Think about Finn, Jake and Oggy. What about Paula – your employees?'

Bennett stuck his face close to Keith's nose. 'Toilets now,' he snarled, leading him in. He looked ready to thump him one and flew through the toilet door that fast, it nearly swung off its hinges. Running his fingers vigorously through his wig, he banged his fists on the vanity unit and slammed a toilet seat down. 'Sit.'

Keith became increasingly hot under the collar and undid his top buttons, doing his best not to aggravate Bennett further by speaking.

'I spent my early teens crying myself to sleep most nights, not knowing whether I was coming or going. Since Daniel died, I've always felt alone, *until* I bumped into Ronny again and met Farooq and my good friends at the Birdcage. They're my family, Keith. Being with them is the one time and place in this cruel, nasty world where I get to be me. Then all this happened. I've been so against it from the start, and not for the reasons you think, but playing alongside you, Oggy, Jake and especially Finn made me feel alive just like Daniel did.'

'Me too.'

'So how do you think I felt, hey, when Daniel's mam asked you to read "The Dove" at his funeral? He wrote it with me in his back garden. When she asked you to ride in her car after laying Daniel to rest, I died inside. All through spite because she caught us in bed together.' Bennett wiped a tear from his cheek, taking some of his eyeliner with it. 'We used to rehearse in his cellar too when his mam was out. I'd play his Blue Sparkle, and he'd sing, write, or draw that naked Vitruvian bloke, asking if I could see our oppressed divine feminine beauty within, longing to be a part of the show. He called me his benevolent bonobo and told wild stories about mystical messengers flying through his bedroom mirror at three a.m., wanting to whisk him off in a super-magnesium zinc alloy ship to the land of love.'

Keith couldn't bear it any longer. 'Wait here a minute. Please.' He left the gents in a hurry and hauled his rucksack from its peg before rushing back across the dressing room to the toilets. He closed the toilet door behind him, and Bennett finished relieving himself at the urinal. Waiting for him to wash his hands and dab his eyes with a paper towel, Keith plucked Daniel's white origami swan from its envelope. 'Does this little fellow belong to you?'

Tears streamed down Bennett's face. 'Where did you find *her*?'

'Don't kick off. I'm telling the truth, I promise. I found it in Daniel's Blue Sparkle case. I never would've had the courage to open it after all these years if you hadn't given me grief about losing my touch. Charlotte had deep concerns about me relapsing.'

Bennett held out his hand and Keith laid the white swan in his palm. Bennett grabbed some toilet tissue from the nearest cubicle and wiped his eyes. 'The night before Daniel's eighteenth birthday, my dad came home pissed and gave me a black eye and a thick lip for being different. I escaped to Daniel's through my bedroom window, and he made me this swan, naming her Mona. He *spurned* my invitation to go fishing next day. I left her on his windowsill and stormed off to Chorlton, then he invited you to go camping in Rhyl. I assumed Daniel took his own life because I dumped him the night before Rock Heaven. He admitted cheating on me with Ronny and apologised. It hurt like hell. There hasn't been a single day since where I haven't blamed myself for his death.'

'You knew? Why didn't you say something?'

'He slept with everyone. Yes, it was humiliating, but who could ever say no to Daniel? It wasn't Ronny's fault. I need to find him and apologise. Can't believe I threatened to piss on Daniel's chin. Who even says shit like that? You think he'd look down holding a grudge?'

'Very much doubt it. I told Daniel I was leaving the band to settle down with Charlotte and we argued just before I fell asleep on the beach. He told me he didn't belong. He spoke of Rock Heaven and wanting to be free.' Keith handed Bennett Daniel's journal. 'I haven't read all of it. Don't think his guitar, swan or journal was ever meant for me. He loved *you*. I'm so sorry for your loss.'

'Charlotte whispered those exact same words to me. I'm really sorry for yours and hers. I wish I knew sooner.' Bennett gazed at the Great Sphinx and the Pyramids of Giza sketched on the front cover before flicking through the pages. '*Forest Fables: One hot, sunny afternoon millions of moons ago, an immoral species with more advanced DNA than humans entered Earth's atmosphere, seeking to create their own slave race. They detected a large troop of brown female, hamadryas baboons, having fun beneath the Phoenician juniper. Beautiful, somewhat impressionable mammals, attracted to the sound of music, were relentlessly pursued along the Nile River through what is now known as Ethiopia, Eritrea and South Sudan. They cowered, cringed and held on to the branches of those trees to no avail, eventually sucked up to the stern of that ship.*'

Keith and Bennett stared into each other's eyes and screamed, '*Juniper Suction.*'

'There's more. *White, male baboons turned their backs on expectant mothers with diverse infants, leaving them to nurse their offspring by the flooded riverbanks in the Giza Plateau alone, but interbreeding soon spread from old world monkeys to orangutans, gorillas, bonobos and chimpanzees, creating human beings. If it wasn't for our imagination, we'd still be swinging from tree to tree.* What's this slapdash fill-in-the-blanks list?' he asked before reading it out. '*B_ _ N _ _ _ and B_ C_ _ the bonobos. R_ _N_ the orangutan. G_ A_ _ the gorilla. C_ I_ _ O_ _ the chimpanzee. G_ _ N_ _ _ Y_ the gibbon. S_ L_I_ the silverback.* I'm one of his bonobos. Ronny we know was his orangutan. The gibbon's our old headteacher Gwendolyn. Daniel got in trouble purposely so he could knob her in detention.'

'Does Becky's name fit?' Oggy asked, interrupting. He stood at the door with his hands in his pockets. 'Sorry, I heard shouting. Can I see?'

Bennett handed him Daniel's journal.

'Thought as much. His Aunt Grace was his gracious gorilla, and the silverback is most likely my mum, Sylvia. As you know, she was an amputee. I found Daniel sunbathing in my garden one afternoon when I returned home from football practice early. I heard them giggling. He called her his one-legged, super-sexy silverback. It knocked me sick.'

'I'm so sorry.' Keith approached Oggy and placed his hand on his shoulder. 'It was *you* who wrote that nasty note.'

'Afraid so.' Oggy lowered his head in shame. 'I still remember his pain-stricken face. He hurt me. I wanted to hurt him back. I didn't want him dead, I swear. When Judy cheated on me, everything came flooding back and I needed my friends. I wanted to make amends. It's *my* fault Daniel killed himself. *I* ruined our lives. I'm so sorry.'

Bennett patted Oggy's back. 'It's not your fault, same as it wasn't mine for dumping him or his for quitting our band. He wasn't called dirty-dick Daniel for nothing.'

'Not sure that's helping,' Keith said. 'Daniel simply felt like he didn't belong to this world anymore. He realised how much pain he'd caused. He refused to hurt anyone else.'

Oggy handed the journal back to Keith. 'I'm tired of all the secrets. I knew something happened at Reading Festival. Becky was beside herself; Clifford was so protective of her. They shut me out, but I knew it had something to do with Daniel. Becky dumped me the next day with no explanation, then moved away straight after his funeral.'

'Wait. There's still one unidentified name on Daniel's list. The chimpanzee, look.'

Bennett peered over Keith's shoulder and hit the roof. 'All this time. That slimy, cheating, chug-eyed chimp. I'll kill him.'

TEN

Saturday, November 5th, 2011 – 22:00

Finn swaggered through the cheerful crowd in search of the pink cuckoo, gaining pats on his back, posing for photos and soaking up all the attention. He spotted Niamh in a classy coral dress, shuffling away from two enormous speakers, and blew into his hands, sniffing them to make sure he didn't have dog breath.

Her mates smiled at him before stepping away, and his dreamy lady spun around. 'Na then. Gone all professional with the glittery guyliner, have we? What do I call you?'

Finn flicked his curls away from his eyes, saying the first thing that popped into his head. 'Depends. If you're here for work, I'm Marc. If you have the hots for me, I'm Finn.'

'Ge'ore,' she replied, giggling. 'You've changed.'

'You said don't be shy.' Finn shook her hand, grinning like a lovestruck teenager.

'I also remember saying something about you being an awful singer at the Ship. Sorry.' Niamh sipped her vodka lemon and lime. 'Sothis Media's tab. Pretty sure it's my round.'

'Water, please. Need to focus. You left the Ship in a

hurry, and I'm sorry I didn't get the chance to speak to you at the Printworks. What do you think of our journey so far?'

She leant towards his ear and whispered, 'Can't comment.' Plonking her drink on the table by the column, she ran his feather boa through her fingers. 'Looked like you were avoiding me. It's fine. I get it.'

Finn stuttered. 'No, no. So, could I maybe get your number and take you out after this competition?' He tilted his head back and puffed out his thumping chest, his thumbs in his trouser pockets. 'Is that a yes?'

'I can't date lads who wear more makeup than me. Sorry, stud.' Niamh blushed.

'This is all *your* doing, remember.' Finn twirled his corkscrew curls through his fingers, pouting, and mimicked Beryl's voice. 'You'll need to make it fast. Once I win this competition, my phone will be red hot with all kinds of offers.'

'Shut up bragging. All this T. Rex stuff's gone to your bonce. You ain't no big-time glam rock superstar yet. Maybe I'll ask my judges to rein you in a bit.'

Finn stepped a little closer. 'Seriously, though, I've been dying to meet you again. Thanks for your help at the Ship. The last thing I want is to make you feel uncomfortable at work, but I like you, and I'd love to find out just how wild and crazy you really are.'

Niamh passed Finn her phone and smiled. 'Tap your number in. That's my brand-new work Mini. What you reckon?' she asked, showing him a photo.

'I can't date birds with loads of money, sorry.'

'Oh, I'm a bird, am I? Who said we were going on a date?'

Finn's mouth kicked in before his brain and he blurted out the most pathetic thing ever, wishing to take it back. 'If you're a bird, I'm a—.'

Niamh split her sides with laughter. 'Love that film. You sure I'm your type?'

'What film's that?' Finn asked, brushing it off by acting numb. 'You're stunning. We're a perfect match. I love your smoky eyes too,' he said, teasing.

'Never been told that by a lad before. Still worried.' She glowed even more. 'Where would you take me on a date then, Bolan?'

Finn smirked. 'Maybe go to a rough bar, head to the strip club in Chinatown, then grab a kebab and munch it on a frozen kerb at the taxi rank. Sound romantic?'

'Sure. This Sheffield lass can help warm a nesh Mancunian up.' She giggled at his open-mouthed expression and slapped him on his upper arm. 'Oi, I didn't mean it like that.'

'What do we have here?' Clifford asked, resting his hands on their shoulders. 'Look how smitten you both are. Some might say this is a conflict of interest, but not me.'

Niamh pushed his hand away. 'Shouldn't you be backstage?'

'My offer still stands, Finn. Knowing how good the Wall are, I doubt you'll even make the final round. Face facts, your none-hit wonders are nothing but a flash in the pan.'

'Shove your offer. All you care about is power, not people. Isn't that what my mam said to you?' Finn asked through gritted teeth.

Clifford stepped back, gobsmacked. 'Josie Finnegan

was your mother? She always said you had stars in your eyes. How did I not realise? My sincere condolences. Finn, I'm truly sorry for your loss. There isn't a day that passes by where I don't think about her,' he said, bowing his head before waddling off in a trance.

'You okay? I'm so sorry about your mum.' Niamh's radio buzzed, and she unclipped it from her belt and lifted it to her ear. 'On my way. I need to go. There's trouble backstage. Let's meet after the final. Talk properly then. Good luck.'

Fans wanting selfies mobbed Finn, putting a stop to his funeral face, and by the time he returned backstage, Clifford had a bloody nose and his sister Becky was sitting on the steps crying, with her son Antoine comforting her. Physical Graffiti pitched up in front of them, gobbing off. Juniper Suction retaliated, and security showed up, doing their best to keep them apart. The biggest bouncer took command. 'Go back to your dressing rooms now or you'll be disqualified from this competition and escorted off the premises.'

Ronny snapped, 'All Daniel wanted was to be himself and none of you let him. In some way you're all responsible for his death. You should be ashamed. He enjoyed sex – so what? He was just trying to find out who he was, who he felt comfortable with and who he could trust. Isn't that what we all want?'

Becky shot up, striking Clifford again and again with her handbag. 'You convinced me to dump Oggy, dump Daniel and move in with Dad away from the drama all because you were screwing Daniel yourself. You knew how much I blamed myself for his death and you said nothing in case I found out. Who are you? What are you? You better leave.'

'It's all lies. Oggy, you should've told me about Josie.' Clifford leapt at Bennett, trying to snatch Daniel's journal for himself, putting Niamh's security staff on the back foot. 'Give it me. He loved me.'

'Not what it says here, bug-eyes.' Oggy did his best to stop Bennett punching Clifford's lights out, and Finn dived in front of Keith to protect him but failed to hold on to his suit. He tumbled to the floor, taking everyone with him before a loud yelp from the bottom of the pile put a stop to the ruckus. Niamh returned with more security and, one by one, they made the heap smaller by pushing and shoving people to opposite ends of the corridor. Keith surfaced, nursing his swollen hand, which had been trampled on, but he never said a word. He just gave Finn a worried look before being helped up by Oggy and Bennett.

Niamh stripped Clifford of his backstage pass and Physical Graffiti headed back to their dressing room with Becky. Finn, fearing the worst, dragged his feet to the medical room behind Oggy, Bennett, Jake, Farooq, Ronny and Sadie to check on Keith. They listened to the Wall's 'Stairway to Heaven', waiting for news. A first aider opened the door twenty minutes later. 'Now, remember, rest, ice, compress and elevate. I'd get an X-ray too. If you continue to play before your wrist heals, you could cause permanent damage. Don't chance it.'

Keith nodded and exited the medical room wearing a worn-out wrist brace. Before anyone spoke, Niamh announced Physical Graffiti had made it through to the final round and a chorus of boos filled the venue. Finn pulled his T-shirt over his head and slid down the cold brick wall with his arms folded, escaping into his beat-up thoughts as Niamh revealed that Juniper Suction would join them. The crowd went ballistic.

'What's wrong?' Keith asked. 'In case you didn't hear, we just made the final round.'

'All our dreams and ambitions just went up in smoke,' Finn replied. 'I can't go out there without you. I won't do it.'

'You all can, and you all will, especially you.' Keith pulled Finn's T-shirt down, uncovering his face, and knelt in front of him. 'Did you need me in the Church or at your audition? So stop feeling sorry for me. Besides, Bennett is much better than I am.'

'That's bollocks and you know it.'

'Bennett, you're three weeks away from eviction. The Blue Sparkle belongs to you. You must set the tempo. Daniel and I always tuned our instruments together. We played what our souls wanted to hear. Use Daniel's capo. Keep it simple. Open mind. Open chords. Accommodate Finn. Focus. Clifford may have scarpered, but if we give up on our journey now, he'll keep coming back again and again, haunting and tormenting us.'

'We should do this *together*,' Jake said. 'That's our motto.'

'He's right, Keith. So is Finn. It won't be the same out there without you.'

'Guys, stop with your excuses. I never wanted fame and fortune. Going off his journal and what you said, Ronny, Daniel didn't either. To him, the purple heart trophy exemplified the courage and bravery it takes to be ourselves. He just wanted to be himself in a world of like-minded beings where he belonged. I'm more than happy with what I've achieved. Being a part of this journey with you lot has been an amazing experience, and I'm so thankful. I might not be on stage beside you, but I'll be in the audience on the front row with my wife as a proud spectator. Please stop moping. You're not blaming me this time, so go out there, win this bleeding competition and bring our purple heart trophy home.'

Oggy jumped up. 'Keith's right. Let's give it our all. Ronny, Sadie, Farooq, we have work to do. Bennett, Jake, let's give these two a few minutes and get ready.' He dragged them to their feet. 'Physical Graffiti have two songs to perform, then we're up.'

Finn spread his legs across the corridor. 'Everything you just said is bullshit. How can you not want to be out there performing in front of that crowd? We need you. I need you.'

'Tonight's the night you'll realise you don't need anyone else, whereas I get to watch the most gifted young man I've ever met perform. It's been an absolute privilege. I can't wait. Daniel used to say, "It's all about the journey, not the destination," and as always, he was right. For years I believed I couldn't play without him by my side. I was wrong and so are you. I won't let you make the same mistake.'

'We want Bolan! We want Bolan!'

'You hear that, right? That's not rejection. That's unreserved acceptance. Remember why you wanted to be here. Remember who you wanted to be here for. Your mum's energy isn't here in this icebox of a corridor. Her warmth is out there on stage. That's where she belonged, and so do you.' Keith held out his hand. 'So are we going back to our dressing room to get you looking the business or are you going to sit on your backside, having given up, and ignore your wonderful fans?'

'*Our* fans.' Finn let Keith pull him up, then hugged him. 'You're still weird.'

'I know. Wipe your face. You don't want Niamh to see you like that.'

Finn sang along to 'Light My Fire' by the Doors at his dressing table. 'I fancy a change, Sadie. Keep the silver stars, but everything else neutral. I want to be me.'

She gripped Finn's chin with her thumb and finger, working her magic one last time in the competition, and Ronny set his corkscrew wig in place, tinkering with it. In waltzed Farooq, unwrapping a snow-white suit, complete with shiny sequins, a plunging neckline, flared trousers and a sky-blue velvet choker.

'It's ace. You shouldn't have,' Finn said in a squeaky voice. 'Thanks.'

Ronny squeezed him tightly. 'We'll give you a minute to yourself.'

Admiring his new clothes, Finn ran the smooth velvet through his fingers and threw them on, having a proper good look at himself in the mirror, then pressed his hands on the dressing table. Inhaling through his nose, he filled his lungs to twenty-five per cent capacity and held his breath without releasing for nine seconds. He did the same to reach fifty per cent, then seventy-five per cent before finally mastering one hundred per cent lung capacity.

Closing his eyes, powerful waves of energy flowed up from his spine, working their way through his groin, the pit of his stomach, and his heart, throat and forehead before settling beneath his crown. He floated through a tunnel surrounded by twinkling stars, swirling coloured patterns and flashes of light, then opened his eyes and winked at the man in the mirror. 'Thanks for everything, Electric Warrior.'

'Who were you talking to just then?' Keith asked, sneaking up behind him.

'Myself.' Finn spun to face his friends.

'That's all you need to focus on tonight – being yourself. Look, I'm shaking more than you. That's me, guys.' Keith embraced each of them. 'Together.'

'My pixie prince,' Ronny yelped. 'I'll keep saying it year on year and shout it from the rooftops for the entire world to hear. Daniel believed femininity to be the ultimate form of sophistication, dear.'

'Right, everyone. That's the five-minute call.' Oggy handed Finn the microphone. 'There ain't no better time to light that blue touch paper, son of Josie. Love you, kid.'

Juniper Suction headed off, and Finn saw the crowd gathered below the glitter balls through the circular windows. Adrenaline worked its way through his body, and Ronny, Farooq and Sadie wished them good luck, giving Finn one last squeeze at the back of the line. The audience quietened down, and the rotating platform spun to reveal a four-foot white chrysanthemum swan, like the one at Marc's funeral, with Finn's microphone stand in the centre. Oggy, Bennett and Jake dived into position.

'I don't know if Manchester's ready for this,' the DJ bawled. 'Let's find out. Please welcome back on stage for the last act of Love Is the Drug: Juniper Suction and the incredible Marc Bolan.'

Oggy gave Finn that all-important wink and he bowled in beneath indigo strobes, kicking off 'Ride a White Swan' in spectacular fashion. He gave the thumbs-up to his dad, who was pushing Mace in his wheelchair. The crowd went nuts and he high-fived Bennett at the front of the stage, banging his arse against his. 'You and me.' They sang into the same microphone, making sure their voices carried to the far ends of the dance floor, before Finn bopped and jived the full length of the stage, interacting with Oggy and Jake. Feeding off their energy, he encouraged everyone to join in, clapping their hands, then scanned left and right in search of the pink cuckoo. When her amazing smile penetrated his line of sight, he dropped his shoulder, kicked out his leg and winked.

Oggy tossed Finn a bottle of water. 'Show her what you're made of this time and there's every chance you'll lift the pissing roof off this place. "Bang a Gong. Get It On."'

'Hang on a sec.' Finn attached his microphone to his stand, making direct eye contact with members of the audience. 'How's everyone doing tonight? You good?'

'*Woo! Yeah!*'

'Before our final song, I thought it'd be a good idea to introduce ourselves properly. Give it up for Oggy – drums. Bennett – bass. Jake – percussion, and finally Keith,' he roared, pointing to him in the audience. 'Show some love to my dad, Mace, Charlotte, Farooq, Ronny and Sadie too. I wouldn't be here if it wasn't for these guys. Love is the drug, right? If you don't know the person next to you, introduce yourselves. That's what I'm talking about.'

'Bolan! Bolan! Bolan!'

'Thank you, Manchester. My real name's Finn, by the way.'

'Finn! Finn! Finn!'

'I'd like to say a massive thank you to Lucas and Inner Vibrations over here for the wonderful work they do for people like you, me and our band. Show them some love. If you're struggling with your mental health, feel alone or feel like you don't belong and need to hide, our last song is for you. A great man once told me every life is a journey. Every journey once recorded is a story, and each one is as valuable as the next. Our stories matter. I've been hiding away for the past nine years, so believe me, I know how you feel. We see you, we hear you and we love you.' Finn whipped off his stovepipe hat and wig and launched them into the audience. His bandmates did the same. Red, orange, yellow, green, blue, indigo and violet strobe lights lit up his arms. 'How's about we just be ourselves for the next few minutes and generate a boatload of electricity together? Sound like a plan? Could you please lift Keith up and hand him back to us? He belongs up here. You can have him back at the end, Charlotte, I promise. Careful, he injured his wrist. Bang a gong. Let's "Get It On".'

Finn helped Keith on stage to wolf whistles and cheers, then acted all cool and macho, giving his dreamy lady the curly finger. Niamh's face glowed as she scrambled to the front and his dark brown eyes locked on to her beautiful big blue ones. Strutting his stuff better than ever, he aimed Bolan's lyrics directly at her, blowing her a kiss. Keith, Oggy, Bennett and Jake joined him at the front of the stage and linked hands, bowing their heads to a unified, electrified audience. Physical Graffiti and the Wall applauded from the sidelines and Becky threw Finn a towel.

'What a night, reyt? I'm shaking.' Niamh made her way on stage with her microphone, flanked by her judges, waiting for the screams to die down before pulling a rainbow envelope from her handbag. 'Sothis Media would like to thank all tribute acts for taking part in this fantastic contest. Landlords, landladies and all you music lovers, we'd be nothing without you. You've been marvellous throughout, and I'd like to say a massive thanks to our judges, staff and tonight's finalists. Show your appreciation.'

The audience wouldn't pipe down.

'As you know, only one band can win. Drum roll, please.' Niamh signalled to the DJ and the thumping stopped. 'I'm thrilled to announce the winners of this year's Love Is the Drug Guy Fawkes Sextravaganza are … *JUNIPER SUCTION!*'

'*Yes!*' Finn howled. He dropped to his knees, loving the fans' deafening roars.

Keith, Oggy, Bennett and Jake lifted him up, going berserk, screaming and bouncing about. Becky, Physical Graffiti and the Wall congratulated them before stepping aside, and Oggy collected the purple heart trophy and two cheques for £25,000 from Niamh with tears in his eyes. 'Wow. This is unbelievable,' he said, speaking into her microphone with passion. 'You wouldn't believe what we've been through to get here. These guys are so musically and vocally talented. Touching on what Finn said earlier, it just goes to show, if you be yourself, stick together and fight for what you believe in, you can achieve anything. We'd like to thank our team behind the scenes, Farooq, Ronny and Sadie, who provided dance lessons, costumes, makeup and above all, unconditional friendship. Our cheques will be split between our team, ADDER Dystonia – a charity close to Sadie's heart – and Inner Vibrations. We dedicate this trophy to Daniel Saunders and Josie Finnegan, two beautifully gifted people who passed way before their time. Finn, thanks for bringing us so much closer together. From the bottom of our hearts, thank you. We love you all.' Oggy, Keith and Bennett took turns kissing their repossessed trophy.

'Your friends are understandably emotional right now, Finn,' Niamh said. 'What does winning this competition mean to you?'

Jake dived in. 'Can I just say how much I love this guy? I'm so full of love for everyone right now. I can't explain it. His voice gives you goose pimples, right? Me too. Look. How do you do that? Just so you know, Niamh, he's got the hots for you big time.'

Finn shrugged, covering his beetroot face with his towel till the whistling died down. 'Thanks, mate. The last few months have been the best days of my life, Niamh. I mean it. Oggy, Bennett, Jake, you've helped bring the best out of me, and Keith, you gave me an opportunity young lads rarely get – especially where I lived. If it wasn't for you showing up at my door late one night waving a flyer in my face, I honestly don't know where I'd be right now. So thank you.'

'Shock!' Bennett gave Keith a massive kiss on the lips. 'Revenge is sweet, you absolute beauty.'

'And thanks to everyone for supporting us. We needed it. Six months ago, I'd never have believed I'd be here now, performing on this stage with this amazing group of people. Believing in yourself. Believing in others. It can make all the difference. Your love was our drug tonight. For my mam and Daniel. Gone too soon.' He lifted the purple heart trophy into the air and waved it at his dad, who looked the happiest he'd been in nine years, then spotted Clifford wiping tears from his face and clapping his hands high above his head. 'Many of you over the past few weeks will have now heard of Daniel Saunders, who tragically died thirty-four years ago on Bournemouth beach when the Magnesium Gurus were about to take on the world. If it's okay with Niamh and Sothis, we'd like to stay and play some more hits, starting with "Metal Guru" for Daniel and his best friends here.'

'Shall we let the audience decide?' Niamh held her microphone towards them. 'Pretty sure that's a yes. We'll leave you to it.'

'Hang on a sec.' Finn passed Oggy their purple heart trophy. 'You look stunning, Niamh. Any chance I can take you out for a meal or a few drinks?'

Wolf whistles rang out all around, and Niamh blushed. 'I can do better than that.' She gripped Finn's collar and kissed him, taking him completely by surprise.

'Wow! "Metal Guru", then how's about some "Hot Love"? Take it away, guys.'

***

Juniper Suction signed their recording contracts with Sothis before Finn waved his dad and Mace off, wearing the black and gold *Electric Warrior* T-shirt Niamh had bought him as a present. He headed through the lobby of the Midland Hotel, made himself comfortable on a gigantic sofa and did his best to let the past few months sink in.

'Morning, Marc,' Keith said, teasing. He shuffled up next to him with a rolled-up newspaper. 'Every muscle in my body is aching. Has Niamh left for Sheffield already?'

'Not yet,' Finn replied. 'She's sticking her bag in her new Mini, dying to show off.'

'Good for her.' Keith sat back, admiring his surroundings. 'This place is magnificent. Them rooms must've cost a blooming fortune. Your dad and Mace get away okay?'

Finn nodded, showing him his phone. 'Look. Mace keeps messaging pics of mansions with massive gardens and sports cars.'

'It'll take some getting used to. Exotic holidays, plush restaurants, chauffeur-driven limos and no more getting out of bed at six a.m. to work on freezing cold construction sites. Our lives are about to transform. The fancy suits are in there now touting us for the Christmas number one spot. Who'd have believed? I'll never forget last night's performance as long as I live. Breathtakingly brilliant. We witnessed the real you shining through. As for Bennett, I take it back. He still has a long way to go to be better than me.'

Finn shook his head, grinning. His phone bleeped, and he checked his message from Niamh. It read: *You coming with?* 'You sound well excited for someone who didn't want the fame and fortune. Does any of this frighten you?'

Keith sat up. 'Are you okay? If you're not, I'm not. What is it?'

'Dunno. Our lives have just been flipped, and I don't know if I'm ready. My mam wasn't. Last night on stage felt like the real me; I felt the closest I've ever been to my mam too. But this morning the bright lights, contracts, photographs and interviews hit me all at once. It feels like I'm under pressure again.'

'Hey, hey.' Keith rested his hand on Finn's shoulder. 'It's new and it'll calm down. Take a breath. You're not alone in this. We all have a say in decisions. Oggy made sure of that before we signed our lives away. He knows this industry inside out.'

Finn rubbed his face with both hands and exhaled. 'I know I'm not making much sense, but what if these men in suits are the real vultures my mam and dad wanted me to stay clear of? What if they don't have our best interests at heart?'

'This isn't like you. You trust Niamh, don't you?'

'Course I do. That doesn't mean I trust the people she trusts.'

'Okay. What's really worrying you? Come on, don't shut me out. I'm all ears.'

Finn sighed. 'Niamh wants to beat the traffic over the tops. She's asked me to go with her. Maybe I want to stick around for your interview with Elaine.'

'Come off it. You know everything there is to know about us old codgers. This will be like your first proper date. It's what you wanted.'

Finn checked his phone. 'She just pulled up outside. Truth is, I'm scared.'

'I get it. You've been through one of the most traumatic experiences known to man, so here.' Keith dropped his newspaper in Finn's lap. 'If you can't stomach the wonderful views across the Pennines, we're on the front page. Guessing you have your inhaler? You can listen to some of Niamh's music to take your mind off things, find out more info on what Sothis have in store for us. What? She'll put your mind more at ease than I can. Do not get stressed, though, you hear? Why not pretend you're going on stage? Do your warmups? No, scrap that. You'll freak her out.'

Finn laughed.

'That's more like it. Less thinking, more enjoyment. You better scarper before Jake grips you. You'll never get away. Any issues, call me. It's no problem.' Keith shook Finn's hand, then hugged him. 'Remember, Charlotte wants you both round for tea next weekend. The kids can't wait to meet you. Hang on. Where's your stuff?'

'Reception. Niamh checked us out. I'll grab it. Two secs.' Finn approached the desk and handed his ticket in. 'Could I get my case, please?'

'Of course, Mr Finnegan,' the porter said. 'This package just came for you.'

Keith popped his head over Finn's shoulder. 'Another gift. She's a keeper. What does it say on the tag?'

'*Congratulations, Glam Rock Superstar. Fully deserved.* Hey, what were you and Bennett chatting about earlier? Heard my name mentioned a few times.'

Keith grinned. 'If you must know, we were discussing the one thing missing from your armoury. Don't tell

Bennett I gave you the heads-up. But how would you like us to help add another string to your bow by teaching you some riffs and licks on a fancy Flying V?'

'Are you being serious?'

'Deadly. You know we'd never have achieved any of this without you. We were all so lost. You not only brought us all closer together, you brought the colour back into our lives. I just wanted to say on behalf of us all, thank you for being Bolan.'

Finn's eyes welled up. 'Do you honestly think Daniel was right about life being more about the journey than the destination?'

'Daniel held a firm belief in life after death. He had our final destination tagged as the land of love. Who are we to dismiss it? I know it's hard. Life was never meant to be a walk in the park, so try shutting everything else out and enjoy yourself. I knew I'd talk you round.'

'You can have some credit. The rest goes to Marc and the sailors of the skyway. I'll call you later and let you know what's in the box.' Finn put on his hoody and made his way to the main door of the hotel. His phone bleeped and he spun round, giving Keith the thumbs-up before reading the message. It was from Jake: *Have you got off, you fanny? Fone me when you get to dee dah land, duck. Heard two Sothis men-in-suits chatting shit about binning us off once the hype dies down. Do some digging. Bennett wants to open a chain of knocking shops. I kissed Sadie. Think I'm in love. Keith's punching well above his weight. He told me all about his NDE. I was right about ETs. Oh, and the magnesium goo woo's been snogging the head off Webecca Decker. Peace out, lady boy.*

Finn creased up with laughter, put his phone in his jeans pocket and strolled down the steps to the kerb, waving to fans and paparazzi. Niamh pulled up in her fancy black Mini to save him, and he dived in, a little light-headed. Although it gleamed and had a brand-new smell, he fastened his seatbelt and tugged on it, making sure he was strapped in before rubbing his hands together. 'Turn them heaters up. How long till we get there?'

'Just over an hour, mardy bum. Got you some water.'

'Cool. So, what's Sothis really got planned for Juniper Suction? Can your colleagues be trusted? I mean, if something wasn't right, you'd tell me, wouldn't you?'

Niamh nodded. 'Where's all this come from? Has someone said something?'

'Just asking.' The thought of winding roads over Woodhead gave Finn the chills and a crawling sensation beneath his skin. He opened Keith's newspaper, flicking through the aftereffects of Love Is the Drug, and came across a reprinted article with a black-and-white photo of his mam from the morning she died.

'Is that her?' Niamh asked. 'She's beautiful.'

'Was.' Finn folded it up and shoved it in the door panel, praying Niamh wouldn't hit him with a thousand questions about his past in case he went all woozy. He watched the rain bounce off the windscreen on the M67 before fog swept in when leaving Tintwistle. 'Where did that come from?' he asked, grabbing the handle above the door.

'Be reyt.' Niamh travelled less than twenty miles an hour on the straights and less than ten miles an hour on the curves, sipping her Fanta lemon. Her full beams were on, as well as her fog lights. 'What's in your mysterious box?'

'You tell me,' Finn replied, wiping sweat from his forehead. 'Reception gave it me. You didn't have to, you know. My T-shirt was more than enough.'

'It's not off me. Might be sexy underwear off your groupies.'

Finn's phone rang, and he let go of the grab handle to answer it. 'Keith. Hello. Keith, can you hear me? No signal.' He tried calling him back, but no joy, then turned the volume up on the radio, aiming to take his mind off his nervy trip. Nothing came through the speakers except interference. Giving up when none of the stations worked, he switched it off and opened his mysterious gift with tingling fingers. 'I feel weird.'

'*Don't* throw up in here,' she said. 'You've lost the colour in your cheeks. You want me to pull over?'

A message from Keith made it through. *Call me as soon as you can. We need to talk. Think I know who the sailors of the skyway are.'*

Niamh tapped Finn on the knee. 'Well, do you want me to pull over or not?'

'No, no. I'll be fine in a sec. Keep going.' He tooted on his inhaler to overcome his shortness of breath and guzzled his bottled water to cure his dry mouth, then clutched his chest. The hills and large parts of the road had vanished beneath a blanket of fog, and Niamh slowed right down, approaching a tight bend in the road. Flipping open one side of his box, Finn pulled out a CD with *TIB STREET JAM SESSIONS* scribbled on it and gasped. 'Here, put this on.' He unfolded a note from the back. It read: *Daniel Saunders and Josie Finnegan were the only people I ever really cared for on this planet. I miss their vibrant, electromagnetic energy every single day. You made two troubled souls, who held mighty powerful beliefs of reincarnation very proud. Having watched you perform; I share their beliefs unequivocally. Take care, Marc – lots of love, Clifford.*

'Finn, talk to me. Finn.'

Multicoloured blotches appeared before Finn's eyes, the scent of gardenias filled his nostrils and his spine warmed up the moment his mam's voice filtered through the speakers, singing 'I'll Be Seeing You' by Billie Holiday. He slackened his seatbelt and shuffled further forward in his seat, trying his best to reach her when a bright white light flashed through the windscreen. 'Mam.' His hand slumped, striking the steering wheel.

'Finn,' Niamh screamed, slamming on her brakes. 'Tree!'

If it wasn't for our imagination, we'd still be swinging from tree to tree.

This book is printed on paper from sustainable sources managed under the Forest Stewardship Council (FSC) scheme.

It has been printed in the UK to reduce transportation miles and their impact upon the environment.

For every new title that Troubador publishes, we plant a tree to offset CO_2, partnering with the More Trees scheme.

MORE TREES
LET'S PLANT A BILLION TREES

For more about how Troubador offsets its environmental impact, see www.troubador.co.uk/sustainability-and-community